I0708317

LOVE HOLDS TRUE

A SHADES OF BRAMLEY HALL REGENCY ROMANCE NOVEL

MICHELLE HELEN FRITZ

Love Holds True: Shades of Bramley Hall Regency Romance by Michelle Helen Fritz

Copyright © 2023 Michelle Helen Fritz

All rights reserved.

Cover Design: Wanderlust Ink & Tome LLC

Chapter Heading Art: Samaiya Art

Developmental & Line Editing: Bre' Davis Edits

Proofreading: Brittany Smith & Cathey Nelson

Published by Clear Spring Books LLC of Clear Spring, MD

DEDICATION

For Faith who is the sweetest lady, the kindest friend, and one creative maven!
May your dreams always flourish and may love always hold true.

CONTENTS

Chapter 1	1
Chapter 2	9
Chapter 3	15
Chapter 4	21
Chapter 5	25
Chapter 6	35
Chapter 7	41
Chapter 8	51
Chapter 9	55
Chapter 10	67
Chapter 11	77
Chapter 12	83
Chapter 13	89
Chapter 14	93
Chapter 15	99
Chapter 16	105
Chapter 17	113
Chapter 18	119
Chapter 19	125
Chapter 20	133
Chapter 21	139
Chapter 22	145
Chapter 23	151
Chapter 24	155
Chapter 25	159
Chapter 26	163
Chapter 27	169
Chapter 28	179
Chapter 29	183
Chapter 30	189
Chapter 31	195
Chapter 32	201
Chapter 33	215
Chapter 34	223
Chapter 35	227
Chapter 36	231

Chapter 37   239
Epilogue   243

A Note from the Author   249
Acknowledgements from Michelle Helen Fritz   251
Also By Michelle Helen Fritz   253
About Michelle Helen Fritz   255

1

THE DOCTOR IS IN

*D*r. Gideon Carrow twitched the reins as he scanned the well-traveled lane before him. The afternoon was waning as he made his way home to his countryside manor. The physician had been paying calls upon his elderly patients delivering tonics that he had procured from the apothecary earlier that morning. He had also dispensed helpful advice to bring his patients relief from their various ailments.

"Walk on," Gideon commanded from atop his mahogany-colored horse, Perseus.

The autumn day was turning out to be quite blustery as he burrowed deeper into his greatcoat. The sun had been playing peek-a-boo with the wispy clouds ever since Gideon departed his home earlier that morning. The sounds of leaves rustling in the wind had been a constant companion as had the birdsong that met his ears.

"'Tis a very fine day with no threat of rain," he remarked to his horse, whose ear wiggled in response.

Hearing the sound of hooves trotting along the lane, he looked up to find the Earl of Bramley seated astride his horse, Brutus. He was making his way into the town of Bramley, which was the direction from which Gideon had just come. When the Earl caught sight of Gideon atop his horse, he called out a genial greeting.

"Good day to you, my good man!" Lord Bramley's sea-colored eyes were lit with open friendliness. "Which has occupied your morning? Broken bones, chills, or the plague?"

"Good day to you, my lord," Gideon remarked as he reined Perseus to a halt. He shuddered. "Never mention the word *plague* to me again, I beg you. One Scarlatina outbreak this decade has sufficiently been enough to last me a lifetime."

Nodding his head, His Lordship angled his top hat to better protect his eyes from the waning sunlight as he replied, "Indeed, I can quite agree with that."

Gideon felt secure in the regard that the Earl held for him. They had formed a friendship of sorts and the Earl never stood upon ceremony with him.

"I've just treated a nasty dog bite that the ever-precocious Felman lad received from his father's best hunting hound." Gideon smiled bemusedly while His Lordship flinched. The man could not stomach ailments or bodily fluids. But he was not alone in his revulsion to such matters. Many a titled gentleman tinged green when presented with that which adversely affected the body.

"Ah, playing with them again, was he? Terrible business, that of a bite wound." Wincing and switching the topic he inquired, "Will you dine with us this evening? It will only be Mariah and me."

Gideon nodded his head. "I shall be delighted to. Thank you for your kind consideration."

"You are always welcome at the Hall. Perchance, would you have me send around an invitation for another to dine with us?" Lord Bramley lifted one dark quizzical brow at him.

"As it is your home, I will leave the invitations to your wise counsel." Gideon's own brows furrowed as he noted the smirk lining the other man's face.

"There are no young ladies you are currently courting? Tell me, my friend, when will we welcome a Mrs. Carrow to your abode?"

"Not anytime soon, my lord. I have had my fill of conniving debutants and matchmaking mamas to last me a lifetime. Besides, I find that I rather enjoy my freedom to come and go as needed within the community without the hindrance of a wife." Not to say that he was too much of a confirmed bachelor. If he happened upon a lady who managed to capture his heart, he would be more than willing to settle down. Being held in high esteem within *the ton* had never been of interest to him. There had been a lady or two in the town who had held his regard but his affections would not take root, and so he let the flirtations fall away.

"You may naysay all you like, but when a certain set of fine eyes find yours, you too shall become a lost man. I don't envy your bachelorhood." The Earl shook his head at him.

Was that pity he saw on the Earl's face?

Why should I be pitied? I have a full life with many pleasures and a purpose.

"Pity me not, Your Lordship. Whenever my eyes discover this fair lady, I shall move heaven and earth to be forever by her side. For now, though, I am content to be as I am. Tending to those who require my services and dining with you and your lovely lady."

"I see you are resolved to deny me the pleasure of welcoming you into the fold," Lord Bramley stated in a droll tone.

"Pray tell, what fold is that?" Gideon leaned forward to pat Perseus along his neck as the stallion was growing antsy.

"That of the wedded bliss club. Hathwell and I need a new member with fresh blood."

"Have you both become bored of each other?" He quirked a blond brow at the Earl.

"Never. Only we long to see you join our ranks. Having a wife is quite entertaining." His Lordship leaned forward in his saddle.

"Oh no," began Gideon as he tilted his head. "You sound like some other fellow I know. And speaking of Simon, is he not in your elite club?"

"*Simon*? My brother-in-law you mean? That *Simon*?"

Gideon gingerly nodded.

"I am suddenly feeling quite ill indeed to be compared to that *Simon*. No, he has not been taken into consideration for membership. And truly I bear the man no ill will for he's as pleasant a fellow as any." Lord Bramley frowned at him. Simon was ofttimes a ringleader in chaos and was quite known for making a muck out of things. The poor man always meant well, but sometimes he erred. Simon was a doormat for bad form to trod upon.

"I see," Gideon spoke, looking contrite. He cleared his throat, which had suddenly gone dry. "Well now that that has been cleared up, what time shall I arrive to dine?" Gideon had meant no disrespect with his comment, which was made in jest. He suspected that his unease was plainly marked upon his face.

Lord Bramley seemed to regain his jovial manner and said, "We shall see you at seven as I well know your schedule is quite full." Brutus stomped his foot, showing his impatience to be on his way. His Lordship nodded his head at Gideon and directed his restless horse to continue along the lane.

Gideon smiled at Lord Bramley's back and let his horse lead them home as he ruminated. He found that he was looking forward to an evening of amusing company and diverting conversation. In his humble opinion, there was no better hostess than Lady Bramley. Her beauty and grace added to the charm that was Bramley Hall. Gideon urged Perseus to trot toward home more quickly. With such wise and caring benefactors, he considered himself blessed to be so happily settled within the town of Bramley. When it had come time to find a town that was in need, Gideon had sent out inquiries along with a recommendation from an esteemed physician. Dr. Abrams had readily accepted his presence in the town of Bramley as the older gentleman was longing to spend his days by the seaside in happy retirement. Lord Bramley had happily welcomed Gideon in thanks to the warmth of Dr. Abrams's introduction.

While his residence had not the grandeur of Bramley Hall, nor the cozy dimensions of the parsonage, it was entirely suitable for a bachelor and his modest number of servants. It was general knowledge that his earnings as the town doctor far lacked the accommodations of this lifestyle. Gideon was a second son and had therefore been granted a generous allowance from his older brother who had assumed the Marquessate upon their father's passing. Gideon did not mean to live above his simple country income. With the insistence from his family, he purchased a small estate and the servants to keep it. He did not see a reason to thumb his nose at the kind and well-meaning gesture of familial affection. It ensured that his home could also serve as his office and made his position easier. He was situated near enough to the town that it was effortless to reach by foot. All he needed at any hour of the day, or night, was right within his reach, whenever calamity or illness might strike.

Gideon had always known that one day he would need to choose a living. The regiment was not to his liking, nor his family's, and he had never considered himself studious enough to lead a parish. He disliked endlessly debating and found it exceedingly tiresome, so choosing to become a barrister was firmly set aside, much to his maternal grandfather's consternation. Once he had bid his last tutor goodbye, he was allowed to attend Oxford and there he had become enamored with the idea of medicine. Gideon found the human body fascinating. His grandfather, the Duke of Sutton, was adamantly against this pursuit as he feared diseases and whatever else could take Gideon's vitality, or very life, and squander it. The older gentleman did not desire to see his grandson become a surgeon, as so many of those who called themselves such were more apt to remove any offending limb at the slightest of complaints. Even after assurances that that was not the practice Gideon had in mind, the Duke still balked. The allowance that was provided for him by his brother was more than enough to cover his studies, so Gideon had settled his course and read every tome known pertaining to doctoring and herbal medicines. He was ready to earn his entire family's displeasure in order to follow the calling of his heart.

However, Gideon's older brother, the Marquess of Netherfield, was in favor of the decision and became Gideon's staunchest ally. There were only three years in age separating the brothers, and they had always been close. As Netherfield was located in Sussex, there was a span of more than half a day's hard ride between their residences, more if traveled by carriage, or plagued by inclement weather. They had normally met regularly, but the past few months had seen a decline in their visits. They had both become exceedingly busy in their daily lives.

When Perseus halted before the stable, Gideon brought himself back to the present. He looked around his estate and took in the withering landscape. Darkening English ivy and clematis climbed the stones of his home, Lakewood House. The oak trees and shrubs lining the lane gave him privacy unless someone came farther up the driveway. The garden was situated in the back of the estate and was barely visible from the lane. Gideon often broke his fast on the terrace as he found the fresh air to be enlivening. After late nights tending to ill patients there was no better way to begin his day. Fresh air fed the soul and nurtured the body. The Lord provided so much richness in the world to be savored, and Gideon delighted in discovering each treasure.

There was a small lake off to the east of Lakewood House that provided excellent sport in both fishing and rowing. He remained in perfect health due to his exercising almost daily by rowing across and back along the lake's shining surface. Gideon believed that one needed to exercise their body just as much as their mind. He had already spent time there very early this morning before setting out for his rounds. Once Gideon had dismounted, he handed over the reins to one of the grooms and began the short walk to his oak front door.

Upon reaching the door, he was greeted by his butler, Murdock, as the servant opened the door. Murdock was a spry fellow in his early golden years and had peppered gray hair that was combed over the balding middle section atop his pale head.

"You've a letter from your brother, sir. And Mr. Kirkman has inquired whether you will be dining in this evening. What shall I tell him?" His inquisitive blue eyes met Gideon's as he patiently awaited his reply.

"I shan't be home. I have received an invitation to dine at Bramley Hall. Please send my regrets to the chef. Have any new medical supplies arrived?" Gideon removed his charcoal-colored greatcoat and handed over his topper to Murdock. His gaze traveled to the chandelier hanging from the high ceiling where its crystals were glittering prisms across the walls and ceiling. The decorative plasterwork that continued throughout the house was simple but elegant. The taste of his home suited his character perfectly. Clean lines and orderly.

"Very good, sir. No, nothing has arrived. I shall let you know once it does," Murdock said as he hung up the outerwear.

"Would you direct Delaney to see to the categorizing of it once it does arrive? He can stock the supply shelves as well. Please let anyone who calls know that I am at home and receiving patients," Gideon informed the butler, who bowed to him.

Gideon made his way to his study, passing painted landscapes that hung along the papered wall, and opened the door. After he closed it, he strode to his mahogany desk and, rounding it, sat down heavily into his leather chair.

Resting atop his desk was a cream-colored letter addressed to him in his brother's elegant handwriting. He was not due to receive a letter yet, as the last one received still sat on his desk, awaiting his reply. Thinking that the new letter must be of import, he did not delay in reaching for it and breaking the red wax seal.

GIDEON,

GRANDFATHER REQUESTS THAT YOU RETURN HOME IMMEDIATELY. *I HAVE displeased him and he wishes to have you set me straight. We are all at sixes and sevens here and I need the support of my dearest friend and brother. I have shocked the old man and our dragon of a grandfather threatens hourly to suffer a cardiac episode of some sort. If we cannot come to an agreement, I fear that life as we both know it will be forever changed. Know that my actions are the sole cause, and I will happily bear the brunt of displeasure. But I do caution you, my decision shall not be swayed and while I am resolute to earn your ire, I pray that you will forgive me. The one thing I will beg of you is your forgiveness.*

YOURS,
Francis

GIDEON RUBBED HIS HAND DOWN HIS FACE AND READ THE MISSIVE AGAIN.

What could this mean? he wondered.

He was a man of action so, after taking a deep breath, he stood and walked over to the bellpull to summon Murdock. He had paced the span of his study and back before the butler knocked once and entered.

"How may I assist you, sir?" Murdock bowed.

"It seems I am needed in Sussex at once. I shall set out first thing on

the morrow. Please direct Gibbons to ready and send for Delaney."
Gideon continued to pace.

"At once," Murdock said as he left the room.

When the door closed, Gideon halted and then strode back over the Aubusson rug to his desk. He took to his chair and awaited Delaney's presence. While it wasn't customary for physicians to take on apprentices, Gideon found the entire experience more than a worthwhile endeavor. The lad was sharp as a thorn and tender-hearted, and he had been invaluable with his attention to detail and organizational skills. Since Delaney was such a quick study, Gideon had even allowed him to aid in treating patients, under Gideon's watchful eyes.

The lad can manage for a day or two without me.

Gideon looked over his study and his eyes locked onto the massive bookshelves that lined the side wall. The medical texts could aid Delaney should he require additional knowledge. Gideon disliked having to leave so abruptly, but his brother needed him, and he would not let him face their *'dragon of a grandfather'* alone. The Duke was used to being obeyed instantly and Francis was not one to court trouble. Something large was afoot.

2

SURPRISING NEWS

The rain was abysmal and added to Lady Everleigh Winslow's great displeasure as she sat before her father. Her presence had been requested without the accompaniment of Miss Owens, her former governess, and now companion. Everleigh's attention was veering to the lead windowpane where the raindrops were falling in zigzag patterns. It had been raining since yesterday and she was tired of being cooped up indoors. She was longing for the rose bushes that had been her sole focus since her Mama had passed into Heaven's gates three springs past. Tending to the roses in the vast garden where so many beautiful memories had been created somehow made her feel close to Mama still.

"Are you listening?" huffed the Marquess of Thornwhistle. From his irate glare in her direction, Everleigh knew that he was quickly losing patience with her. His dark eyes were tired and weary from age as his square jaw ticked in irritation.

"Of course. Do go on," she directed with a wave of her hand and then lowered her jade eyes to the carpet in a meek, mild manner. The carpet's brilliant fibers were woven in dark burgundy and navy with a floral pattern and braided scrollwork along its edges.

Frowning at her, her father continued, "This is the appropriate choice for you. Her Majesty has even approved of the match; the family has long been held in high esteem and the Marquess is one of Prinny's closest friends. The entire male line has served the Crown in one capacity or another. You shall be a *Marchioness*. Such a match is just what your Mama and I dreamed of for you. You could have even reached the rank of a *duchess*, but as this entire matter is time sensitive, with the Queen's approval, I see the good sense in settling you into a position such as this."

"I understand, Papa. But have you considered that the Marquess of Netherfield is older than I and has never shown any indication, at St. James's Palace or anywhere else for that matter, of having the slightest idea who I am?" Everleigh resisted the urge to squirm upon the burgundy satin padding of the settee. She was not accustomed to challenging her father's decrees. She allowed her eyes to trace the patterns as she listened to her father. That the Queen was in favor of the match did nothing to banish her fears.

"That is but a trifling matter. His grandfather, the Duke of Sutton, has decided that the man must attend to the matter of gaining heirs. You're as pretty as any other young lady and our family pedigree is exemplary," Papa readily answered.

Everleigh felt as if she were a broodmare or some sort of prized hound.

Pedigree indeed! I do not want to leave my home, especially to wed someone I know I shall never please. Besides, who will attend to the rose bushes?

She knew perfectly well the gardeners were capable of tending to every flower on the estate, but Mama had maintained that love was what made the roses flourish so. The paid gardeners would not love the roses, not as well as she did.

Besides, I feel closer to Mama when tending to the roses, almost as if she were standing over my shoulder, guiding me.

"Everleigh, my sweet daughter. You must see the sense in such a well-made match." Papa's ramrod posture remained intact even while seated in the rococo-style armchair.

"I do. I thank you for the consideration you have taken on my behalf. I only wish I had more acquaintance with the man I am to wed. 'Tis a silly wish, I know." She felt dejected and knew that no matter how she felt, or what she thought, her future was set in stone and completely unchangeable.

"We shall be dining with the Marquess and the Duke later this week. That will give you plenty of opportunity to meet with the man. You are younger, 'tis true, but age doesn't matter. You shall be a *biddable* bride and easily handle any task set before you. I would not give your hand to a man *unworthy* of you." The Marquess of Thornwhistle said in finality, letting her know that the discussion was at its conclusion. He smiled at her once again, showing an abundance of straight teeth, and then rose.

Everleigh watched her father leave the sitting room and then, when he softly closed the door, she slumped forward with relief, as much as her short corset would allow. At eight and ten she was not too young to wed, just too young for a man so much older than herself to make her his bride. Everleigh felt emptier as her spirits sank lower still. Surely a man of one and thirty who much preferred more worldly women did not want a miss who was so much younger than he.

That is exactly what he should *desire. A shy miss who he can mold as he wishes.*

What really frightened her were the rumors that shrouded the titled gentleman. Not only did he keep company in the same social circle as the Prince, but he was also involved very passionately and publicly with the opera singer Miss O'Brady who was the current favorite of *the ton*. Their affair daily fueled the gossip sheets.

Miss O'Brady was one of the leading performers at Covent Garden. She was also a widowed lady but chose to retain her professional name after her husband had passed on. Her performances were always sold-out events and the lavish parties held after each performance were scandalous; filled with revelry and debauchery. It was not unheard of for titled men to take to the theater to court paramours, some very publicly, but a performer was strictly off limits to the peerage in seeking a spouse. True, she was a brunette beauty with vivid purple eyes and the voice of an angel, but respectability within *the ton* was a hard thing to attain when one had fallen so far. The lady could marry a titled gentleman who could give her status and wealth, but the poor creature would still be ostracized within certain circles no matter how far she rose.

My peers would think it ridiculous to ever make a comparison when a marquess's daughter was so far above the singer.

Everleigh would have a comfortable home with Netherfield being her due. Her husband's actions would be his own.

Perhaps it is the principle of the thing.

Miss O'Brady and she were not just social circles apart, but worlds apart. Everleigh did not possess the level of talent and poise the singer possessed. The Marquess of Netherfield was sure to find her lacking and would grow bored with her. Mayhap even send her off to an estate far away. Everleigh wasn't opposed to rusticating in the country, but missing out on so much that London had to offer would bring her such unhappy. Her future was bleak indeed. She had been raised with the understanding that her one duty was to marry well. Her most valuable assets were her virtue and bloodline. She didn't believe that a love match was even a possibility for herself, she merely hoped to esteem her future husband and in return earn his regard.

Dear Mama, how your guidance is sorely needed. I miss you, endlessly. How would you advise me now?

Taking a deep breath, Everleigh wondered if she would have a season and officially be presented at Court. Would she simply be wed and then presented? Either way, it was not something that she had any say in. Everleigh had the next few days to forget about what was to come and let her fears subside, if that was possible. Her presentation to *Society* had been delayed by two years with her father's blessing. Had this match been in the making the entire time?

Everleigh had been to St. James's Palace a number of times as King George and Queen Charlotte were her paternal great-uncle and aunt. It was expected that she and her father would attend all festivities there. While it was not a wholesome atmosphere, that of the Court, she had been privy to outrageous gossip and events; it was an unavoidable part of her upbringing. Mama had said that she had learned the proper way to curtsey before she ever took her first steps.

While she did not truly understand what happened behind the closed doors of the Princes' suites, she had heard enough to know that it was all highly immoral. That her betrothed was a party to all that entailed, had been for quite some time, didn't help to ease her anxiety at the unsuitability of the match. Still, what titled male, or one in the line of succession, of a similar age as he hadn't been privy to the Prince's company?

Not only was her intended the grandson of a duke, his father had also assumed the Marquessate when he had discovered a plot against the Crown. The family line was comprised of heroic men. Even if they were free to behave as scandalously as they liked, the pedigree was undeniably incomparable.

The sitting room door opened and in glided Miss Owens, whose peaches and cream complexion blended wonderfully with her pale pink morning dress. Her blonde hair was arranged atop her head in a serviceable knot. A smile graced her face as she spied Everleigh. From her youthful manner and effervescence for life, one would never know that Miss Owens was nearing forty. Sitting down beside Everleigh, she reached over and patted the back of her hand.

"Is all well?" her companion inquired.

"As well as I can expect. Papa has decided that I am to wed the Marquess of Netherfield." Everleigh frowned as her blonde brows drew together.

"I see. That is not unexpected news…"

"Even so, I do not think it a wise decision. I shall pale in *every* comparison to his paramour."

"You are superior in *every way* to that woman," Miss Owens stated emphatically.

"You know I adore you, but neither your good opinion nor anyone else's matters when it comes to what the *Marquess* believes. My entire happiness rests on his shoulders, and if I cannot charm him, what will become of *me*? Of *you*?"

Everleigh felt a single tear trickle down her cheek. She hastily brushed it away with her fingers.

I don't wish to be such a mulish creature. What is wrong with me?

"You are a well-bred lady and you have been expertly raised as such. You know how to run a household and you will be the consummate hostess. You have nothing to fear, so set these fears aside and approach this with a clear head and heart." Miss Owens nodded as she met Everleigh's eyes.

Everleigh straightened her shoulders and replied, "You are right. I am being a poor-spirited miss. I know nothing until I meet with the

Marquess. I shall do as you say and reserve all judgment until I have at least met the man."

"That is a very wise course of action and I commend your resolve." Miss Owens beamed at her.

Rising, Everleigh made her way over to the window and peered out. Through the drizzle, she could see the beloved rose bushes.

Just like my beloved roses, I can weather any storm. I should like to take a few clippings with me to plant in my new garden, should permission be given to do so. For I cannot bear the thought of leaving them behind.

3

EXCELLENT COMPANY

fter ensuring that all was ready for his departure the next morning, Gideon directed the footmen to have his copper tub filled and summoned his valet, Gibbons, to attend to his attire as he bathed. While he was more than capable of putting his wardrobe together himself, he preferred to leave it to Gibbons to handle so he could focus on his patients above all else.

Gibbons is apt to suffer a fit were I to leave the manor in a state not befitting my invitation to Bramley Hall. Having been chastised before, I don't relish the scolding again.

Standing before his full-length mahogany mirror, Gideon inspected himself. He was not adept at tying a complicated cravat, so he patiently watched as Gibbons saw to the task. His trousers were black, as were his polished boots. His white linen shirt and burgundy waistcoat would pair nicely with his black fitted tailcoat. His wardrobe consisted primarily of black as it was easy to hide the stains of his profession when needed. Stains from bodily functions were a bugger to remove and he disliked handing over such duties to his housekeeper. Nodding at his reflection and thanking his valet, he made his way from his bedchamber, down the staircase, and came to a stop in the foyer before Murdock.

"Good evening, sir," greeted Murdock with a dignified bow of his head.

"Good evening, Murdock. Has Delaney taken care of the medical supplies yet?"

"He has and was whistling a merry tune as he went off to see to the task. I rather believe he likes to do the organizing, and the thought of being the one in charge seems to enliven him."

"Indeed. He is an amiable enough fellow." Gideon stated as he awaited his outerwear.

"Very well, sir, you are in fine form this evening. I have given instructions to have your buggy readied." Murdock handed over his charcoal-colored greatcoat and assisted his master in donning it. Next, he reached to the left to lift the beaver skin top hat from the small table where he had laid it. Once the butler passed it to Gideon and it was in place atop Gideon's golden hair, Gideon cast an appreciative smile at his butler and waited as he opened the door.

Stepping through the door, Gideon briskly trod to his buggy and climbed into it. He never minded driving himself wherever he was to go: it was easier to drive himself than wait on another man to fill the role as there were many times when he was needed urgently. There were many late nights that came with being a physician and his guilt would have pummeled him if he knew that somewhere in the dark nights, a servant waited to drive him home. It simply would not do, so he drove himself.

At the quick click of Gideon's tongue, Perseus began a trot down the gravel driveway and came out onto the lane. Twilight had crept across the sky and the blue and purple clouds that were embracing the moon allowed a little glow to shine down to light his way. The sound of frogs greeted his ears as an errant bug or two flew within his view. Soon, he caught sight of the manor home of the Earl of Bramley. Gideon took the slight curve of the lane and let Perseus lead them up the driveway to the main entrance.

This stone Hall was a tribute to those who had come before. It was maintained with extreme diligence and was a vital piece of history for the nation. Kings and queens had slept within its walls. Lord Bramley had invited Gideon into his study one evening after dinner and the pair had pored over a diary of one of His Lordship's grandfathers who happened to be heavily involved in espionage for the Crown. Further diaries gave accounts of the succeeding male heirs dabbling here and there in covert assignments. When Gideon had closed one leather journal, he had inquired whether Lord Bramley was also involved in the family tradition. With a gleam in his eyes and a shrug of his shoulder, the man had refused to answer. Gideon's respect for the fellow had grown ten-fold.

A liveried groom met him as he halted the horse and buggy. Gideon alighted from his conveyance and handed over the reins. With a nod to the groom, he removed his leather driving gloves and laid them atop the seat. Then taking his white evening gloves from his waistcoat pocket, he pulled them on. He adjusted his tailcoat and patted his neckcloth. Gideon was pleased that, though padded shoulders were all the rage, he had no need for such cumbersome things.

Gideon was thankful that the Lord and Lady of the Hall neither stood upon ceremonious airs nor upheld the strictures of Society; one could be at complete ease in their presence. Gideon had been raised as a gentleman, though, and manners had been ingrained in him from a young age. He would not be remiss in his social graces.

Using the golden knocker affixed to the ornate wooden door, Gideon thought it odd that Billingsley had not opened the door before he had to knock.

We're all aging as the days pass, some more than others it seems.

The butler opened the door within the next few seconds and greeted Gideon with a dignified grace. Once Gideon stood in the foyer, he handed over his outerwear.

"If you would follow me, Doctor, the lord and lady are expecting you in the drawing room," Billingsley informed him with a bow of his gray head.

"Thank you," Gideon nodded his gratitude and followed after the butler. He noted a few new pieces of landscapes that lined the walls and stopped a moment to inspect one. Seeing the familiar signature of Lady Hathwell gave him a reason to smile. The lady was indeed talented and he was glad she freely shared her art.

Perhaps I shall commission her to paint Netherfield. 'Twould make an excellent addition to the collection there. Francis could have no objection to such a project.

Hearing a throat being cleared, Gideon turned back to follow Billingsley, and within a few more steps they stood outside of the drawing room. He waited for the butler to open the door and announce him, then walked through the door and closed the distance to the Earl and his Countess who were standing before him in welcome.

Gideon beamed as he took Lady Bramley's gloved hand and kissed her knuckles. He bowed to her and then turned to Lord Bramley and bowed before him as well.

"So good of you to join us," His Lordship warmly spoke.

"I thank you again for the invitation. 'Twas timely since tomorrow I shall be departing for Netherfield. My grandfather has summoned me to my brother's estate and I have no inkling why," Gideon confided. His eyes scanned the golden hues of the drawing room before returning to his hosts.

"Please make yourself comfortable, Dr. Carrow," directed Lady Bramley. She indicated an ornate armchair with gold padding. When she took her own seat across from him, he sat as his host claimed the chair beside his wife's.

"I say, seeing one's family is always a good reason to return home. I do hope you find whatever awaits you to not be terribly disagreeable," replied Lord Bramley. The gentleman wore a dark green tailcoat and tan-colored trousers. His silk waistcoat was a sage green with tiny golden embroidered flowers. He was far from a dandy but his mode of dress served to show his rank within the aristocracy.

"I shall soon discover the answer. I dislike the idea of the Duke and my brother disagreeing and I'm shaking in my boots at the idea of having to intervene in whatever has caused the concern to arise." Gideon smiled wanly.

"You have my support, no matter what you discover," stated His Lordship.

"You are most kind," Gideon nodded his thanks.

"Will you be gone long, Doctor?" inquired Lady Bramley. She was stunningly attired in rich blues and the high-waisted cut of her dinner gown almost hid the curve of her swelling stomach. Her bright sapphire eyes were lit with curiosity.

"Have no fear, I shall soon be returned. Your little one's arrival is not due for months yet and you have always been the picture of perfect health," Gideon offered his assurances. "And Delaney will be in attendance should anything occur." Lady Bramley had safely birthed two other babes, and he had no reason to believe that the next one would be cause for concern once the time arrived.

"Excellent news. I thank you for your consideration for all of Bramley," Lord Bramley said with a genuine smile.

Billingsley entered the drawing room and announced that dinner was served. The trio rose and made their way to the dining room. Gideon felt peaceful. Dinner among his friends was exactly what he needed to bolster his low spirits.

4

DAILY TASKS

Bright sunlight cast its glow across Everleigh's bedchamber the next morning as her abigail arranged her hair in the usual style. Picking up the curling iron from its resting spot in the pan situated over the hot coals of the fireplace, the ladies' maid lifted the hair alongside Everleigh's right cheek and twisted it around the rod. The heat was not bothersome to Everleigh. She welcomed it as she tended to chill no matter the season excepting summer, of course. The abigail unwound the curl and proceeded to use the tongs on the other half of her hair that lay straight against her cheek. When that task was complete, the maid returned the iron to its place and fussed with the curls hanging down Everleigh's nape.

"You are all finished, my lady," the abigail said as she backed up a few paces. The white cap covering her head bobbed as she moved.

"You are a wonder, thank you," Everleigh expressed her gratitude with a smile.

"Will you be needing anything else?"

"I am set to meet with Mrs. Rowley in a few minutes. I shall await her in my private sitting room. There is to be a delivery from the modiste this afternoon, please see that the gown is pressed and stored appropriately." Everleigh stood from her dressing table and moved over to her full-length mirror. She turned her head one way and then another.

I suppose I shall do.

Her morning gown of pale blue shimmered in the reflected light. The wide midnight blue ribbon situated just under her ample bosom tied in with the darker blue flowers the abigail had woven into her hair.

"Yes, my lady, I will see to it at once," the maid said as she began to put away pins and other odds and ends that littered the dressing table.

Everleigh nodded to her, then glided over to the small table beside her four-poster bed. Resting atop the table was her diary where she kept important details relating to the running of the household. The small leather volume also contained her thoughts about dresses and pairing her jewels with her attire. Some pages contained her feelings about the latest book she was reading as she rarely had another to confide in other than Miss Owens.

Today, Everleigh would be meeting with the housekeeper alone. This was a task that she felt she could easily perform without aid. Miss Owens had been instrumental in guiding Everleigh with learning how to properly run a household as the lady herself had been a gentleman's daughter. When the family became impoverished, Miss Owens had been brought into their employ.

Everleigh's mother had already imparted a wealth of knowledge to her, but there had still been some things Everleigh felt she was ignorant of and she did not wish to err. Having Miss Owens by her side to rely upon had eased her nervous heart and mind.

On silk-slippered feet, Everleigh made her way through her bedchamber and toward the adjoining room that served as her private sitting area. The rosewood desk sat prominently upon the large rug which was decorated in hues of blue with a floral motif. Everleigh pulled the chair from underneath the desk and sat. She leafed through her notes, then set her book aside. She longed to be outside amongst the roses, but Everleigh had duties that must be seen to first.

Turning her head to the window behind her, she let the sun's warmth shine upon her as she basked in the silence of the room, and let her worries fall away.

A soft knock at the door pulled her attention toward the other side of the room.

"Do come in," she softly called out.

Mrs. Rowley entered the chamber and closed the door behind her. She walked to the desk and curtsied. "Am I interrupting, my lady?"

"Of course not, as this is our arranged hour. I trust that you are well?"

"I am, thank you. And you, my lady?" Mrs. Rowley straightened.

It wasn't customary for the lady of the house to inquire after the health of her servants, and when in Papa's company, Everleigh never would have dared to. Everleigh was of the opinion that kindness never hurt a situation and while she may, she was pleased to show goodwill and hoped that in her new role as Marchioness she could continue along in this manner.

"In fine health. Will you not be seated?" Everleigh waved her hand toward the chair situated opposite herself. The housekeeper sat and placed her own diary on the desk before her. Her gray hair was styled in a severe bun and her black dress made her pasty skin look even more pale, almost to the point of bearing a sickly tinge.

"What shall we discuss today? The menu has been prepared and approved of by Mr. Hendrick for the week," began Everleigh.

"We shall need to hire a new maid and replace the footman that was let go last week."

Everleigh nodded in agreement, then proceeded to discuss other mundane household issues as well as which agencies would provide the best references for the new employees. They went over the ledgers for household expenses and soon an hour had passed by.

"Goodness, I do believe that we have managed to go through both of our lists quite effectively, Mrs. Rowley," Everleigh spoke warmly to her.

"Indeed. Thank you for your time, my lady," said the housekeeper as she rose from her seat and closed the brown book in her hands.

"It has been quite a productive morning." Everleigh watched as the housekeeper reached the door and opened it. Once they bid each other a good day, Mrs. Rowley exited the room and closed the door behind her.

Everleigh picked up her diary and rose from her chair, tucking it under her arm. Leaving her chambers, she padded down the staircase and made her way to the formal sitting room where Miss Owens sat reading the morning paper. Her companion looked up at her entrance and smiled at her.

"How did everything go?" Miss Owens inquired from her spot before the fireplace. Her kind brown eyes searched Everleigh's face.

"Well. I am happy to have that done for the day. Now, what else do we have for today?" Everleigh came to sit beside her on the settee.

"Well, Signor Marino will not be here until this afternoon for your dancing lessons, so we have the morning to ourselves. We arranged the flowers yesterday and embroidered as well. Today, we could delve into watercolors or go for a stroll in Hyde Park." Miss Owens ran a hand over the folds of her lavender morning dress and then met her gaze.

"What are you reading?" Everleigh reached her hand over to pick up the morning paper. Bringing the papers to her own lap, she let her eyes trail down to the society pages. Miss O'Brady was performing tonight at Covent Garden. An idea began to form in her mind.

I do hope that I can bring Papa on board with my blossoming scheme...

Everleigh felt bold, but her mind would not be swayed from its current course.

5

COMING HOME AGAIN

Gideon was prepared for all manner of calamities to greet him once he stepped booted foot into his brother's home. Whatever was currently sending his grandfather into a fit was sure to have some weighty importance. The man was not altogether unreasonable, and it was Gideon's hope that this crisis could be calmed. However, when his thoughts drifted to the cryptic nature of his brother's missive, he felt uneasy. How could the actions of his older brother affect him in such a way as to alter his own life? He would support his brother no matter what; he had earned that loyalty. As Perseus gained the distance, Gideon's nerves grew more fraught.

Before long, he was trotting up the gravel driveway of Netherfield Hall at last. Crisp-leafed oak trees and fading wisteria lined the sides of the vast estate. Withering ivy still clung to the stone facade. It was the perfect picture of a country mansion. The trees were just beginning to brown, starting to take their autumnal slumber.

A footman dressed in forest green livery approached Perseus and reached for his bridle to stay him. Gideon climbed down from his mount and nodded his gratitude to the servant. He moved quickly up the steps and was soon standing before the open door. Mr. Collins, the butler, was standing silently with a ramrod posture. He was not the butler from Gideon's childhood, as Mr. Mayhew had retired. Mr.

Collins was a replacement that Francis had elevated from senior footman to the esteemed post of butler.

He was a fine choice, Gideon scoffed. *If being lax at times and given to ignoring orders and doing the opposite of what was directed were indeed qualities to praise. He really should be replaced. I recall my last visit when I requested a brandy and he brought me tea instead. Then there was the other visit when he placed me in the wrong bedchamber, much to Lady Agatha's dismay.*

Gideon had barely escaped with his dignity intact.

'Twas a mercy the lady was already wed and had also been a victim of the butler's bumbling ways.

"Welcome, Doctor," droned Mr. Collins with a bow of his head. His dark hair was styled in the Brutus fashion, cropped close to his scalp. The man didn't have one errant wrinkle, in either garment or face.

"Thank you. I believe the Duke and my brother are awaiting me," Gideon replied.

"Very well," the butler held out his hand for Gideon's greatcoat and topper. Gideon passed them along to the man. Then Mr. Collins stowed the outerwear and indicated that Gideon was to follow him. A groom would deliver his saddlebags to the house in short order, where a footman would store their contents away in the bedchamber that he usually inhabited while in residence. Though he had spent his youth at Netherfield, those chambers had been in another wing of the manor.

Mr. Collins led the way to the study where he knocked once, and when a muffled "enter" was issued, he opened the door and stood aside. Gideon cautiously stepped one foot after another until he had reached the middle of the room. He stood upon the large ornate Aubusson carpet and looked from one unhappy face to the twisted scowl of another. His brother was seated behind his mahogany desk with his ledgers out before him. Their grandfather was seated on a cream-padded settee near the fireplace, where the blazing fire was illuminating the room with a soft incandescence.

"Here you are at last. I'm counting on your good judgment to sway your brother from his current path," said the Duke with an authoritative tone.

"Indeed? And am I to know the particulars before I endeavor to undertake this task, Grandfather?" Gideon queried with one blond eyebrow raised.

Here begins the trouble.

"He is absconding with a *light skirt*! He means to wed the *trollop* and make her a *Marchioness*! An *opera singer* to be the next lady of the house! Can you imagine such sordid business? And let us not fail to mention that she is divorced!" The Duke rose from his place by the roaring fire and came to stand beside Gideon. His grandfather looked older than his age of three and seventy. His skin was pale and papery as frown lines marred his face. His gray hair was immaculate despite his agitation. He was dressed all in black a la Beau Brummell, the current leading arbiter of male fashion. His grandfather looked every inch the titled peer posed from a fashion plate.

Even at his advanced age, he carries the look well.

"That is *enough*, Grandfather, I beg of you. Please do not dishonor my beloved with such a colorful narrative." Francis's tone was gruff as he brought his right hand up to rub his face in a gesture of frustration.

He does not deny this. How has this come to be?

Gideon felt ice flowing through his veins as he attempted to stay silent and glean all he could before reacting.

"What I am saying, young man, is no different than that which the gossip columns write. She is inferior to your title and rank. She shall bring ruin upon us all. You must think of your *family*, your progeny." The Duke stood his ground.

"This is my future happiness at stake. Miss O'Brady will be my wife and the mother to my children. She is due respect," groaned Francis with fatigue.

"There will be no future whatsoever *if you take her for a bride!*" bellowed the Duke.

"Then you leave me no *choice*. I shall renounce my title and leave everything behind!" Francis stated as he rose from his leather chair. He held his blond head high with resolve and purpose.

"You would be so selfish and cruel?"

"You would have me be so! I *cannot* exist in a world where Shannon lives and I am not with her. I am doing my best to solve this issue, but you are thwarting me at every turn. Grandfather, where is your heart?

Have you none?" Francis soundlessly moved over to stand a few inches from the gentlemen.

"*Pah!* Why do you speak of matters of the heart? What does such a thing matter where *duty*, *honor*, and *respect* are concerned? You shall be the ruination of this family! I will not stand meekly by and watch you take down the entire Marquessate! You will set this all aside and attend to what matters most!"

"And what is that? What is *duty* and *honor* if I'm to spend the rest of my life without the woman who makes me come alive? Who brings me joy and gives me purpose? You expect me to turn away from her. This I cannot do! I'll not be swayed."

Gideon reached out a hand to lay upon the Duke's shoulder, but the Duke batted it away. Concern for his aged family member seized his heart.

He will do himself real harm if he cannot calm himself.

"Mark my words, young man! When your passions have cooled and she has lost her beauty, you will be a great *nothing* of a man. You will have given up everything and your ardent *love* will be nothing but bitter ash! And where will you be then?" The Duke turned his back and walked over to peer from the window.

"Then so be it, Grandfather. At least then you will have the very great pleasure of knowing you were right, yet again." Francis looked defiant with dark smudges under his gray eyes.

Waving his hand in the air, the Duke spoke, "Perhaps you can make him see reason, Gideon. For if he fails us, the *family line ends with his idiocy!*" The Duke turned to face the brothers.

"I am not sure what can be done, Grandfather. I mean to counsel my brother, but he seems determined in this course of action." Gideon softly spoke.

What has come over my brother? He has always been so devoted and loyal. Were I to believe in such nonsense as witchcraft, I would be tempted to lay the blame entirely at her feet. An opera singer? But perhaps, she's angling for a title? Is it possible that Francis has been completely taken in by her?

"Then you must give up your generous allowance! Are you prepared for that? To lose your practice, your patients, your ambitions? For you certainly cannot afford your current lifestyle on a doctor's wages. I cannot summon another marquess from thin air; Francis must be made to see reason and do his duty." The Duke slammed the tip of his walking cane down on the carpet in anger.

Gideon swallowed and gazed absently around the study. Was he capable of picking up the pieces after his brother destroyed everything?

What has become of Francis's dedication and duty? To see our ancestral home, our proud lineage be lost because of him, wounds me deeply. I never expected the day would arrive that he would throw it all away... And for what? An inferior love match?

"I shall leave you to it. I am a tired man. This... has all been too much for my constitution. I fear that at any moment I may perish right on the spot," the Duke dejectedly sighed. He looked crestfallen and, though he had always been in the best of health, he now bore a broken quality like a discarded porcelain doll.

Fear filled Gideon's heart as he observed his grandfather.

I can't lose him too...

"Let me examine you, Grandfather?" entreated Gideon. He did not desire to see his grandfather so affected by his brother's actions. When death came to call upon the older man, he longed for it to be a peaceful passing, not brought about by disappointment and regret. He was the only remaining family member that Gideon now had whom he could esteem to be like.

After all he has done to ensure that Francis and I have been well-cared for, I cannot turn my back on him. I must seek to bend Francis to his will.

"No. I do not need to be attended to. I am not some doddering weakling. I shall lie down and try to forget ungrateful grandsons who seek to be the end of a legacy." The Duke glared at Francis, then shuffled over to the door. He rapped the door with the golden griffin head of his cane. Mr. Collins promptly opened the door and ushered him from the room.

Gideon ran his hands through his golden hair and exhaled.

What am I to say? How am I to sway Francis when he has so completely made up his mind? How can he be willing to throw his entire life away?

"I do apologize. You must know that I don't do this lightly. I can no more say goodbye to the woman who holds my heart than I could sever my own arm from my body." Francis stubbornly regarded him.

"I cannot pretend to understand your feelings..." Gideon trailed off. He felt sick inside. His stomach was churning over.

"My feelings? I think I have duly stated them."

Gideon's shoulders drooped as the weight of his family's legacy settled onto them. He remained silent as he walked to the desk and sat in one of the armchairs before it.

"You have not heard the worst part that Grandfather had inflicted upon me."

"What is that?" Gideon watched his brother close the distance to take his own seat behind the desk.

"He has arranged a marriage. I could not in good conscience be wed to another when my nights, my passion would belong to another. I've not led a Godly life, but I would not wish to wed another when I can offer her only unfaithfulness. I shan't begin a marriage that is doomed from its very beginning for I shall never stand another's touch. 'Twould be unfair of me. Heirs are needed and *I won't* produce them. I do not want to be the villain that I would surely become were I to let Shannon go," Francis confessed as he glared at the fire.

"How do you know that the woman Grandfather has chosen would not suit you?"

Francis threw back his head and laughed. "You, my dear little brother, have never been in love. For if you ever had been, you would know that to love is to be consumed by fire. Loving is to burn, to yearn with every particle of your being for another. Someday you will burn for someone and then, and only then, shall you truly understand."

"I very much doubt that. I consider myself a man of Science. I approach things differently than most of my acquaintances. I've never felt this fire you speak of, and in truth, I hope now I never will." Gideon's top lip curled in disgust.

Love should not make one weak, or turn them away from their responsibilities. If that is to be the case, I shall wash my hands of the entire thing here and now. Never will I allow my heart to lead me to ruination! Even if a union were to be passionate, I would not desire this damning flame that has turned my brother away from all he was expected to do and be.

Gideon was growing morose with this discussion. "Perchance you could learn to love her in time."

"*No*, that I will never do. I must follow my heart, even if it leads to my ruin." Francis clenched his jaw.

"I would spare you any hardship that was within my power. But this… it means giving up your legacy. Will you not come to regret such a monumental decision as time passes by?"

"I have thought of little else. Gideon, please, please try to understand."

"I don't mean to distress you any more than you currently are. But this has landed me in unfamiliar territory. I never expected you to turn your back on the family. Surely, there are other options?" Gideon implored his brother to reconsider. "We must have hope that-"

"I wish that I could see the world as you do. God has not been too kind to me. He has given my heart to someone *Society* loves to see on stage, but spurns as one of their own. If there was a *just God*, he would have made a way out of this mess, for all of us. But He is silent when I pray. And brother, I have prayed and begged and pleaded upon my knees. You are my only hope. Do not ask me to go through this life leg shackled to another when my true love is forever separated from my side." Francis sat forward in his chair and brought his hands to rest atop his desk.

"So you must give up everything and follow your heart," Gideon said solemnly.

I love my brother, but how will he not come to regret this? 'Tis his duty to produce an heir and ensure the family name and holdings. This was always his destiny!

"That is the way of it. Don't make unfair judgements, not until you meet Shannon. Tonight! We can attend Covent Garden and, after her performance, we can retire to my townhouse. That's all at present I will ask of you."

"I shall meet this request of yours; I am eager to meet this woman you would toss everything aside for. But I am undecided on championing your cause."

Francis rose to his feet. "That is all I am asking! Meet her." The hopeful tinge to Francis's voice was like a dagger to Gideon's soul.

"I can agree to that as well. Does the lady who holds your heart know that you mean to give up the title?"

"No, no one does." Francis walked to the liquor cart and poured them each a glass of brandy, then brought the glasses back to his desk and handed one to Gideon. He raised his glass and toasted. "To the unexpected endeavors we all must embark upon."

Gideon tried to smile, but it felt disingenuous. His heart was not in it.

Directly after finishing his drink, Gideon left the study and took the staircase steps two at a time to reach his grandfather's bedchamber. After he had rapped upon the door and been bid to enter, he closed the distance to the lounge where his grandfather was reclining and bowed at his waist. Gideon then bent down on his haunches and addressed his grandfather who was looking at him expectantly.

"I came to see how you are faring," he softly spoke.

"That depends entirely upon you. Have you managed to talk sense into my grandson?" the Duke peered up at him through pinched eyes.

"I have not. Not yet at least. We are to make haste to the theater, so I may meet this goddess."

"*Pah!* You will not let me down? You would not turn your back on familial responsibilities? I say, I cannot quite understand the youth of today. Shunning their duties and thinking of their own selfish desires before all else." His grandfather turned his head and stared at the papered wall to his left.

"I shall do my best," Gideon assured him as he reached for the thin hand of his grandfather and began to count his pulse. The older gentleman allowed it but would not turn his head to face him.

"You will send me reports regarding your progress? I shall depart on the morrow for Sutton."

"I shall if that will alleviate some of your distress." Gideon set his hand back down beside him.

"What will alleviate my distress is to have a grandson that will do his *duty*! You must step in and make him see reason. 'Tis entirely unfair to ask you to take this responsibility on your shoulders, broad as they may be. You and Francis have always been so closely knit, if there is a chance that he will listen to anyone's council, it is yours."

Gideon did not reply as he stood.

What is there for me to say?

He smiled tightly at his grandfather and bowed before him, then he turned and exited the room. He made for the library on the first floor of the house and sat heavily in one of the leather chairs, ruminating on life choices and undesired titles.

I won't make judgments until I have met the lady and gathered all the facts. Only then may I form a true opinion. But how I fear that no matter what courses this decision sets us on, things will never be as they once were.

6

PERSUADING PAPA

*E*verleigh studied her reflection in the mirror above her rosewood dressing table as she turned her head from side to side. Her abigail had arranged her golden tresses in the current Greek fashion. It was gathered atop the crown of her head with cascading ringlets hanging down either side of her face, tickling the delicate flesh of her bare shoulders. But it was a small irritation to endure in order to look her best. Her jade eyes took in the elegant tilt of her nose and the graceful slope of her neck. Her gaze settled upon her full lips. She had seen women who had either the upper or the lower lip larger than the other, but hers were perfectly matched in size. Her alabaster skin was blessedly blemish free. Everleigh was pleased with her appearance; she could find no discernable flaws.

Lovingly, she touched the necklace resting upon her clavicle. The sapphire gems and diamonds were a perfect match to the earbobs hanging from her small earlobes.

Mama had loved these jewels that Papa had gifted her with upon their honeymoon.

Everleigh could feel her mother's presence when wearing the jewels, and this gave her some comfort, aiding in soothing her nerves for whatever the evening may hold. She was pleased that Papa had retrieved them from the vault and allowed her to wear them for this one occasion.

Rising from her cream upholstered bench she padded over to her full-length mirror. The carved mahogany roses were smooth to the touch and appealing to behold, especially when the winter snows covered her beloved garden. Everleigh twirled in place to ensure all was well with her ensemble. The bedecked evening gown was a sage green that was embroidered with tiny golden flowers. Matching green slippers peeked from beneath the hem and made her feel exquisite in their fine silk.

She took a deep breath and took a few steps back to her dressing table. Reaching it, she bent forward to retrieve her matching reticule and lace fan.

Everleigh left her bedchamber and traveled the short distance along the corridor, then down the mahogany staircase. Once she reached the foyer where Mr. Ashburn, the butler, waited by the front door, she saw that her father was already in his outerwear. He looked every inch the proper marquess from his polished shoes to his gleaming black topper, and he was ready to embark upon the night's entertainment. If he thought her choice of venue, Covent Garden, was odd, he didn't voice it. Her father who could be oblivious at times, and he wouldn't ever discover that the coming entertainment was to satisfy her unending curiosity about Miss O'Brady. Everleigh had never attended the theater before and hoped her excursion would relieve the unpleasantness and fear she had been suffering from since learning of her upcoming nuptials. She had gently persuaded her father by voicing that it was an opportunity for her to cultivate her tastes.

Feeling a sudden case of nerves assault her senses, Everleigh let her thoughts tumble around in her mind.

Would I be any rival for her beauty? Her poise? Her many charming qualities?

With effort, she forced her fears to subside. She accepted her father's arm and allowed him to lead her from the townhouse to the awaiting carriage. A footman assisted her ascent into the conveyance, and she took her forward-facing bench seat. The royal blue velvet cushions were comfortable and matched the drapes in ostentatious elegance. From the gold-rimmed carriage wheels to the sleek pair of gray horses, they made a statement of wealth. Once her father was seated opposite her, he rapped upon the ceiling with the handle of his walking cane and off they went.

Their townhouse was located in fashionable Mayfair, in the West End of London. It was a neighborhood occupied by the elite of *the ton*, and near many of Papa's like-minded peers within the House of Lords.

They soon reached Covent Garden, located on Bow Street, and waited in the line of carriages for their turn to alight. Her father had been silent for the entirety of the ride, and she had followed his lead. Everleigh found it was often simpler to remain quiet in his presence, but at times she wondered if doing so made her seem simple-minded. Certainly, she had thoughts and opinions, but unless pressed for them, she preferred to keep them to herself, lest she cause any offense or embarrassment for herself or another. Only her companion heard the majority of her ideas and hopes.

The groom opened the carriage door, and she took his gloved hand to climb down the polished wooden steps that awaited her. Her father followed behind and, once he reached her side, Everleigh took his arm. Her palm rested on his forearm as he led her from the street, past the statues, and into the vestibule. The patent lamps and elegant chandeliers cast a glow that illuminated the fine silks and glittering jewels of the patrons.

A grand staircase and its landing were the central third part of the hall that would lead to their box, but their progress there was slow. Several elegantly clad lords and ladies stopped to greet the Marquess and engage in light conversation. Her presence was occasionally acknowledged with the slight nod of a head, but as she had not yet been debuted, conversation was withheld. Tonight, Everleigh was merely a decoration upon her father's arm.

And I am happy to remain within his shadow.

Conversation soon waned and the Marquess was able to ascend the staircase and enter the anteroom. He turned to Everleigh with a benign smile and patted the hand that still rested on his forearm. Everleigh's gaze fixed on the statue of Shakespeare, which rested upon a pedestal. The Bard remained a celebrated playwright and she wondered if even the shifting sands of time would ever change his impact upon the theater. She had read his plays and sonnets and had enjoyed them, though she secretly was more inclined to lose herself within the pages of a gothic novel. Though her father was not a promoter of women's education beyond household duties, he had grudgingly allowed Miss Owens to introduce her to the world of Shakespeare. Her mother had fully approved of reading for pleasure and edification, and had encouraged her to pursue it and fill her mind with a variety of ideas.

Thank heavens for the pin money that allows me to purchase my novels.

The strong heroines were delightful and Everleigh was fascinated by the very idea of women being equal to men. She was content to let her father dictate her life, and she did not envision herself ever putting on airs regarding her own importance. Not only did she lack the fortitude to do so, she rather liked knowing what was expected of her fulfilling those expectations well. She could applaud the women who defied convention, but she would not ever be one of them.

Is it wrong that I only wish to tend to the roses and make a good match? I find contentment in the simple joys of my life.

In London, an evening of entertainment was far more about being seen attired in the latest fashion rather than actually taking in the performance one attended. It was a test of social skills, manners, and grace. It was about fashion, but also about presentation, and either avoiding the gossips or encouraging them, if that was a person's desire. How one presented oneself would be noted and whispered about within one's social circle. Being out, but not having been officially debuted, filled Everleigh with a distinct nervousness. While she had never erred in her limited interactions amongst *Society*, to do so now would put a blight on her reputation that would remain irregardless of whom she married or what title she assumed.

Everleigh calmed herself by remembering her mother's gentle grace, which she had always sought to emulate.

No one shall engage with me, really. I have merely to smile and nod and all will be well.

She was soothed by those thoughts.

Her father led her to the right, and soon they were entering the box-lobby. After they were ushered into the square box and had taken their seats, Everleigh smiled delightedly. The light blue seat padding was hidden beneath her sage gown. The gray wall panels surrounding them were decorated with wreaths of honeysuckle and golden accents giving their setting elegance. The subdued tones allowed the glittering gowns and wafting feathers of the patrons to be viewed without obstruction. Everleigh directed her attention to the large stage. With the curtains still drawn it looked as if the entire building was in the shape of a horseshoe. Looking up, she took in the painted cupola and square compartments. Quickly averting her gaze, she scanned the crowd below her. As she did not wish to be caught staring or, even worse, gawking, she stopped looking around and rested her gaze on the box opposite theirs.

Seeing her gaze had drifted to that box, her father leaned toward her and said, "Ah, you have spied that your Marquess is just across from us, have you, my dear?"

"I had not," Everleigh protested with a frown.

"I shall send word for his party to come and sit with us. That will make for a pleasant evening, I should think. After all, you did wish for an opportunity to better acquaint yourself with him, did you not?"

She felt horror chill a path from her heart all the way to her toes.

No! Having the Marquess sitting in our box would ruin everything!

How could she surreptitiously study the singer if her betrothed was watching her watch her?

Without waiting for a reply–what could she possibly say to stop him anyway–her father summoned the attendant to relay the invitation. He returned and patted her hand again.

I suppose this is his way of acknowledging my concerns and seeking to allay my fears?

This was foolish. How could I have imagined that all would go well according to my wishes alone?

Quite a foolhardy thing to do when the eyes of *the ton* were ever watching.

Everleigh began to wonder if word of her engagement to the Marquess had already been revealed and been spread through all of *Society.* Would they be expecting her and the Marquess to sit together? Or would this be something completely surprising that would make the gossip sheets tomorrow?

She remained quiet and, when the performance began, turned all of her attention to the woman on the stage as the lights dimmed and the curtains parted. She was lovely, even from a distance. The white

Grecian gown and its golden sash that she wore showed her figure to perfection. Her creamy skin was accentuated by the vivid scenery around her. Her hair, which was the color of burnished mahogany, cascaded in curls from atop her head, fell around her face, and rested gently on her shoulders. Dark lashes rimmed her luminous eyes. The singer moved in perfect timing to the practiced and perfected notes of the aria. She was a goddess, and there was no comparison between them, thought Everleigh.

7

INTRODUCTIONS & EMBARRASSMENTS

Gideon could finally take a deep breath. He and his brother had ridden from Netherfield to the London townhouse in record time. After a harried undertaking of baths and preparations, they were finally seated in the theater box belonging to the Marquess of Netherfield.

Gideon's thoughts kept returning to the last conversation with his grandfather. He felt a distinct and lingering pain of concern at the strain this was all putting upon the older gentleman. Though he could be prickly and at the best of times exacting, the Duke was one of his few remaining family members and respect and duty were his due. Gideon felt the pressure of expectations from both men resting heavily on his shoulders.

What a quandary! How am I meant to defuse this situation and bring us all together again? All the more reason to calm these violent waters and bring peace into the light again. This stress between all of us will do none of us any good.

When the lights dimmed and the curtains parted, Gideon was finally allowed a view of the woman at the center of all the upheaval. She was certainly a beauty, that could not be reasonably denied, and the rapt attention his brother paid her even from this distance left little doubt the man was smitten. He may even be in love with the woman, as he claimed. Gideon closed his eyes and leaned his head back.

This is a disaster. What can I possibly do to make Francis see reason? Even if the love he feels for Miss O'Brady is genuine, it does not require such foolishness and disregard. I fear anything I say will fall on deaf ears. He is too blinded by passion to consider any other view.

The door behind them opened and an attendant walked to his brother's side. Bowing low, the man engaged in a whispered exchange with the Marquess. Seeing the scowl on his brother's face, Gideon feared that it was news to do with Grandfather and made ready to rise. Francis stayed him with a wave of his hand and whispered something to the attendant, who then bowed and withdrew from the box.

"We have been summoned by The Marquess of Thornwhistle, whose box is located directly across from ours," Francis explained with a glower, marking his sincere aggravation.

"A summons?" inquired Gideon, tilting his head. "Who is the Marquess of Thornwhistle to you that he may issue such a summons?

"My future father-in-law, if Grandfather were to have his way," Francis responded darkly. "And as such, I can neither ignore him nor disregard his *invitation*, so you shall accompany me."

Gideon rose dutifully and followed in his wake. They left their current box and began the arduous walk to the other side of the theater.

"I am losing my patience with overtaxing marquesses and dukes who seek to control my life and every movement. My attention to Shannon has been abruptly interrupted and I am in a foul temper. Will they not just leave me be? Would that I could give them all the cut direct." Francis was uttering oaths under his breath which caused Gideon to raise an eyebrow as his narrative became more descriptive the further they progressed.

Along the way, Gideon spied women he assumed were prostitutes leaning against the walls, looking for gentlemen who had become bored of the performance. He felt their presence was a disgrace to the beautiful building, but knew also that it was a way of life for both these women as well as the *gentlemen* who eagerly paid for their attention. It was an immoral behavior that he alone was powerless to stop.

As a doctor, he knew the darker side of these arrangements; he knew of the diseases and the illnesses, and the other equally horrific consequences of being so free with strangers. They were not among his favorite ailments to treat, but neither could he turn them away.

Thank God Bramley is more wholesome and untouched by the vices of London.

The two finally stood outside of the box where the Marquess of Thornwhistle waited. An attendant opened the door for them to pass through before announcing them. Francis made his way to Thornwhistle's side and greeted him tersely.

Gideon entered in time to hear Thornwhistle say, "This is extraordinarily good fortune, meeting you here tonight."

"Indeed. May I introduce you to my younger brother, Dr. Carrow?" Francis moved aside and allowed Gideon to move forward. Gideon bowed to the older gentleman.

"A pleasure. Will you not both be seated at once?" Thornwhistle directed the attendant to situate two additional chairs in the space.

Gideon nodded to him and watched as the additional seats were arranged.

"May I introduce you, Dr. Carrow, to my daughter, Lady Everleigh?" Thornwhistle nodded his head to the young woman who sat toward the front of the box. She was a beauty although she was still very young. Her hair shone like burnished gold in the lowlights of the theater and her eyes were kind as they met Gideon's when he turned to bow.

Lady Everleigh remained seated as she inclined her head to him. She was graceful and slender in frame. She slowly turned her attention to his brother and then gracefully rose as she awaited his acknowledgement.

Francis stepped forward begrudgingly, and taking her hand, kissed the air above her knuckles. She smiled up at him. Hers was not the smile of a cunning miss with marriage on her mind; in fact, the lady did not even seem capable of either deviousness or deceit.

Francis did not return her smile or offer her any other greeting. Gideon was sure he felt the slight as keenly as she did. Lady Everleigh stood blinking for a moment, regained her seat and then directed her attention back to the stage.

Why is Francis so put off by a woman this charming? And why do I have the urge to shield her from the coldness of my brother?

In fact, his brother quickly turned his back to her, dismissing her entirely; all without a civil word spoken to her. Instead of taking the chair beside her, as would be expected, Francis opted for the one behind her next to her father, leaving the other for Gideon.

Her eyes continued to blink and he wondered if she was attempting to keep her emotions at bay.

Tears are certain to be quite an embarrassment for her, most especially when in full view of Society.

"I say, this is cozy," the Marquess of Thornwhistle cleared his throat. "Quite a merry way to begin your courtship. Would you care to exchange seats?"

"No, I am quite content," Francis replied with a biting tone.

Gideon felt his own temper flare as he took the seat beside her and he wondered why the older man allowed such poor behavior toward his daughter. Did she have no one to guard her honor? Mayhap the man was just as flummoxed by the predicament as he and the lady seemed to be.

What could have possibly caused my brother to give her such a cut? The poor girl...

The humming din of conversation could be heard from the sea of *Society* who were more entertained by gossip than by the opera. Gideon wasn't bothered by the noise. He watched the drama play out on the stage until he looked over his shoulder at his brother. Francis was sitting forward in his chair with an intent stare fixed upon Miss O'Brady. Gideon wondered how his dolt of a brother could dare to stare so blatantly at his mistress while in the company of his betrothed and her father. He felt embarrassed on his brother's behalf and fleetingly wished he could do something to defend Lady Everleigh's honor.

"Do you often attend the theater?" he asked, feeling it was his duty to draw her out from the charged atmosphere.

"No. In fact, this is my first experience. I am not yet out, so I don't attend many events. I had to persuade Papa to allow me to attend tonight," she confided as a blush crept into her delicate skin.

"Ah well, I do hope you find it favorable."

"It has been most enlightening. I see that your brother seems enamored," she observed as she peeked back at Francis and then at the stage again.

"Miss O'Brady is very talented," he allowed, not daring to offer any further response.

"She's also quite lovely, is she not?" Lady Everleigh arched a delicate brow, as if daring him to disagree.

"Yes, she is a beauty. However, some prefer a more refined elegance and the ease of manner that comes with being a *true lady*," he said as he leaned closer to her.

Gideon found that he didn't care whether his brother should overhear his flirting, but it was not his intention to purposely upset Francis either. He merely wished to pay Lady Everleigh the address she deserved.

"Would you be one of those 'some'?" she whispered.

His only answer was a smile before he turned his attention back to the stage. He felt her eyes lingering on him for a bit longer, then she turned her attention back to the performance.

She had a quick wit and was clearly intelligent. How could Francis dismiss her so callously?

Then he found himself wondering what color her expressive eyes were and hoped for a longer look into them, but her attention remained focused on the stage. He gave himself a mental shake.

Best to stop these thoughts right there, old boy.

"WELL, HERE WE ARE. ARE YOU READY TO BE INTRODUCED TO MY LADY?" Francis's eyes sparkled with eagerness.

After the performance, the brothers had bid the Marquess and his daughter a good evening. Gideon watched his brother's interaction with the lady, and it was bordering on the uncivil side, unwarranted regardless of what she may have said or done. Lady Everleigh, much to her credit, met his disrespect with grace. Having conversed with her, he knew that she was not an obtuse chit, and suspected she felt the snub from Francis most acutely. She was just too well schooled in the art of doing the pretty to falter before such blatant rudeness. It was a credit to her upbringing. Gideon did not envy the battle his brother would put them both through if he could not exorcize Miss O'Brady from his soul. Lady Everleigh deserved care and respect from the man who made everlasting vows to her.

The door opened to a dressing room where Miss O'Brady sat before her dressing table, clad only in a red robe. There were ladies on either side of her, in various stages of removing their garish makeup. When she caught Francis's reflection in the mirror, her face lit up with a beautiful smile. She quickly stood and made her way toward them. She reached up upon her bare tiptoes and kissed Francis's cheek.

"My love, may I introduce you to my younger brother, Gideon?" Francis took her bare hand and pressed his lips to her skin, letting his lips linger a moment longer than customary.

Miss O'Brady's eyes trailed from Gideon's boots to his topper before she bestowed that same beautiful smile on him. "How truly wonderful to meet you, at long last. Francis has shared his fondest memories of the two of you."

Gideon bowed to her and touched the brim of his topper. "Do not believe a word he says, I beg of you."

The singer laughed and Francis pulled her to his side as his arm wrapped around her waist.

"We shall all become better acquainted this evening. Hurry and dress so that we can set off for the townhouse. I have invited some of our friends as well," Francis told her with a wink.

"Always a merry diversion," Miss O'Brady remarked to Francis and then padded back over to her dressing table.

Before another dressing table, one of the other ladies rose, and let her dressing gown slip from her shoulders, revealing an expanse of creamy skin. Gideon quickly averted his eyes, just suppressing the unmanly flush that threatened to rise upon his skin. He was not averse to the human body; he had studied it in all forms in his medical texts and had seen enough while treating his patients. But he was not a man used to witnessing such vagrant displays of flesh. He had never taken a mistress and while most of his friends and acquaintances had spent time during and after their studies in brothels and in pursuit of light skirts, he had not. It was not in him to view women as entertainment. He had learned respect for the fairer sex from his mother, and knew a woman's heart was a fragile thing to be handled with the utmost care.

Perhaps it is the healer in me that makes me wish to cherish those within my care? I do not have it in me to take advantage of those who could benefit from my aid. Though I am not immune to women's charms, I can't bear to be a part of their ruination. I will not see them as sport.

"Have a care would you please, Eldie. Cover yourself at once!" admonished Miss O'Brady, who had turned to face the woman. The two began to argue while the other women in the room cackled.

Francis was chuckling at the scene before him as he rocked back and forth on his heels. Gideon had no doubt that Francis found the situation highly amusing and was not at all ashamed of *not* averting his gaze. A flush colored Gideon's face, but it was more for his brother's lack of decorum than for any lingering embarrassment he might feel at the woman's blatant exposure. After all, he was a gentleman; when had Francis stopped being one? He had always admired his older brother; now watching how low he could sink almost caused him physical pain.

Once Eldie had re-donned her dressing robe, the room settled down. Gideon blew out a deep breath. He did not really care what his brother thought of him. He was in new surroundings and woefully unprepared for the company his brother kept. Gideon was becoming more and more inclined to join his grandfather in his distaste for Francis's lifestyle.

"I say, brother, why don't we make our way to the carriage? There are friends we can converse with while we wait." Francis gave his full attention to Gideon.

"Capital idea. Let us be off," Gideon said as he walked to the closed door. It was thrust open from the outside, nearly hitting him in the process. It smacked his topper from his head and when he bent down to retrieve it, a stocking-clad leg came into his view. He moved his eyes to his hat, but before he could grasp it, the woman was bent before him giving him a very intentional view of her overflowing cleavage. She picked up his hat and waved it before him, smiling seductively as she did so. When Gideon reached for it, she quickly hid it behind her back. He took notice of her bright red lacy corset and straightened, allowing his hand to fall to his side.

I can always purchase another top hat. That may actually be the wiser course of action, in fact-

"Missing something, are you?" she asked with a seductive purr.

"Indeed. An item which I believe you now have possession of," Gideon told her brusquely.

"*Tsk!*" she scolded him.

"For heaven's sake! What is wrong with you lot tonight?" Miss O'Brady cried incredulously. She stood from her dressing table and strode over to the woman, wiggling her fingers for the hat. The other woman rolled her hazel eyes and handed the top hat over to Miss O'Brady, then turned away as if she had grown bored anyway.

Gideon accepted his topper back from Miss O'Brady with a grateful smile. Francis patted him on the back and exited the room. Gideon followed behind him as they left the interior of the theater behind.

Once on the street, gentlemen chatted with one another and made hedonistic plans. Those who did not wish to partake of the merriment promised at Miss O'Brady's townhouse sought out other means of entertainment. The Covent-Garden Nuns, tainted ladies of the night, who offered their services to the gentlemen eager for merriment and pleasure, paired off with the ones they seduced to action. When a trio of them veered toward Francis and himself, Gideon averted his gaze and turned his back to signal that their particular company was not desired. The women walked by them calling out lewd suggestions. Gideon cringed. This was the unseemly side of the gentlemen who pursued titled misses in ballrooms. That was only duty; the real entertainment came from performances at places like Covent Garden.

He learned that Francis spent most of his time at the house he had leased for Miss O'Brady. Francis spent the time while waiting to regale his younger brother with tales of the lavish and outrageous parties he hosted. Rather than be amused, Gideon's mood sank further.

When Miss O'Brady finally joined them, they took to the carriage and set off. His brother and his lady were cozily situated forward facing while he sat across from them. Viewing his brother engaging in such salacious behavior left a sour taste in his mouth and a hollowness in his heart. As a younger noble, Francis had been expected to sow his wild oats, but this blatant disregard for decorum and propriety was beyond the pale. He was no longer a young buck and it was past time to shelf his urges and transgressions.

Gideon feared what varieties of debauchery he would discover once they disembarked the carriage and entered the townhouse. If he could bow out now, he would. But he had promised his brother that he would spend time with his friends before forming any opinions and he meant to keep his word. Still, he held hope in his heart that his brother could be redeemed to good sense and sound judgment, and could be persuaded to perform his duties as the Marquess.

Perhaps a dangerous hope to cling to…

After the carriage stopped and they had descended from it, they entered the townhouse and paused taking in the scene before them. Gideon almost turned and fled into the night at the different and debauched scenes taking place before his shocked eyes. The party had long ago begun and couples, trios, and sometimes more, were engaged in carnal acts throughout the house. None of them showed an ounce of shame, and pleasure seemed to be the chief pursuit. The house was loud with sounds he'd rather not hear and his head began to pound.

This is too much!

Every step he took to try to find a moment of peace was a battle he lost. The stairs were in use as were the study, drawing room, and every other corner or crevice. Disgust roiled through him. He had lost sight of his companions almost as soon as they stepped foot into the house. He shook his head and stepped over writhing bodies as he tread heavily up the staircase.

Was everyone exposed?

He meant to locate his brother and inform him of his immediate departure, but he could not find him anywhere. Even the master suites were occupied by others.

Dejectedly, he retraced his steps and was soon standing in the foyer.

"Here's to the night! May your passions burn bright and your tempers low!" Gideon heard his brother's voice from the dining room.

Gideon strode to the entryway and peered in cautiously. His brother was seated atop the dining table, bare-chested, and drinking from a crystal goblet as a crowd surrounded him. A doxy who was *not* his Miss O'Brady was kissing his hairy chest. He found the singer in one of the room's corners, her head thrown back in laughter as the drink in her hand spilled onto the carpet. Gideon rubbed his chest as if to ease a real pain and lowered his head. This was a scene he neither wished to have ever witnessed nor was likely to forget.

Not bothering to address his brother, he turned around and stalked from the townhouse. Disgust and revulsion accompanied him to the other townhouse his brother owned. He hung his head as his leather soles pounded the ground. Lady Everleigh's smiling face flitted across his thoughts and he almost tripped. How could he subject her to such a life as what his brother led? If she were to actually wed Francis, embarrassment was sure to be her constant companion. Were she simple, she might not understand what the gossips whispered, but she was far from being dull-witted. Already she knew of her intended's obsession with Miss O'Brady; she would feel all of his brother's misdeeds and be expected to feign ignorance to them all. How could he stand by and let that happen?

What a wretched situation. To think that my brother has fallen so low leaves a gaping hole in my heart and I can scarcely breathe. Dear Lord, what am I to do?

8

MORNING'S LIGHT

The dazzling morning light greeted Everleigh as she blinked, attempting to remove the sleepy haze from her mind. The cheerful illumination shone from around the heavy blinds and cast its glow so that she knew it was well into the beginning of the day. Thoughts of the splendor of the theater and the dismissiveness of her intended had vexed her mind for most of the night. Covent Garden was every bit as beautiful as she knew it would be from the accounts she had read in *The Times*. Even after the devastating fire that had destroyed it, it had been rebuilt even more grand and impressive in opulence. Her evening had almost been a complete ruin when her father had insisted that the Marquess and his brother join them. It was clear to her that she was merely a duty that her intended husband took no pleasure in. When the Marquess had turned his back upon her, it took every ounce of grace she possessed to act as if nothing was amiss, even when the obvious slight made her want to give in to the tears that had pooled in her eyes.

When Dr. Carrow had shown her kindness, she had felt a surge of gratitude swell in her heart. Where one was brash and unfeeling, the other was warm and inviting: two very different gentlemen to be sure.

Too bad the titled brother was the one Papa sought to match me with. The doctor seemed kind and unassuming. But what was he like in private, when the eyes of Society were not scrutinizing his every action? The kindness in his eyes leads me to believe that he truly is a good man.

When her ladies' maid, Avril, came into the bedchamber to open the drapes, Everleigh sat up in bed. Today, she was to be measured for her Court dress. The modiste was to arrive midmorning with a few of her best seamstresses in tow. Everleigh was not nervous about her presentation as many of her contemporaries were. After all, the King and Queen were close relatives, and she had paid attendance upon them many times. Although she was close to Queen Charlotte, it had been some time since she had seen her great-uncle. Rumors abounded from St. James's Palace regarding him, but Everleigh had not ventured to ask her aunt to distinguish fact from fiction for her.

The only thing that did cause her any consternation about her coming out was the idea of standing for hours, waiting for her turn. As the Queen herself had set the date of Everleigh's presentation, she would be making her debut in late October, among the first wave of titled ladies entering the marriage mart. It would mark the first time she would be an equal to her peers as opposed to a relative of the King and Queen.

"May I bring your breakfast tray, my lady?" Avril inquired as she walked to the side of the massive four-poster bed and curtsied.

"Yes, thank you." Everleigh came out from under the coverlet and stood so that Avril could drape her dressing gown over her shoulders. She slipped into it at the same time she slid her feet into her slippers and made for her sitting room to await breakfast.

Everleigh padded to the large window and peered out. The street was already bustling with men on horseback and carriages going hither and thither, attending to whatever business had them out and about. Her thoughts strayed to the Marquess again. She would have a life of luxury as the Marchioness of Netherfield, but there would certainly be no love between them; she would be a fool to believe otherwise.

Dreaming of love at all shall do neither of us any good.

Avril came into the sitting room, bearing the silver breakfast tray. Everleigh sat at her desk as the tray was set before her and watched as the maid lifted away the domed cover from the plate. Everleigh eagerly tucked into the sausage, fluffy eggs, and toast that greeted her.

"Thank you," she said, after the first bite.

"I shall set out your morning gown and other things to ready for Madame Genevive's visit," Avril informed her as she stepped briskly through the connecting door to the bedchamber.

EVERLEIGH WAS PERCHED ON A STOOL AS MADAME GENEVIVE TOOK HER measurements. It wasn't a painful process, but it did take a fair amount of patience and standing perfectly still. Since she was a relation to royalty, they had been given leave to forgo the standard white and opted instead for a flattering pale pink satin that shimmered at every turn. Tiny gold embroidered flowers would add to the elegance, and a wide lace-trimmed gold rope would complete her gown. With the wide hoop skirts underneath the ensemble, Everleigh was sure to look the part of a regal young lady. She had delighted in choosing from the beautiful fabrics and sumptuous lace. There was a bouquet of color that had overtaken the room.

While she had no nerves about her presentation to her aunt, she did entertain fears about tripping over the wide hoop skirts from the stifling layers she would have to don. She had heard of such misfortunes befalling other young ladies, and their reputations had taken decided hits. Everleigh had no wish to mar her reputation or Papa's, or her husband's for that matter, should she be a Marchioness the day she finally made her bow before the Queen.

"You are all finished, my lady," Madame Genevive informed her with a heavy French accent. It was widely known that Madame was no more French than any other modiste currently residing within England. But as *the ton* desired all things French, it behooved the modistes to cater to such whims. Those who could maintain a French illusion saw their businesses flourish.

"I think once we have procured the right number of white ostrich feathers and jeweled adornments you will look absolutely exquisite," enthused Miss Owens, coming to stand behind her in front of the mirror. The two shared a smile.

Everleigh turned to step down from the stool and, once she was steady on her feet, she allowed her lady's maid to drape her dressing gown back over her shoulders. Then she turned to Madame Genevive.

"Thank you so very much for your time, this morning, Madame."

Waving a delicate hand in the air, Madame Genevive tutted at her. "You are most welcome." She turned to her assistant and began issuing commands and instructions which the younger woman quickly added to her notes, as the other assistant worked efficiently to remove all signs that a fitting had taken place.

Everleigh quietly stepped away toward Miss Owens and the pair made their way to the settee and sat. Miss Owens retrieved the teacup she had been served earlier while Everleigh had been measured. She took a delicate sip as Avril led the modiste and her seamstresses from the room.

"My, what a flurry of excitement this morning has been!" exclaimed Miss Owens with a sigh.

"Yes, it has, but that is one less thing to see to for my coming out. I do hope that I can manage the large hoop skirt." Everleigh rose and walked over to her desk where the tea tray had been placed. She carefully poured the tea into the flower patterned teacup and then added a drop of cream. She gingerly blew into her teacup to cool the liquid before she took a careful sip.

Why does tea seem like such a treat after one has been poked and prodded, she wondered.

"And you shall certainly be set apart from the other young ladies. Think of all the white and you in the midst, in that romantic shade of pink." Miss Owens smiled at her brightly.

"The privileges of my station are ever-present," quipped Everleigh. She leaned against her desk and waited for her lady's maid to return to help her dress.

If only the privilege did not come with quite so many expectations.

9

DAWNING CONFESSIONS

The proclivity for rising at dawn was not an attribute possessed by many of the gentlemen who resided in Town. But when the morning light greeted Gideon's tired and bleary eyes, he could not resist rising from his bed.

'Tis a good thing I have no title this morning, Gideon thought cynically.

His thoughts had not been kind to him while he had tossed and turned the entire night. At some point, he must have finally succumbed to sleep because he didn't remember seeing the footman deliver the paper currently resting on the armchair beside the bed. He wasn't used to seeing the paper before he broke his morning fast, but it was welcomed.

Perhaps it will divert my thoughts to other matters.

Gideon climbed from under his coverlet and sat up on the side of the bed. His feet searched the floor for his slippers, which he quickly slipped on. Rising, he closed the short distance to the armchair and retrieved his dressing gown. He quickly threw his arms into it and tied the sash before striding to the bellpull to summon his valet. He was impatient with waiting for a maid to stoke up the fire, so he saw to the task himself. He wasn't above such mundane chores and would never put on airs, especially when his comfort was something that he could easily see to himself.

But what of our circumstances? I cannot side against my grandfather; my brother's behavior is appalling, true, but do I have any right to condemn him for it? What a rotten mess!

Gideon hissed out a frustrated breath and ran his hands through his hair.

Gibbons quietly entered the bedchamber and strode over to the windows as he drew the drapes aside to welcome in the morning light. "Good morning, sir," he said as he greeted Gideon. He was just about Gideon's age and had a dark head of hair. They were similar in height and demeanor and Gideon was eternally thankful to have the man in his employ.

"I do not think I need to ask, but has my brother returned?" Gideon straightened his shoulders, as if steeling himself for the answer.

"No, not as of this morning." Gibbons walked to the dressing area and, searched the closet, until he began to pull Gideon's clothing from within. He arranged each article in the dressing area, rustling fabrics as he went. He then turned toward Gideon and awaited further instruction.

"I am not surprised in the least," Gideon said with disgust. "Very well, I shall meet with him at his other address and then we will set out to meet with the Duke."

Gibbons nodded his head and then followed Gideon when he strode to the dressing area. He poured fresh water into the basin and Gideon began his morning ablutions.

When Gideon was dressed, he strode from the townhouse and began a brisk walk to Miss O'Brady's townhouse. Since it was still early, the streets were busy with only servants and those country gentlemen who only came to Town to conduct business and were eager to return home. Mounted men on horseback rode in the direction of Hyde Park and Rotten Row. As it was just before the fashionable hour for parading, he suspected that either nefarious business was afoot, or the gentlemen were simply embarking early for their own pleasure. Duels were not unheard of but were frowned upon by the Crown: the punishment was severe and few were willing to face a murder charge and all that it entailed.

Shaking himself from his macabre thoughts, Gideon found himself standing before the front door of Miss O'Brady's townhouse. He rapped upon the door and waited for the butler or some other servant to open it. The door was opened within a matter of moments, but it wasn't by a servant. A gentleman in a great state of disarray came tottering out and almost fell into a heap at Gideon's feet. He laughed uproariously as he straightened himself, tipped his hat to Gideon, and went on his stumbling way.

He will do himself real harm if he does not regain control soon, he thought to himself as he watched the man stutter down the steps.

Gideon entered the townhouse and stepped over articles of clothing, and even unconscious individuals. His journey to locate his errant brother took him through the drawing room, study, dining room, music room, and other assorted areas. While he saw many revelers in various states of consciousness, sobriety, and undress, none of them were the one he sought. His shoulders dipped when he suspected that he would find his brother on the next floor in his personal chambers. Given the hour, he hoped that all amorous activities would have been concluded, so that his presence would not interrupt anything untoward. It was his opinion that various amounts of alcohol affected one's arousal or lack thereof differently and the headache to follow, were one to suffer from such, was never an eager counterpart to another foray into passion.

I suppose that I shall just have to hope for the best that he is indeed afflicted with an ailing head.

Gideon had seen his brother in many states of undress through the years, but the thought of Miss O'Brady thus made him cringe in embarrassment. His mission could not wait until later in the day, though; he had responsibilities and his presence was needed back at Bramley without delay.

Gideon ascended the staircase, and once he reached the last step he braced himself for what he might encounter. Saying a silent prayer for mercy and much-needed guidance, he approached the master suites and rapped at the door. He waited for some time with his arms crossed over his chest. Rolling his eyes, he turned the knob and pushed the door open enough to peer in. His eyes met bare flesh that was sprawled upon the massive bed as a thunderous drunken snore filled his ears. He grimaced and closed the door, resolved to wait, as he had very little choice. He found the closest empty sitting area and sat in one of the rococo-style armchairs, wishing he'd brought the morning paper with him. Weariness and utter boredom warred over him and he bowed his head.

At least the furniture is comfortable.

An hour passed and Gideon grew more resentful. He had never had cause to feel such loathing before; it was not in his nature to dwell on things he could not change. But this… This entire situation made his blood boil.

How could my brother be so callous and unfeeling? Has he no regard for my welfare? Did he even bother to discover what became of me last night?

When a liveried footman strode by him, he asked for tea. It was brought quickly, for which he was grateful.

I will count all my blessings today, because today is not a day that I will ever likely forget. I do not desire for anger and malice to take root in me. But swaying Francis will not be an easy task.

He sighed, trying to relieve some of the tension that had his body tied in knots.

I cannot allow myself to be controlled by ire. I must remain calm, no matter what buffoonery I face.

He poured himself a cup of tea and added a lump of sugar. He took a sip and then another. He was reaching for a biscuit when the door he had been watching so intently finally opened. It wasn't Francis who appeared, though; Miss O'Brady was wrapped in a silk dressing gown. She closed the door softly behind her and turned. She started when she saw him and brought a hand up to lay against her chest as a soft sound of surprise escaped her.

"Dr. Carrow! How early it is! You are an industrious man, I see. If you are waiting for Francis to rise, I warn you it shan't be soon," she said as she clutched her robe closer to her.

"I believe you," he said ruefully.

She looked around as if to ensure they were alone, then moved softly to the wingback chair beside him. He had not anticipated her approach; the tea and biscuit were still held in his hands and he did not rise to greet her. Her appearance was disheveled; her loose hair was tangling down her shoulders and back. She was lovely, true, but she held no temptation for him. He was pleased with that knowledge.

"Now we have a chance to speak with one another," she began hesitantly.

"We do. What is it you wish to discuss?" Gideon set his teacup and biscuit down and gave her his full attention.

"Why, Francis, to be sure. He thinks very highly of you. He speaks of you often and with great pride," she replied, and smiled at him almost shyly. He briefly wondered if it was a practiced mein. She looked sincere, but she was a trained actress.

"I feel at a disadvantage. Prior to yesterday, he had never made mention of *you* to *me*."

"Ah. Well… I do hope you do not view me as a sycophant. I tried to dissuade Francis from his pursuit; I know that I am not what he needs. He kept insisting, though, and how could I resist that charm?" She tilted her head to the side.

"I do not take issue with you. I blame my brother for his own behavior and choices."

"You are here to upbraid him, then?"

"I am waiting to speak with him. Our grandfather is quite put out with things as they are with Francis thumbing his nose at his birthright." Gideon looked down at the carpet.

"What do you mean?"

"You realize he means to make you his wife?"

Miss O'Brady gasped and covered her face with her hands. "You cannot be serious! My God, I mean… *Me*? Are you certain?" Her violet eyes were round as tea saucers.

"Indeed. He has informed our grandfather and myself of his plans."

"But… *I* cannot marry him. He cannot marry *me*. In truth, I don't even wish to marry anyone. I do very well as I am now. I would not give up my freedom. Yes, I adore him and I know he adores me, but men are fickle creatures and his affections will soon alight elsewhere."

"Nevertheless, his mind and heart are fixed upon you. He means to give up his title, if need be, in order to make you his wife." Gideon locked gazes with her.

She wrung her hands in agitation. "Oh, sentimental fool! I am not meant for drawing rooms; I am meant for the stage! Long before my looks fade and my voice tires, he will have come to resent me and regret turning his back on the life he was meant to live. Foolish man! Marry indeed! This is only infatuation!"

The two were so focused on themselves that they didn't hear the bedchamber door open, or notice that Francis was only a few steps away. Servants were all around performing their morning duties, and they had not noticed his arrival in the bustle.

"Do I not have a voice in this matter?" Francis queried with a wave of quiet anger in his tone.

"My love!" Miss O'Brady jumped from her chair and held out her hands to him. He made his way to her. He had taken time to don his trousers and shirt, but his feet were bare.

"Francis, I would talk with you–" Gideon began.

"This is your plan, then? To turn my love against me by whispering my intentions?" Francis's glare was cold, as if there were no longer any affection for Gideon in his heart.

"Forgive me. I was only attempting to bring a solution to these complicated matters."

"By frightening her?" a quiet fury emanated from Francis. "Was it your hope that she would pack her trunks and run from me?"

"You are angry and cannot see reason. It wasn't even my intention to speak to Miss O'Brady. She approached me while I was waiting for you," Gideon calmly explained.

"Do not seek to patronize me! You had no right to inform her about my plans or my intentions! Those were spoken to you and Grandfather in confidence. Does loyalty mean nothing to you?" Francis shook his blond head with disappointment.

"You question me about loyalty? What of your loyalty to your family, your rank, your duties? What about Grandfather? You are the one who seems to be taking loyalty for granted." Gideon refused to back down. This was a fight for their futures, for the future of the family line. He disliked being at odds with his brother, but this was not something he could approach idly.

"I brought you here to stand by my side! I thought I could trust you..." Francis swallowed and then locked his eyes onto Gideon. "Hear me now brother, I love this woman and I intend to make her my wife. You have never been in love; you cannot possibly understand."

"And this life of debauchery suits you? This is what you want to be? How you seek to go on?" Gideon incredulously replied.

"'Tis not a life befitting a marquess, is it?" Francis wiped spittle from his mouth with the back of his hand.

"What am I to do, Francis? How am I meant to not agree with Grandfather? You are living as a wastrel!"

"If I am, then it is *my* life! Unlike you, I was never given a choice! My course was set at birth; I am the heir, only that and nothing more. While you have had your freedom to marry whom you wish, to choose your own living, I remained fixed in my destiny. Duty, honor, and progeny; they have been drilled into me and I was content to follow along before I met Shannon. I cannot, nor will I, continue on without her by my side." Francis wrapped his arms around his lady and drew her close.

"I do not want this!" she cried as she tried to pull away from his chest.

"You do not want me?" Francis allowed her to ease back a little and looked into her eyes.

"I do not want the life that comes after you turn your back on everything you were meant for. What will become of us when you realize it was only ever infatuation and you have no other choice but to continue along with it? You shall resent me. You may even come to hate me. I would rather never see you again than allow that day to ever dawn. I cannot let you do something so immensely stupid!"

Francis lifted her chin with the tip of his forefinger. "Do you love me?"

Her face grew taut as tears shimmered in her luminous eyes. "You're not being fair."

"Do you love me? It's a simple question, Shannon. Answer honestly."

"If you are such a great idiot that you don't know what my feelings are for you, then you do not deserve an answer!" She stomped emphatically.

"We would not be destitute! There are investments and holdings that are not part of the entailment. We wouldn't flounder. I could support you. Even if you decided to retire, I could support us. I would give you choices. Why would I ever desire to live a life where I must call someone else 'wife'?" Francis spoke furtively as if he were attempting to change her mind, before she had even fully made it up.

"I want to be yours, but–"

"No! Do you love me or not?" Francis kissed her forehead as he closed his eyes waiting for her reply.

"You know I do! But I cannot condemn us both to shame and an uncertain future. I can't bear to see you so disgraced."

"You wouldn't my love. Not in a million years would I ever regret choosing you." Francis met Gideon's eyes over her head and Gideon saw nothing but determination and will reflected in them.

Gideon shook his head, realizing that nothing he said would have any effect. And in the raw moment, he wasn't sure he wanted to interfere; the feelings between his brother and his paramour seemed very, very real. It was burning passion, but how long until the flame burned itself out? How long until Francis's heart turned from flame to cinder?

He turned on his heel, making his way down the staircase and into the foyer, barely able to breathe. His chest tightened with the realization that there would be no swaying Francis from his current path. Gideon was nearing the front door when a scantily clad woman burst forth from one of the rooms along the corridor. When her eyes met Gideon's she halted as her hands rose up toward him, beseeching him for aid.

"Please, help! You must do something! *He's going to die!*" her words came out coherently despite the trail of tears coursing down her face. Her blonde curls were in disarray as they clung to her shoulders and cascaded down her back.

Without delay, Gideon crossed over to her and allowed her to catch his forearm as she pulled him into the room. He caught the sound of choking as he entered and rushed over to see Prinny, who was staring up at him with wild eyes. The Prince had turned an alarming shade of purple as he clutched his throat. The woman let Gideon's arm go and sank to the floor beside Prinny. Gideon followed suit and with a few well-placed raps upon the Prince's back, dislodged what appeared to be a grape. Prinny spluttered but soon caught his breath. The woman smoothed his dark waves, cooing as she did.

Prinny's dark eyes returned to Gideon as he spoke, "You did me a great service. Will you not tell me who you are?"

Gideon nodded his head, clearing his throat, and replied, "Dr. Carrow, Your Highness"

"Carrow, yes! I knew I remembered you! You're Francis's brother. I can promise that I shan't forget this."

"Thank you, Your Highness. It's my duty to be of service where I am needed." Gideon leaned forward and assisted the Prince to rise to his feet. Prinny was unsteady, and it took only a moment for him to flop down into a wingback chair. Gideon had met the Prince before. Gideon and his brother had been in his company when their father had still been alive. He'd never much liked the Prince in his youth; he was exacting and spoiled. He liked him even less now as he felt Francis's current situation owed much to the man's ruinous influence.

After ensuring that the Prince was comfortable, he took his leave.

What a trying morning. I can hardly wait to return to the normalcy of Bramley. However, there is still one more task that I must attend to.

The thought of his next conversation with his grandfather had him shaking his head. He would have no news that the gentleman would wish to hear.

Gideon sat with his head between his hands in his grandfather's study three days later. He was at a loss for words. The piece of paper that changed his entire world now rested between Francis's hands as he read the writ of summons. The tension between the brothers had lingered; Francis had yet to forgive him for the conversation he had with Miss O'Brady.

"Gideon," began his brother.

Gideon lifted his head and let his hands fall to his sides, coming to rest in his lap. "Don't say it! *'Tis ridiculous!*"

"What was your response to the messenger?" Francis raised an eyebrow in question.

"I said, 'thank you' and promptly rang for the butler to show him out. What was I to do, Francis?"

The Duke laughed once and then leaned forward from his wingback chair as more laughter completely overcame him.

Gideon and Francis shared a concerned glance and then watched on in silence.

Well, now we've truly broken the poor man. Bedlam awaits.

The Duke withdrew his handkerchief from his waistcoat and dabbed at his eyes as he composed himself. His words were mirthful as he spoke. "*You* shall have to take up the title. I am thankful that you were educated alongside Francis to prepare for such a day as this."

Gideon had worked hard to become a doctor. 'Twas his calling; it flowed through his veins and the very air he breathed. Now, it was no more. One good deed and his entire world was forever changed. Now he'd be entrusted with the running of an estate and tenants and heaven only knew what else.

An earl? This life that I have made for myself has been everything I ever dreamed of. Can I set it all aside and not have regrets? The thought alone brings me grief; if it were to come to pass, I might wither away. What becomes of my dreams?

"I know that the life of an earl is not what you would like. But I must ask you to think about it. I understand what taking on the title would mean to you. The loss of your hopes and dreams. But will you consider what you may gain from it?" The Duke met Gideon's eyes.

"What do you mean?" Gideon queried, tilting his head to the side.

"Think of all the aid you could offer to those in need. You could establish your own hospital or charity. Monetary gifts to those who need the funds the most, even pay tuition for those who could not otherwise procure the funds. You could have a hand in establishing a university for physicians. The possibilities are virtually limitless."

"You could even wed Lady Everleigh yourself, if Grandfather and Thornwhistle agree to the switch. She would still be marrying into our family pedigree," mused Francis. He sat down in the chair across from Gideon and leaned forward as he waited to hear how his words would be received.

Gideon wanted to wince at the desperate longing that laced his brother's words. It was almost painful watching Francis grovel.

A pair of arresting eyes flitted through his mind and the longing to once again discern their color took up his thoughts.

"Not so fast, young man!" The Duke frowned at Francis. "Marrying an earl is a step down from a marquess; her father agreed to match her with you. The contract is binding, unless you can persuade the Marquess to dissolve it."

"I would spare you any hardship that was within my power. But this… it means giving up my entire life. My life's passion is medicine." Gideon reaffirmed his feelings on the matter. It seemed he needed the reminder just as much as his brother; unbidden thoughts of Lady Everleigh swirled in his mind. But he was called to treat the ill, not contemplate the eyes of a very alluring lady.

"It still can be! Only in a slightly more distant manner. You could approach the matter scientifically. The lady is very becoming and modest, from all I've heard. She's young but can be trained. You may seek to distance yourself and she would know no better." Hope shone from Francis's gray eyes and it pricked Gideon's heart.

"I like my life as it is. I feel purpose in what I have been doing. Treating the ill gives me hope." Gideon implored his brother to see his point of view.

"Hope?"

"That God still sits upon His throne. That no matter what ravages a body, there is still a greater plan in place." Gideon placed one foot over the other.

This was never my destiny!

He felt like he was teetering on the edge of a great abyss with no way to slow his downward momentum.

The Duke folded his hands atop his cane and considered his grandsons. "I shall give you my full support if you can manage to change the Marquess's mind about who his daughter is to wed. Keep in mind, you also have the Queen to sway to your side. I do not care any longer to dwell in this depressive state; worrying over what will become of you, Francis. I have stated my wishes and my disappointments; neither has done any good. I am tired of arguing with you."

Francis hung his head and closed his eyes. When he opened them, he turned to look at Gideon, choosing to ignore his grandfather. "She is lovely and in this new path you are set to walk, she would be the ideal candidate to have by your side."

"Even Grandfather has said that she could do better than an earl. What makes you think her father will ever agree?" Gideon questioned him. He was once again irate at Francis's callous behavior towards their grandfather, but refrained from voicing it.

"We would not suit. Given time, he would come to understand that. You are honorable and good, Gideon. The chit could not do better than you." The pleading was back in Francis's tone.

"If I am to do this, you will respect her," Gideon told him with a steely tone marking his displeasure.

Francis only gave him a nod in response.

I only hope that I do not grow to resent or even hate my brother after my dreams are mere dust. After all, if not for his actions, I never would have been there to save the wastrel Prince. It seems as if there is no fleeing from the Earlship now.

No longer could he be a simple country doctor, living the life he felt called to and purposed for. No, his value now would lie in how many sons he sired and how full the family coffers were upon his death. He had no desire to be bitter, but how could the Lord allow such things to happen? He had only done his duty in saving the Prince and this was his reward. An Earlship that would strip away his entire purpose. His heart was aching for the dreams he could no longer hold onto.

10

A UNEXPECTED CALLER

"*H*ow has it been a week since the Covent Garden fiasco?" Everleigh inquired of Miss Owens as they ate the trout placed before them. She had taken to labeling the night, the *fiasco*, because her mind often returned to that evening, and at times, her feelings about it changed just as easily as she did her dresses through the days after. It had been quite the trying evening and was sure to be one that she wouldn't forget.

"Time has certainly passed quickly," Miss Owens affirmed with a nod of her blonde head. "But it usually does when one keeps busy." They had spent several of the days since the theater shopping in Bond Street for ribbons and lace. On several occasions, they had even patronized several tea houses. Though Everleigh was not yet out in *Society*, the fashionable *ton* knew who she was. She had been greeted pleasantly in the shops and at tea.

"And to think of all the matrons who have made it a point to extend well wishes and congratulations. And yet, the Marquess has not once even acknowledged the match or paid a call upon me." Everleigh took a sip of her wine and swirled the pale liquid in her fluted goblet.

"But my dear, hasn't *that* been your deepest wish? That he would

67

stay away?" Miss Owens raised an eyebrow at her while she cut a dainty piece of the fish.

"Well yes. But he does not know that. And really, were he to suddenly appear with frost in his eyes and his haughty bearing, I'd be tempted to tell Ashburn to bar him entrance. Although, his lack of interest does show, at the very least, that he does not seek to deceive me in any way."

"Now, that is a blessing to praise. But his inaction will never pave the path to matrimonial bliss. You must be the one to try, dearest." Miss Owens ate the bite from her fork then dabbed her mouth with a white linen napkin.

"Oh yes, I do understand that. I just would be so crushed to be unwanted and forever held in disdain. I know the Marquess prefers his lady love and I am standing in the way. How else am I to feel?"

Miss Owens placed her napkin back on her lap as her gaze sought Everleigh's. "You can only control your own actions. You are no more responsible for his folly than a stranger would be. Believe me, I have the added years of maturity to examine this entire affair from a different point of view. You are deserving of your own happiness and, the Lord willing, you will get it, somehow. Have faith."

"I shall try." Everleigh set her napkin atop her plate and looked at the landscape that hung on the wall directly opposite her. The colors were dark from age and the gold frame was ill-suited to it. An errant thought entered her mind. "What do you suppose Papa does while at White's Club every evening? He has not once taken his dinner with us."

"Oh, the male sex is mysterious indeed. Though, I have been told by my brother through our correspondence that they place bets on inane things such as who is set to wed whom and whose horse will win the next race. I suspect mostly that it's all just posturing." Miss Owens lowered her voice and spoke as she lifted a hand to her eye as if peering through a quizzing glass. "Now see here you overgrown putrid puppy! I am the more important titled gentleman here. How could you fail to notice me what with my preening as if I were a veritable prized peacock, you bacon brained humgruffin imbecile! I shall have my wiley way and you will expediently vacate my favorite seat at once. How dare you put on airs and place a bet against my best hunting hound's illustrious litter."

Everleigh attempted to keep a straight face, but peals of laughter broke from her. Her companion was not ridiculing her father, merely an insipid nameless member of *the ton*. Papa assuredly thought he was above and better than most others, but to her knowledge, he had never uttered such outlandish words before.

Miss Owens smirked at her and rose. A footman rushed to grab her chair. Everleigh allowed another footman to give aid with her chair and was soon at Miss Owens's side. They linked arms as they made their way from the dining room to the sitting room. They seated themselves comfortably on the settee for the evening.

It wasn't too long after they both had taken up their embroidery when Ashburn entered the drawing room and announced a visitor. Rather than fear or offense at the intrusion at so late an hour, Everleigh felt her interest piqued.

With her eyebrows raised, Everleigh requested that the guest be shown into the room. Her mouth formed a perfect "O" as the newly conferred Earl of Fairfield, who she had last met as Dr. Carrow, was announced and entered. The butler bowed before exiting.

How is it that he seems even more handsome than I recall? With his hair shining so brightly in the light, he looks like he could be Adonis or mayhap even Zeus himself.

Everleigh just stared at him saying nothing until Miss Owens elbowed her side. She was so surprised that she rose to greet him. Miss Owens followed suit as the Earl came to stand before them.

"What a most unexpected visit this is, Lord Fairfield. I trust all is well?" Everleigh tilted her head in curiosity.

Gideon bowed before her and took a moment before he replied, "I wish it were the case. You are well?"

"Yes, thank you," she answered at a loss for something sensible to say.

"I have been informed that your father, the Marquess, is not currently home. I had wished to speak with him."

"Oh?"

"But, as my business affects you, I felt it may be pertinent to discuss it with you. If you might spare a few moments of your time?" Gideon cast a beaming smile her way.

Everleigh looked at her companion in bewilderment. It was highly irregular to receive gentlemen callers at so late an hour. Scandalous even! In return, Miss Owens delicately shrugged a shoulder letting Everleigh know that the choice was hers. Making up her mind, Everleigh nodded.

"Please allow me to introduce my companion, Miss Owens," she said as she directed his notice to the other woman.

"I am pleased to make your acquaintance, Miss Owens." Gideon nodded to her.

"The pleasure is all mine, your lordship," replied Miss Owens with a slight flush to her peaches-and-cream complexion.

"Please do be seated." Everleigh motioned to the wingback chair located a few spaces away from the settee where she and Miss Owens sat once again. When the Earl had taken his seat and began gathering his thoughts, Everleigh began a surreptitious perusal of him. His black trousers hugged well-defined legs and the forest green fitted tailcoat emphasized the muscles of his forearms. He did not look like any of the doctors she had known in Town. Her eyes met his and she thought she saw hesitation in them.

Gideon cleared his throat and addressed her, "My dear Lady Everleigh, I have some alarming news to share with you. My brother has decided to give up his claim to rank and title."

Everleigh felt his words assault her senses. It took her a moment to direct her thoughts.

"Extraordinary! Has anyone ever given up their title before?"

What does this mean for me? How does this affect the Marquess's family? My father will be highly displeased as this certainly affects the state of the marriage contract.

"Not to my knowledge. One usually aspires to rise in *Society*, not sink below its notice," he replied dryly.

"May I ask why? It simply cannot be because he bears such a great loathing for me. There must be other circumstances in his way?" Everleigh blinked at him uncertainly. For what man would give up his birthright simply because he disliked his bride?

There must be more… and perhaps his mistress plays a part in all of this?

"It seems he has determined that it does not suit the lifestyle he desires to lead." A severe frown marred Gideon's face.

"Oh dear. And naturally, this affects me, because we are betrothed." Everleigh drew her bottom lip between her straight teeth and nibbled it. After a moment she became aware of Gideon's gaze which was focused on her mouth.

"As you are aware, I have recently assumed an Earlship."

"Yes, I read about it in *The Times*. Your brave actions are the talk of the Town it seems."

Gideon dipped his head and said, "Indeed. It's all still rather new to me," he swallowed. "My grandfather feared that Francis would take drastic measures to circumvent a marriage."

Everleigh felt a blush begin in her chest and creep up her throat, coming to rest on her cheeks.

He means the Marquess has no desire to wed me.

It took a moment for Everleigh to gain her composure.

"You must mean that your brother opposes the match so much that he seeks to disassociate from *Society* altogether." She gave a nervous titter. "How mortifying."

"My lady, please know that his decision is for his own reasons. He is the one who is turning his back on all he knows, his values, and the family. His poor decision was made before it was even hinted that a match between you two would be considered." The earnest look in Gideon's eyes did little to assuage the sting to her pride.

"You mean to say that he prefers the company of Miss O'Brady, although he's yet to take advantage of the chance to enjoy mine?" She asked with an arched brow and a hint of wry amusement in her voice. "Well, that can be understood, I suppose, when you consider her beauty, her grace, and her talent. How could any lady seek to compare?"

This is a living nightmare! Papa will likely sue for Breach of Promise.

She had spent the last week gracefully accepting the congratulations of those around her, even though she wanted to shriek and run in the opposite direction. Though the engagement had not been printed in the society pages, it had been widely circulating. She could recover from this as *Society* would readily take her side. After all, she was the one being thrown over for someone quite inferior. But, how the entire affair stung.

"My dear lady! You cannot be serious! She is merely, forgive my language, but a kept woman. She is *not* your equal! You sit on a pedestal she could never even hope to climb!" the Earl of Fairfield exclaimed with a burning intensity ringing in his voice.

Everleigh was momentarily flummoxed. "A pedestal? Nonsense!" She shook her head, smiling shyly. "What is to happen now?"

"I am here to offer a solution; one which I hope you will not take offense to and think beneath you. Would you consider a marriage with me, instead? I understand that the Queen is in favor of a marriage between you and Francis. My grandfather wishes for the change to take place, only if it pleases you and your father. Should your father agree to dissolve the contract and allow another to take its place bearing my name, we shall present the matter to the Queen for deliberation. Unless she is ready to welcome Miss O'Brady to Court, my brother will walk away from everything; I'm attempting to make this as seamless as possible for all of our sakes."

"The Queen is my great-aunt. You must believe me when I tell you–."

Interrupting her, Gideon asked, "Your great-aunt?"

"The Queen, she is my great-aunt. So believe me when I tell you, she will never consent to such a match between your brother and his lady. Your family would fall beneath her notice, and in her ire she may strip your brother of everything before he has a chance to give it up voluntarily. I know very little of business and estate matters, but I do know my aunt."

Gideon rubbed his chin and nodded. "My grandfather and I are also sensible of this. To have a mistress is one thing, to wed her is quite another." Gideon flinched. "I meant to say–."

"You meant to say exactly what you have. I am not ignorant of the Marquess's regard and even his affection for the singer. I must admit that was why I attended the theater a week past. I wanted to view her with my own eyes. When your brother was… curt… to me, I knew there would never be a civil match between us." Everleigh peered off toward the window and took a steadying breath.

"I had no idea you were privy to that information."

"Is not all of England privy to it?" she huffed out a laugh as she turned her attention back to him.

Continue to remain calm as if this doesn't trouble you at all. Exchanging one brother for another... Father shall never agree. How I wish that this decision was mine to decide.

If only she could truly make herself feel better about the entire thing. Her nerves were strung so tightly, it was a wonder that she could relax her jaw enough to converse.

"If the Queen allows it, I will take my brother's obligation for your hand."

Everleigh directed her attention to Miss Owens, who had sat silently beside her the entire time. Miss Owens gave her a soft smile and reached over to take her hand and squeeze it before she let it go.

Everleigh did not comprehend Gideon's words right away. Once they settled and she realized he had said he would assume his brother's obligation, the true meaning of his words sank in. He meant to wed her! Had she not wished all week that she had been promised to him instead of his brother?

She met his gaze and saw his eyes were expressionless. Was it possible he desired the match even less than his brother? She was a duty, a mere *obligation*, according to his words. She felt a moment of self-doubt. Was she lacking in feminine charms altogether?

Drawing upon every ounce of grace and composure she possessed, she straightened her spine and clarified, "And the terms of a new marriage contract would then fall to you to fulfill."

"Indeed. I would be honored to assume that duty." He smiled slightly.

"Well then, if the Queen chooses to allow a change of bridegrooms, we shall see a lot of changes in duties and obligations, I expect," Everleigh stated lightly.

"I dare say we will. Although some changes may be for the better. I will, of course, discuss these things with your father as well. I admit I should have spoken with him first. It was not my intent to cajole you just now; I only wished you to know the truth. I do hope I have not overstepped my bounds or overestimated my own importance?" The earnest look struck a chord in her heart.

"Not at all. I value the transparency. I thank you for coming to me and not leaving once you knew that my father was not at home." Everleigh was feeling tired. Her emotions had been high since his arrival and she was beginning to develop a headache.

"Of course," he stated.

"I only hope that you will not come to see me as a hindrance to your own happiness."

"I have no doubt we shall both enjoy a life of quiet kindnesses and gentility." Gideon dipped his head in her direction.

"Exactly. Now that we are all aware of the situation, I will await word that it has been resolved." Everleigh stood, signaling that their time was at its end. She realized that she was massaging her temples and quickly let her arms fall to her sides.

A lady never implies or shows that she is unwell, she could hear her mother say.

Gideon had risen moments after she had. He watched her with quiet intensity. "You may find that lavender is a great help in alleviating headaches. Do you often suffer from the malady?"

"No. Please don't think that I am given to illness," she assured him quickly.

"I will take my leave. I apologize for causing you any distress. I did attempt to broach the subject with delicacy," he admitted.

"You were superb." She told him with a smile.

Everleigh watched Miss Owens walk to the bellpull and summon the butler. Feeling Gideon's gaze, she turned her attention back to him.

"I will seek your father out on the morrow and we shall begin to navigate this difficult situation. Thank you for hearing what I had to say." Gideon took a few steps toward her and reached down for her hand. His skin was warm against hers and the contrast of his fingers against hers made her want to study them longer. He brought her hand up to his mouth and kissed her bare knuckles. His warm lips left her skin tingling, and she had to bite back the gasp that wanted to escape from her. Their eyes met and she could not make herself pull away from his gaze. She felt butterfly wings brushing against her midsection and an odd sort of weightlessness.

Whatever is the matter with me? Perhaps I am coming down with a malady of some kind. Should I let him examine me?

She gave herself a mental shake.

How improper! I do not think modern medical practices can cure what ails me.

What would he make of her if he knew her current state? He had plainly expressed that it was his *honor* to wed her, not his *pleasure*. She felt the difference keenly.

When the door opened and she heard Ashburn clear his throat, Everleigh blinked and returned to her senses, promptly stepping back from Gideon.

Gideon bowed to both Everleigh and Miss Owens, then turned on booted heel and followed the butler from the room.

Once they were gone, Everleigh and Miss Owens resumed their places on the settee.

"He is a handsome one, is he not?" Miss Owens queried.

"He is," was Everleigh's timid reply.

"I can see you wed to him, and I believe that it would be a match that suits you both well. He is kind and considerate. Is that not what you desire most in a husband?"

"It is." Everleigh felt that her heart may be in danger from the Earl and his attentions. Was it better to wed him and not his older brother? What if her blossoming affections would never be returned? Could she survive a marriage where her feelings were unrequited? Her heart was telling her that she must put faith in the Lord and tread the path that He was setting before her.

I will need to rely upon His grace and trust in Him. I do hope that soon pleasure would overtake honor where Gideon's feelings are concerned. Lord, if this is your will, please make the path smooth and pebble free.

11

A CASUAL CHAT WITH THE MARQUESS?

*D*underhead. Idiot. Imbecile. Cad. Gideon was keeping track of the names he could label himself.

Had I really said honor? That 'twould be my honor to wed her?

It would be so much more. A pleasure. A great adventure. A delight!

But my honor?

He scoffed at himself. Honor was a word used when rakes danced with a bluestocking or when one was to attend some rigid event. Being wed to Lady Everleigh would be a pleasure. She is lovely, well-spoken, and not given to fits of temper. She had met his news with grace and acceptance. What more could a man desire in an ideal wife? Her figure was pleasing and her eyes were a captivating jade hue. He was delighted to finally know the exact shade. Gideon had almost shouted it when he made the discovery.

'Twas the morning after his impromptu visit, and he cringed as he replayed the encounter in his mind.

I must do better!

He thanked Gibbons for the quick shave and assistance with dressing. He was wearing his best attire, but it was not that of a future earl. The hour was not one that was acceptable to pay a call upon his future father-in-law, but, *dash it all*! He had plans to make, and a great deal of those depended on the Marquess. He hoped it went as well as he imagined it would. He would be greeted civilly and shown to the Marquess's private study. They would begin with something banal like the weather or a current bill being presented in the House. Mayhap the man would offer him a drink despite the early hour. Once relaxed, Gideon could segue into the more personal issue at hand. Then he could turn the focus of his concern to the appointment with the Queen. He knew that even with his grandfather by his side, the meeting would be daunting. These thoughts accompanied him all the way to the Marquess of Thornwhistle's townhouse.

Gideon soon found himself in the Marquess's study, standing by the door, waiting for the Marquess to enter. He practiced his speech and straightened his cravat. He was aware that he did not look the part of a minor lord, much less an earl. As looking the part was half the battle among *the ton*, he was already losing.

But always, hope remains. Lord, guide my steps.

His eyes roamed around the study. It boasted a very masculine decor with mahogany furnishings and elegant green accents. A bookcase against the side wall was overflowing with tomes, but the room had a lack of decorative objects. Gideon found this surprising; in his experience, men of the peerage were apt to display their position and wealth in the assortment of art pieces and whatnots they could afford to collect. The entire study was reserved, leading him to understand that this was a room for business only, not pleasure.

It would be perfectly suited to a country parson, if the decor weren't so obviously expensive.

When the door opened and the Marquess sauntered into the room, he passed Gideon without a look, going directly to his desk. Although dressed impeccably as though to receive guests, his message regarding the early hour was heard as loudly as if he had spoken. Gideon frowned. The older man took to his seat behind the mahogany desk and began sorting his correspondence into different columns. Gideon felt the dismissal, but did not have the time to receive it. He cleared his throat and continued to wait for an acknowledgement.

What else am I to do?

After a few more minutes, Gideon began to doubt whether his presence had been noted at all. Although his acquaintance with the

Marquess was limited, he did not recall that the man suffered from either poor eyesight or hearing, but it was becoming apparent that his manners were impaired. He felt slighted and inferior.

Finally, the Marquess looked at him and Gideon felt like a schoolboy facing the displeasure of a headmaster. He schooled his features to indifference. This was not a battle he intended to lose.

"Well, Dr. Carrow, or shall I now address you as Lord Fairfield, we meet again. What has brought you to my doorstep at such an unfashionable hour?" The Marquess of Thornwhistle looked him up and down with disdain clearly marked upon his aristocratic features.

"I have dire business to discuss with you."

"And it pertains to your brother, I expect. Very well, you may approach the desk and do take your seat. I do not wish to crane my neck to see you." The Marquess indicated the two armchairs sitting before his desk, facing him.

Gideon strode purposefully to the armchair on the right and sat down. The seat was lower than he expected, and for a moment he feared he was falling until his backside finally met the padded cushion. *Dear Lord!*

His feelings of fright must have shown on his face, because the Marquess began to laugh until he coughed. He patted his chest and then addressed Gideon.

"An amusing sight to be sure. It gives me the advantage in any conversation; regardless of what my guest has to say, I can still lord it over him. Now, let us have this news that has brought you here." The man impatiently thumped his fist upon his desktop.

"You are aware of my brother's unsavory reputation?" Gideon waited and when he received a nod, he continued on. "He has decided to flout it all and wed Miss O'Brady. As he is the heir, the line would fall away if Her Majesty scorned the match and objected. Naturally, his actions would be cause for you to sue him for Breach of Promise."

The Marquess leaned back in his leather chair. "So that is why you've come today? To forewarn me?" His eyes narrowed as he processed the information he'd been given.

"Not entirely. I mean to offer you a solution that I hope you will not outright reject. I would be honored to take my brother's place as your daughter's betrothed." Gideon met the man's stare refusing to cower to him.

"So, you mean for me to agree to a dissolution of the contract, then, draw up a new contract so that *you* may become my son-in-law?"

"I mean to fulfill all the duties and responsibilities my brother wishes to abandon, concerning your daughter. I assure you that I take them all very seriously." Gideon attempted to lean forward in his chair, but was impeded by his knees hitting his stomach.

The Marquess snorted. "You think it will be as easy as that? You cannot just assume that I will be dancing a jig to agree to have Everleigh wed someone else far below her station, you do understand. And if you think you can weasel your way around the Queen, you can expect to be tossed out instead. Her Majesty has given her blessing to the match with your brother. No matter what I would have to say on the topic, she will still have to be consulted."

"I have no preconceived notions. I only want to do what is right. Up until this point, my life's pursuit has been medicine, and I would have it stay that way. However, if my brother is to abscond from his duties, my future changes as well; it's changing even now due to the Earlship. Fortunately, I was educated along with Francis; my father feared something may happen to the heir, and the spare," here he indicated himself, "would have to be the Marquess. Perhaps we should have paid him more attention. Though I will not be a marquess, I do hope that my conferred title is enough to offer."

"Why should I honor a new marriage contract?" The Marquess folded his hands and rested them upon the desk.

At that moment the idea that he would not was like a blow to Gideon's senses; he felt taken by surprise. Despite his words to the Marquess, he was already anticipating the wedded bliss he hoped for with Lady Everleigh; despite voicing the scenario to the Duke and Francis, that such a match would not be well-received. She was already the cornerstone of the new life plans he was making. He rose, walked to the bay window, and looked out at the busy street, where carriages and pedestrians were beginning to flock. He turned to the man whose support he needed so badly.

"I would spend my life honoring your daughter. Neither you nor she would ever have to question my fidelity or fear any scandal. If I leave for business, that is exactly what I will be seeing to. I would not disgrace a wife by breaking my marriage vows; I would be faithful to her alone and see to her every need and want. If you doubt me now, I ask that you give me the chance to earn your regard in the coming days. I would be a better husband to your daughter than any other candidate."

His words were met with a silence so oppressive, he felt his heart seize. Finally, the Marquess rose and closed the distance between them. When they stood with barely a few feet separating them, he spoke.

"I can honestly say I believe you are sincere in your intentions toward my daughter. However, it's not entirely at my discretion. The Queen is a stickler for propriety; traditions are very important to her. You will need a solid case to present before her, and a strong argument for her to hear. Even that may not be enough. You will need to have my daughter by your side. Everleigh is a particular favorite of Her Majesty's and may be what you need to aid in swaying the Queen. We shall attend the appointment with you. I trust the Duke has already made the arrangements?"

"He has. And your presence would be greatly appreciated." Gideon had nothing more to say. He couldn't help but feel that he had superbly just passed some sort of test. 'Twould seem that he had his future father-in-law's support, and that was something to celebrate.

"Return back at precisely eleven o'clock. We shall begin to prepare our argument and appraise my daughter of the circumstances. If she is amenable, you will have my blessing and I will stand with you through the scandal that is sure to follow. Are you prepared to withstand it and protect my daughter, no matter the cost?"

Gideon nodded at the Marquess. "I give you my word that it shall be so."

Dear Lord, this is the beginning. May I be worthy of my station and worthy of those placed in my care. And, even more, may I be worthy of Everleigh each and every day.

12

PLOTTING BEGINS

The door to the drawing room opened and Papa entered with the Earl of Fairfield trailing in his wake. Everleigh and Miss Owens both rose from the settee in surprise. Everleigh still held her embroidery in her hand, as she had not thought to set it down before rising.

He has returned and father does not seem ready to breathe fire. This could be a very good thing.

The Marquess of Thornwhistle halted his stride before the ladies. He waggled his fingers toward Lord Fairfield who came to stand beside him. "My dear, the Earl of Fairfield has come to call upon us. I've instructed Ashburn to bring tea."

The Earl made a very pretty bow to the ladies but his intent gaze was riveted on Everleigh as she rose from her curtsey.

"How good of you to call, Lord Fairfield," Everleigh enthused as she felt her skin flush with delight.

Gideon stepped nearer to her and said, "The *pleasure* is mine, my lady." Then he reached for her ungloved hand. Her skin tingled where his flesh met hers. Gideon smiled softly as he raised her hand to his lips and placed a warm kiss on her knuckles. His eyes were smoldering as he held her gaze.

Everleigh suppressed a gasp as she felt a pleasant heat warm her from the inside. His gray gaze roved her face as if searching for something. She felt the weight of his stare as his eyes moved from her lips to her eyes and then back again to her lips.

I suppose I should not be so transparent about my delight, but how am I meant to hide my reactions when the mere sight of him steals my breath away? Especially so since I had no warning of his arrival.

When Gideon gently let her hand go, he backed away and the loss of his warmth sent a chill along her spine that nearly made her shudder. Collecting herself, she remembered her manners and indicated the wingback chair he had occupied the night before. "Please, make yourself comfortable."

Gideon inclined his head in gratitude and Everleigh sat back down on the burgundy padded settee beside Miss Owens. Once they were settled, Gideon walked to the chair and waited for the Marquess to take to his chair before sitting himself.

"My darling daughter, we have some delicate business to discuss. As I am quite certain the Earl of Fairfield's visit here last evening was to inform you of the current situation, we will spare you from having to hear the details again," the Marquess began dryly. "We are here now to discuss how to proceed forward."

Everleigh pretended to cough to hide her astonishment from her father. She had not informed him of last night's visit and, from the way his brows now furrowed, neither had Gideon.

"How did you learn of Lord Fairfield's visit?" she questioned after looking briefly at Miss Owens, who shook her head almost imperceptibly.

Her father scoffed. "Do you really think anything takes place in my own home that I am ignorant of? What kind of lord do you take me for?"

"I thought the household was under my authority," Everleigh challenged lightly, one eyebrow arched.

"The servants answer to you regarding the day-to-day operations, however, they answer to me for their wages," the Marquess raised a bushy eyebrow back at her. "Ashburn's in particular, being generous enough to *not* keep secrets."

The topic of finances caused Everleigh to cringe.

How crude to speak of such things in front of a guest!

"It was not intended to be kept secret from you, Your Lordship." Gideon began, casting a glance at Everleigh. "I did seek you out first. However, when I was advised that you were away from home, but Lady Everleigh was not, I made the impulsive decision to speak with her. As it directly involves her and her opinions gave me insight as to how to proceed, I don't regret my rashness."

"Her opinions, eh?" the Marquess rudely scoffed. "Still insolent at the lateness of the hour, however."

Before the animosity could grow, Everleigh interjected. "What's done is done. I do apologize for the slight, Papa. As Lord Fairfield has said, it was not intended to be a secret. May we beg your pardon and move on?" It was unlike her to speak to her father so, and the rise of both his eyebrows let her know that her brashness had been noted. She did not look away, though. The Earl of Fairfield intended to marry her, and she couldn't bear to see the two men in her life at odds.

Papa narrowed his eyes at her and then blinked. "I suppose we must."

Everleigh felt some of the tension slip away and looked down at the embroidery still clutched in her left hand. She smoothed the wrinkled fabric, then set it gently down in the basket on the floor beside her.

If only I could smooth the wrinkles between the Earl of Fairfield and Papa as easily. I cannot alienate my father. I shall have to trust the Earl to pave his own path forward.

Gideon cleared his throat, but said nothing. Her father was equally as silent. Beside her, Miss Owens shifted her body slightly, the only sign that let Everleigh know that she, too, felt uncomfortable in the silence. The clock upon the mantle seemed to grow louder, and her nerves grew more taut with every tick. Just when she thought she would go mad, the door opened and Ashburn entered with the tea. He made his way to the low table before her and settled the tray there. When he straightened, he bowed before them and briskly exited the room.

As gracefully as possible considering her nervousness, Everleigh poured the first cup and asked the Earl how he took his tea. After adding his requested dash of milk, she passed the teacup resting on the saucer to him before cutting a delicate slice of the accompanying lemon cake and handing it to him as well. Briefly, she wondered if he wouldn't prefer something a bit stronger instead. His long tapered fingers brushed hers as he took it and she swallowed another gasp as she wondered if it had been intentional. Meeting his eyes, she barely caught the quick wink he gave her.

Oh my! I do not think such behavior is proper from one that is not one's husband. But... What a delight to know that he is attempting to make our situation better. Perchance this is his way of wooing me?

Warmth enveloped her heart at the tender thought of something beautiful and fragile blooming between them.

The Marquess cleared his throat and Everleigh blushed as she poured the next cup and prepared it to her father's liking, offering a piece of cake which he declined. Moving right along, she poured Miss Owens' cup, adding her preferred two lumps of sugar and a drop of milk. Everleigh cut a generous portion of cake for her companion, knowing it was a particular favorite of hers, before pouring her own cup of tea with a single cube of sugar. Her throat had become parched, and fearing she might choke on the crumbs in front of everyone, she eschewed the cake as well.

Everleigh gingerly took a sip and listened while the silence overtook the room again. After a few minutes of hearing only the delicate sips and the ticking of the clock, she straightened her spine with steely determination.

"It is very fine outside," she heard herself say, then inwardly questioned if the weather was really all she could think of. At least it gave her father an opening to agree with her.

"I'd say, it looks very much like rain," he said instead.

Her shoulders slumped a bit as she replied, "Oh?" and looked out the window to the graying clouds.

"I always say a good rain makes one feel as if the world has been refreshed," Gideon remarked. She cast him a grateful look.

"I'll be sure to pass that sentiment along to my tenant farmers whose crops were recently destroyed by the deluge we suffered last month," the Marquess stated dryly.

"Quite right, Papa. Only the proper amount of rain should be commended." She wanted to smack herself in the forehead, but calmly took another sip of tea instead.

"Well now that the state of the weather has been agreed upon, shall we now move on to the more important topic at hand?" The Marquess raised an eyebrow sardonically.

"Please!" Everleigh exclaimed a little too loudly, then blushed.

How utterly mortifying! He is deliberately being obstinate and I am rising to his bait.

She lowered her eyes and took a sip.

"Your esteemed father has suggested that you should be in attendance with us when we petition the Queen," Gideon began. "He has said that you are a favorite of hers?"

"I do not know about that, but she does spend time with me."

"She is too modest," the Marquess said brusquely. "She found favor with our Queen when she was but an infant."

Everleigh felt another blush. "Why do you believe I should be there, Papa?"

"After the Earl and his grandfather, the Duke, have explained their situation and petitioned Her Majesty to allow the dissolution of the marriage contract, you will let her know that you prefer Lord Fairfield's pursuit to that of his brother's, and petition her to bless this union instead of the one implied in the contract. Mayhap even suggest she set the date for the nuptials herself. She does like to have a hand in such matters," the Marquess added offhandedly to Gideon, who nodded for lack of any other response.

"That sounds reasonable. But what if she rejects the first petition that you and your grandfather put before her?" Everleigh questioned anxiously.

"That is up to her and her alone," her father answered for Gideon. "The Queen is your own relation and you are a favored niece; certainly we can make your wishes known. Her Majesty is not unreasonable."

Gideon spoke, "I think the added support of my friends, the Earls Bramley and Hathwell, will aid in our mission. I have sent word asking them to join us when we go before Her Majesty." He sighed and addressed Everleigh. "'Tis the best solution I can offer. My brother is adamant in his decision and so we shall have to be as well."

"To think, Daughter, you could well make your presentation at Court as the Countess of Fairfield and all without being properly debuted! Consider what a coup that would be! The family is *beloved* by the Crown." Her father clapped his hands, pleased as a Mama scheming to match her daughter to a duke.

"Yes, of course. But.." she trailed off.

"What concerns you?" asked Gideon as he sat forward in his chair to direct his full attention to her.

Everleigh felt tongue-tied and had to swallow before she could answer. "Is this truly what you want? I am so sorry to ask, but our future is not yet set in stone, as it were, and if I can save you from a life you do not wish for, then-"

"You are in no position to make any promises," her father cut in with ire. "It has been decided that you will soon be wed, whether to the Marquess, his rascal brother, the Earl himself, or some long-lost cousin come to make a claim. You will be wed to one of them and our families shall be joined together!"

Ignoring the Marquess's outburst, Gideon answered her solemnly, "Is this not what you desire?"

She waved her hand delicately. "My feelings do not matter," she reiterated her father's dismissal. "I have always known that mine would be an arranged marriage, and I have been content with that," she replied obediently as she lowered her gaze to the Aubusson rug under her feet.

Not that I, or any woman, truly, have the power to change destiny. However, I would not resist this match for all the riches in the world. I am coming to adore this man and my deepest desire now is for him to return my regard, however foolish that wish may be. I cannot stop my heart from desiring him and I shall be inconsolable if he should change his mind and turn from me. Pray, let it not be so.

13

SMITTEN IS NOT THE WORD

Gideon watched as an array of emotions passed over the lovely face of the lady he hoped to make his wife.

What must she be feeling? Thinking?

He discerned that she was unable to express herself freely with her tyrant of a father in the same room. He prayed that she had no wish or desire to end the agreement; he knew he had none. Heaven help him if she did! It had only been a matter of days, but he knew already that he would not be able to let her go, even if she ardently wished it. He desired her, yes, but there was something else, something so much bigger that he could not name. "Smitten" came to mind, but he knew that was too mild a word for what he was feeling.

He was stirred from his thoughts by the Marquess, who stood abruptly. "We have made our plans and now we must see them through. If the Queen agrees to the match, you shall be wed."

Rising to his own feet, Gideon nodded his head toward the man. Then he took the few steps needed to stand before Lady Everleigh.

Everleigh. Even her name enchants me.

He reached his hand out toward her and she placed her dainty hand in his. He gently pulled her to stand before him and they stood there, locked in silent bliss just to be staring at each other.

"Pah!" came the Marquess's voice. "She is not yours yet, young man!"

Gideon gave a self-deprecating grin, released her hand, and stepped away from her.

"Thank you for calling upon us today. I...we," she amended, looking sideways at her father. "We should love to have your company for dinner tomorrow night." Everleigh gave him a dazzling smile as her eyes twinkled.

"I should be delighted, my lady," he assured her.

Nothing would keep me away, not even the dragon that stands fuming in the same room.

Miss Owens rose from the settee and made her way to the bellpull, summoning Ashburn. When the butler came through the door, Gideon felt hollow with the knowledge he must take his leave. He was temporarily unable to make his legs move toward the door, especially when she approached him again and held her hand out to him.

"Until tomorrow, Lord Fairfield."

"The time cannot pass soon enough," he brought her hand to his mouth and let his lips touch her silky skin.

Rosewater and... was that lily? Her scent is divine. Just as captivating as every tempting inch of her.

"Ahem," the butler loudly cleared his throat, letting Gideon know that he was acting like an imbecile once again. Only this time he would suffer gladly in order to feel her skin beneath his. That thought brought other images of skin against skin and he felt his body grow hot. He admonished himself and turned his mind to calmer things, lest he embarrass himself with his ungentlemanly thoughts. Reluctantly he let her hand go and bowed to her. She curtsied to him and when she rose the smile that lit her face made her appear ethereal.

She is a goddess!

"I bid you a good day, my lady," he said. Then feeling her eyes watching him, he turned and exited the drawing room. The Marquess had already quit the room and the butler followed Gideon to the foyer where he handed over his greatcoat and topper. Soon, he was in his outerwear and stepping from the townhouse.

Gideon was not paying attention to where he was walking. He had jade eyes upon his mind and the remembrance of her soft skin against his was a distraction. He shook himself from his thoughts and realized he was almost to Hyde Park. As he had not exercised since being in Town, he felt his muscles could benefit from a brisk walk, so he entered the Park with that intention. He noted the trees with their rustling leaves. The hedges were showing that autumn was beginning to make an appearance here as well as in the countryside. He had never given much thought to the seasons before, and wondered if Everleigh had a particular one she favored. How did she fill her days? He longed to sit with her and spend time discovering all the things that gave her delight, but that would have to wait until she had taken his name. He didn't imagine that her father would welcome his presence too freely in his home before then. The advantages of marriage were looking more and more enticing the longer he thought about them. What would it be like to share his life with her? He would miss his medical practice, it was true, but to share his life with hers would certainly grant him purpose and joy.

He turned onto a narrow pathway and quickened his pace. It felt good to feel the burn in his muscles that exercise brought. He missed rowing on the lake in the mornings and would be glad to resume it, whether he be in Bramley or his new estate, Fairfield. Images of rowing across the shining water with Everleigh facing him caused his heart to fill with warmth. If she disliked being out of doors, he wouldn't know what he would do with himself. He suspected it wouldn't be an issue. Her skin had a healthy glow to it that spoke of sun and fresh air.

Removing his pocket watch from his waistcoat, he saw that he had been walking for half an hour. He had no real purpose to see to at present; not until later when his new solicitor would be meeting with him to detail the holdings and assets that were bestowed upon him as the new Earl of Fairfield. He was set to stay in Town until the week's end. They were scheduled to meet with the Queen in five days' time. Gideon's pupil, Delaney, was pleased as a punch to be overseeing the needs of the residents of Bramley. He had yet to recommend a new doctor for the town; the idea of leaving his practice still stung, though he was growing more accustomed to having to leave it all behind.

Earls Bramley and Hathwell had sent word to expect them within a day or two. They offered their unwavering support for him, and he felt immense gratitude. These men were true gentlemen and truer friends.

He had met many men in his lifetime, but few that he felt an immediate kinship with. These men had welcomed him into their circle with open arms. He knew they would weather any storm with him. It was astounding how the span of a mere few days could shift one's entire world.

And I shall be pleased to be inducted into their fold of blissfully wedded husbands. But, had I not thought the same of Francis? That he would always stand by my side? I saw us growing old together, surrounded by our families, and now that will never be. How it stings and I wonder if that will ever abate. I had not seriously considered marriage before now, though, nor of having children of my own. Now all I can see is her beautiful face and her alluring jade eyes. And she shall soon be mine. She must be! When the Lord showed me this new path, I felt bitterness coat my heart, for all I would be losing. Now, with just the thought of her, it has all melted away. What a wondrous work the Lord was in the midst of.

14

'TIS IN HIS KISS

While she lay in her bed that evening, sleep would not come. Everleigh had felt the daylight hours drag as a restlessness had overtaken her. Now that she could settle into the oblivion of slumber, her mind would not let her rest. It was frustrating. All her thoughts circled back to Gideon.

Should I think of him by his surname? Or should I think of him as the Earl of Fairfield? Will he ever grant me leave to be bolder still and call him 'darling'? Or 'beloved'? Or simply 'husband'?

She could not stop smiling.

Everleigh had never suspected that a man could make her pulse race and her thoughts scatter like leaves in the wind. She had most certainly never expected she would be wed to such a man. She only hoped that in time he, too, would feel as affected as she was.

When she thought of his brother, her blood ran cold. To be married to him and to know that Gideon existed would be pure torture. She would willingly defy her father if the Queen would not grant them favor. She didn't care what became of her reputation; she would welcome a life as a physician's wife. Should he decide to give up his Earlship, they could economize and be very happy together.

If only he feels the same longing that will not let me go.

Everleigh tossed and turned and when her mind finally quieted,

93

she closed her weary eyes and saw a very expressive pair of gray eyes that winked and twinkled at her. They would not leave her thoughts, and she decided she did not wish them to. So, she sighed contentedly and drifted merrily away into dreams.

THE GARDEN BEHIND THE TOWNHOUSE SMELLED SWEET AS EVERLEIGH walked through the rows of roses. She was tending to her beloved bushes and humming to herself. It was a melody her mother used to sing to her, but she had forgotten the words. A pang of sadness clutched at her heart, and she stopped in place to massage the area above her breast. The grief had lessened in the passing years, but at times it came back and pricked her heart as keenly as when her mother had first left.

"Are you unwell?"

Everleigh whirled around as her hand flew to her mouth. Closing the distance between them was Gideon. His face showed alarm as he reached her side and grasped her gloved hand in his. His eyes looked her over from the straw poke bonnet to her half boots.

As he studied her, she studied him as well. His golden head shone brilliantly in the sunshine. The cobalt-colored fitted tailcoat and black trousers only enhanced his masculinity. The gray greatcoat brought out his eyes in stunning detail and the sun reflected off his perfectly polished Hessian boots.

He looks magnificent in this early morning light!

His kind eyes finished assessing her, and she realized he was waiting for her reply. She shook herself mentally and smiled up at him.

"I am perfectly well, thank you. And you are experiencing good health?"

With a wry smile in return, he nodded to her. "I am. Why were you looking so forlorn, so lost just a few moments ago?"

"I was remembering my Mama. How the words to one of her favorite melodies escaped me. I feel like I am missing more and more pieces of her, and I rather dislike the thought."

"I am sorry for your loss." He said as his thumb stroked the point in her wrist where her pulse beat. The action sent a delicious thrill soaring through her.

"You, too, have suffered losses. I know that both of your parents have crossed into Heaven," she stated.

"Indeed. And though I miss them, I find that time has made those losses easier to bear."

"Do you think that time really does heal all wounds? Even the ones you cannot see?" Everleigh stared up at him. His large frame blocked the sun from her eyes that her bonnet could not.

"It must. Or one learns how to cope with it," he mused.

She didn't have anything else to say as she was simply content to gaze up at him. His eyes were twinkling as he stared back at her. She was aware of the impropriety of his hold on her hand, that he was standing much too near, and that Miss Owens had wandered off to only God knew where, leaving them without a chaperone.

"Do you enjoy being out of doors?" he questioned.

"I do. I sometimes stay out most of the day when we are at my father's country estate. I love nothing more than tending to the rose bushes that my mother so dearly loved. As you can see, we have roses here, too. I wonder..."

"Yes," he prodded.

"Would you mind if I brought some clippings with me to wherever we make our home? I cannot bear to leave them all behind. I know the gardeners are perfectly capable of caring for them, but I have such fond memories entwined with them." She resisted the urge to gauge his reaction. 'Twas such a small request to her. But how would he take it?

Will he find me to be silly and sentimental?

The thought hurt.

"Of course! You must bring anything with you that you desire. If I need to purchase another carriage–or two! –it wouldn't matter one wit to me as long as you are happy." She saw the truth of the sincerity and the certainty of his words when she searched his eyes. The discovery stole her breath away.

Her lips parted to say something, but she did not know what.

I should express my gratitude!

Before she could utter a word, he closed the small space between them and brought one of his large, gloved hands up to cup her cheek. The gentleness of the movement made tears form in her eyes.

"Have I injured you?" he immediately asked with alarm once again overtaking his handsome features.

Everleigh shook her head and smiled at him. "No. You just surprise me at every turn. I feel blessed beyond measure to soon be able to call you mine," she whispered, throwing every thought of propriety to the wind.

"My darling, may I kiss you? I know 'tis not proper, but if I don't taste your tempting lips now, I shall always regret such a moment of inaction. I have always behaved as a gentleman, but it's as if all my self-control has failed me, but say the word and I will let you be." His eyes roamed over her face, his gaze settling on her lips.

"Please," she surprised herself by begging, longing lacing her dulcet tone.

What was happening to her? Before she could further ruminate on her shortcomings, his hand came up to the pin holding her bonnet in place and withdrew it. He gently pulled the bonnet from her head and let it hang by its tied bow in the crook of his elbow. He slowly brought his head toward hers. Everleigh closed her eyes and he placed a whispered kiss across each of her eyelids. It was as if the softest rose petals were being brushed against her skin. The action made her feel treasured, and she had to swallow the lump clogging her throat. But then his lips were at the edges of hers. He kissed each corner of her mouth and then placed the full weight of his warm plush lips against hers. Any thought of being demure flew from her mind. Any thought of anything else other than him vanished completely. She brought her arms up around his neck, ensuring that he stayed exactly where he was. She nearly whimpered when his velvety tongue traced the seam of her lips, which parted in surprise. Never had she known such bliss was possible just from touch, and she would have never imagined such a kiss existed. When she didn't push him away, he slowly inched his tongue into her mouth and swirled it along hers. She moaned and opened wider for him. When his tongue kept brushing along hers, she finally chased it with her own. They stood, clinging to each other in the heated embrace. Their tongues danced until she felt like the lack of air would make her faint, or perhaps it was just the heady rush of passion burning between them.

Gideon eased his tongue from her mouth and rested his forehead against hers. They both struggled to regain their breath. Everleigh sought his lips again with her own and he let her, seemingly content to let her lead this next kiss. She flicked her tongue along his bottom lip, and he groaned. He tasted of tea and things instinctively forbidden. His stance shifted and instead of tugging her closer, he pulled her arms from around his neck and created even more distance between them.

He gave her a roguish grin and she couldn't help but respond with a similar one of her own.

His kisses were magical!

Gideon chuckled and said, "Thank you."

Everleigh's eyes grew large as she realized that she must have spoken aloud. She waited for mortification to overtake her, but it never came. Instead, she felt giddy with delight, as if intoxicated from his attentions. She bit her bottom lip and he groaned.

"Do you know that when you bring your bottom lip between your teeth like that, I nearly fall to my knees from want of you?" His voice was deeper. Richer. Needier.

"I did not realize I possess any such power over you, but perhaps you will find it fair to know that I am at your mercy, as well." She laughed nervously. "I do not know what possessed me to allow such liberties, Lord Fairfield."

"Why, my charm, of course," he feigned indignance. "Or perhaps my wit?"

"You are incorrigible!"

"I am many things, my darling, and all of them are yours." He leaned toward her and kissed her forehead which caused her to sigh.

"Is it always like this?"

"What?" he cocked a blond brow at her.

"What happens between a man and a woman? If this is what exists between your brother and his lady, then I cannot fault his actions one bit."

Gideon laughed at that, then turned serious. "No, it's not always like that. There must be mutual feelings between a couple. I have witnessed my brother and his paramour, and they do share that burning passion. But one must be a gentleman and not take advantage of those who are innocent." He held her bonnet out to her, and once she grasped it, stepped away from her.

She tilted her head to the side to study him. He winked at her as he readjusted his greatcoat and ran his fingers through his short hair. He took a deep breath as he studied the rose bushes.

Everleigh attempted to calm her racing pulse as she put her bonnet over the topknot that wound all of her tresses together. Tying the cream ribbons, she realized that she bore no regret for what had just taken place. If anything, this burning passion they shared made her believe that perhaps he did feel something more for her.

Marriage to him would be exceptionally diverting. What on earth is it about his kisses that make me long to never let him leave my side? I just completely lost myself in him, and I am eager to do so again.

From the way Gideon was currently ignoring her, she discerned that next time may be very far away.

'Tis just as well. I will just have to wait and be patient and dream of all the glorious things that marriage to him means. Until I marry him, that is.

15

THE BURN OF PASSION

He tried not to pay attention to Everleigh's soft pants, but the sounds were wreaking absolute havoc on his self-control. He was a gentleman, and she was a lady; he must take care to remember this. How he was being tested! But he would stay a safe distance from her until he had his body and thoughts under control. Though the burn of passion would haunt him until his wedding night, he would not heed its call again.

His ears picked up the sound of light footsteps on the gravel, and his eyes met Everleigh's horrified stare. He walked toward the newcomer in order to give her an additional moment or two to compose herself. Thankfully her hair had been arranged in a severe style and the topknot had held itself in place, despite his amorous attentions. Redonning her bonnet had been an easy feat without the aid of a mirror.

Her hairstyle reminds me of tales of governesses from my childhood chums; all fierce and no-nonsense.

This image was the complete opposite as to how she normally presented herself. He discovered that he found that he admired both looks equally.

His lady's ardor matched his justly, and if he had not known better, he would have thought that she had been kissed many times before.

However, he knew her to be an innocent, and had behaved as such until he continued to woo her with his lips and tongue.

Lord! She had tasted of tea and honey and a most forbidden ambrosia.

The thought set his pulse to racing again.

Gideon chided himself as he came across the oddly absent Miss Owens. She had met him when he first entered the garden through the double terrace doors. After exchanging greetings, she had informed him of Everleigh's location and remembered a task that needed to be seen to. His eyebrows had arched at her lack of concern for her former charge, now friend, but considered it his good luck. Besides, as they were to wed, no harm could really be done to her reputation.

"Did you find Lady Everleigh?" questioned Miss Owens as she halted her steps a few feet from him. Her poke bonnet hid most of her face from his view since she was so petite in stature.

"I did. I believe she will be along presently." He smiled at her.

"Wonderful. Shall I ring for tea to be served alfresco? The view of the garden from the terrace balcony is lovely and Lady Everleigh always enjoys the scenery."

"Splendid idea."

"What is a splendid idea?" queried Everleigh as she came to stand next to him.

"Tea on the terrace. I believe that Mr. Hendrick has just taken fresh scones from the oven." Miss Owens informed them with delight.

"Well, we shouldn't want to miss indulging in that confection. Lead the way." Everleigh nodded to her, and when Gideon offered her his arm, she placed her hand on his bent elbow to allow him to escort her. The feel of her touch thrilled him. He could see many days spent in just the same manner. What an untold joy it would be to experience both the extraordinary and the mundane with her by his side, gracing his arm… And was she squeezing the muscles along his forearm, testing their mass?

Yes, yes, she was!

He hoped his physique appealed to her. He certainly had nothing to complain about where she was concerned. She was lovely and shapely and sharp-witted. There was nothing more he could desire in a wife.

The trio made their way the short distance to the balcony and Miss

Owens rang for tea to be brought. Gideon helped Everleigh into a chair, then waited for Miss Owens. Once she was seated as well, he took his own seat. The rightness of this settled over him.

Here is where I belong, forever by her side.

"We will need to have your Court dress fitted once more, I think," spoke Miss Owens, interrupting his thoughts.

"I believe you are right. We have very little time to have it finished." Everleigh admitted with a slight shrug of her shoulders.

"I do hope you have a strong constitution, Lord Fairfield. The dress is huge, with rope and frills. A lesser man may flee for the hills," teased Miss Owens. Her rich brown eyes were lit with merriment.

"I thank you for the warning. I will be sure to properly prepare myself," he replied.

"At least neither of you are expected to wear what amounts to a small canoe on your person and execute a perfect curtsey in the process," Everleigh commented with a roll of her eyes.

Gideon laughed at her un-ladylike display. He liked experiencing new facets to her personality. That ability to be a proper hostess one moment and then completely at ease the next were traits that he didn't know he needed in a wife. But then, he had never imagined that he would wed a titled lady either.

The butler brought the tea tray out and set it down on the table. He bowed, then took a few steps back to wait for any direction that might come his way.

After Everleigh poured the tea and passed out the scones, she silently watched Gideon as he took a small bite of the raspberry scone. Feeling her gaze, he looked at her.

"You do not care for sweets much, do you?" she asked.

"Only once in a while. I confess I do not possess much of a sweet tooth at all. Sandwiches are more to my liking."

"Should I ask if Ashburn can fetch some?" She blinked her expressive eyes at him.

"No. I am not that hungry, not for food anyway. I find that I am sustained to just be in your presence. Let my eyes feast while they may."

He caught the blush tinting her cheeks as she lowered her head and shook it slightly.

"Well, all the more confections for me, then," Miss Owens said as she reached for another scone. "Everleigh only likes certain desserts. You will keep her happy with chocolate in any form, and fresh fruit over pastries."

"All very useful information; you have my eternal gratitude for it. But how does one dispel her foul humors?" he inquired with seriousness.

Everleigh sat straighter in her chair and looked at him as if he had two heads.

"Oh dear, seems I must have stuck my toe in the tart there. My apologies, my lady," he smirked at her.

"Foul humors?" Miss Owens repeated. "I have never witnessed such a deficiency in Everleigh. Even as a little girl, she possessed the most even of tempers. The only time I have seen her succumb to melancholia was when her dear mother passed away." Miss Owens looked at him thoughtfully.

"I am an angel," Everleigh said, giving him a flirtatious wink. He barked out a delighted laugh and raised his teacup to her. "What of your foul humors? You must possess them to be so concerned over mine. How am I to lure you out of the doldrums?"

He thought for a moment. "Sit beside me and hold my hand. Tell me about your day and your dreams. Look at me as you do now, as if I am your entire focus. That is all that I require."

"The things you say!" she brought her hands up to cup her face.

"What is wrong with stating the truth?"

"Not one thing. But I hardly know how to respond to you. Your words do things to my heart and my mind and I get a bit lost," she confessed in a hushed voice.

"Then rely upon me to find you. I only wish for you to know-"

"Lord Fairfield, back so soon?" boomed the cantankerous voice of the Marquess. The older man came from the house and took the chair beside his daughter. Everleigh effectively made his tea and placed it before him. She chose a scone and placed it on the spare plate at his setting.

"I hope you are not offended by my presence," Gideon told him.

As if I could bear to stay away!

"Twice in one day. How delightful. I can barely contain my joy," the Marquess deadpanned.

"Well, I am happy to entertain him," ventured Everleigh, avoiding her father's stare. She directed her attention back to Gideon. "I do hope you like roasted hens?"

"I do," Gideon told her with a gleam in his eyes. He was not a finicky male and he suspected that all he would ever need was her by his side where he could face anything, be it sweet or sour, that life threw their way.

16

DINING DELIGHTS

wirling around in a full circle, Everleigh critiqued her appearance. Her dinner gown was created from the softest periwinkle muslin, and the effect of the shimmering material made her feel as if she shimmered from the outside as much as she glowed inside. The wide cream ribbon that gathered under her bosom provided a striking contrast in light hues. Her golden tresses were piled artfully atop her head with cascading ringlets on either side of her face. Delicate strands of seed pearls had been entwined throughout her coiffure. The topknot from earlier was no more, though she marveled that the Earl had still desired her despite the severe style. It was as if she were capable of unsettling him, wrecking all of the carefully woven threads of his passions and self-honor. What a thrill to be so powerful and to be so desired.

Feelings for me were stirring in his gaze. How horrible it would be to have to endure such blistering cold if passions chilled once we were wed.

Everleigh focused her attention outward and donned her mother's pearl necklace, completing her *toilette.*

I do hope he gives me that delightful smile of his approval. For when he does, my skin tingles and my breath catches in my chest. And when his lips are pressed against mine, 'tis as if all the wrongs in the world have suddenly been righted. I never knew that two people could show affection in such a startling manner before. Am I wanton and ill-bred to be considering when I may experience it again?

It was time to begin the evening, but Everleigh found a sudden case of nerves overcoming her.

How will Papa behave tonight? He has been so contrary as of late. And the good earl had borne his insults well. He truly is a wondrous man.

She dismissed Avril, then made her way to the drawing room to await her guest and her usual dining companions. When she entered the room, Miss Owens greeted her as they both took to the armchairs nearest the toasty fireplace. The creaking and popping of the burning wood set a warm and inviting atmosphere in which friends could confide secrets in one another. The shadows that were cast inside the long room gave an aura of seclusion.

"Your earl will be prompt, I daresay," began Miss Owens with a teasing twist of her lips.

"He is not my anything," Everleigh protested. In truth she was correct, the marriage contract binding her to Francis had not yet been dissolved, and Her Majesty had not yet approved Gideon. No matter how her heart wanted to dismiss the facts as trifling matters, things were still far from being settled.

"You give no credit where it is due, my lady," scoffed Miss Owens. She was lovely in a pale peach dinner gown trimmed in delicate lace at the neckline and hem.

"I am attempting to be realistic. I long for everything to go as planned, but I well understand how tricky the situation is. I could not bear it if I gave voice to wishes and hopes and then saw them dashed after I had spoken them aloud, even to a friend that I adore. Words are powerful, are they not?" Everleigh smoothed her dress with a gloved hand.

"To be sure. Words do have the ability to both bolster one up and tear one down. I commend you for your sense of self, in knowing what it is that you need."

When they heard an echo of a rap upon the front door, Everleigh's stomach flipped.

What if he regrets his earlier actions? What if kissing me was the worst mistake of his life?

Ashburn soon opened the door to the drawing room and

announced the Earl of Fairfield, who sauntered in with grace, looking every bit like the titled gentleman he was. His cravat was exceptionally knotted, and his dinner attire of black trousers and forest green fitted tailcoat enhanced the cream silk waistcoat boasting tiny golden swirls. He had swapped his boots for laced shoes of black leather. Everleigh felt as if she would swoon just from gazing at him.

How have I been reduced to such a bumbling gel? But my goodness, he is divine!

"You are a vision of loveliness," the Earl of Fairfield greeted her as he halted before her and gave a low bow. He straightened and then reached for her gloved hand and pressed a kiss along her knuckles. While the kidskin of her cream glove served as a barrier between her skin and his warm lips, the memory of their earlier interlude was enough to cause her to blush. He noticed and gave her a crooked smile.

"How wonderful to have you to dine with us this evening. Does not Miss Owens look stunning?" Everleigh drew his attention to her companion; she felt as if respect were due to the woman who was so instrumental in her upbringing. Miss Owens's dinner dress brought out her cream complexion. Everleigh had often been surprised that no man had ever caught her hand. Though Miss Owens was older, she was still striking and turned heads no matter where the two ventured. Her attraction, Everleigh suspected, not only rested in her understated beauty, but in her regal bearing as well.

Gideon let Everleigh's hand go and turned to Miss Owens. He gallantly took her gloved hand in his and kissed the air above it. "You are quite lovely as well. I am a truly blessed man to be dining with such incomparable beauties."

Miss Owens had never been given to flights of fancy; she never blushed when she was the center of attention. But was that not a hint of red coloring her cheeks? It seemed that even she was not immune to Gideon's charming personality.

"Why are you all standing about in this insipid manner when my daughter has decorated a sumptuous table? Are we not to dine?" came her father's irritated voice as he peered into the room.

Everleigh's smile slipped away as she replied, "Of course, Papa. We were waiting on you. Now that you have arrived, and if Ashburn is ready for us, we can adjourn to the dining room."

I do so hope this evening goes well… though as it's entirely up to Papa to behave as a gracious host, I cannot help but worry.

"Excellent. You look rather dandified, Fairfield. Good," acknowledged Papa as he nodded at Gideon.

"Good evening to you, my lord," said Gideon as he returned the gesture.

Perhaps it is just me, but does Lord Fairfield possess a note of wariness lingering in his gray gaze? Smart man to take care where my father is concerned.

From behind her father, Ashburn appeared along the corridor and entered the drawing room. "Dinner is served." he announced, then turned to lead the procession to the dining room. Gideon held out both of his arms to the ladies. Everleigh grasped his right arm while Miss Owens took his left. Papa led the way, not slighted in the least to be unaccompanied, and within a short distance they reached the opulent dining room.

The dining room had always been the most elegant room in the townhouse. A crystal chandelier hung from a ceiling that was molded with rosettes. Frescos of Greek gods almost seemed as if they were staring judgment down at them while golden candelabras lined the room's corners. Cherubs clung to the candelabras with grinning expressions that always made Everleigh feel that if they came to life, they would fly about, making all kinds of mischief where they may.

Gideon led her to her place at the head of the table, opposite her father. Everleigh removed her hand from his forearm and he pulled the rococo-style chair out for her to sit. Once she was seated, he nodded to the livered footman to slide her chair in. Then he turned and retraced his steps with Miss Owens until he reached the spot where the lady would sit on the right-hand side of the Marquess. He allowed another footman to pull out her chair and when she was ready, the servant pushed it in. His eyes caught the Marquess, who was staring daggers at him.

Oh dear! Despite Papa's impeccable manners, he is clearly showing his displeasure.

One hand rested atop the table as his fingers drummed on the mahogany, indicating that he was severely lacking in patience. Gideon quickly strode to his chair, which a footman had pulled out, and sat upon the golden-patterned cushion.

Everleigh signaled to Ashburn to begin serving, and he in turn signaled the footmen to serve the cream-based soup. She looked down at the china bowl. It was elegant with its golden pattern of roses, but it had never been her taste. Nor that of her Mama. Although it fell under a wife's preference, her father had requested that the pattern be a statement of the wealth he had brought to the Marquessate with sound business practices, once he assumed the title. After her second attempt, Mama had chosen one that Papa approved. The china was yet another statement of the affluent wealth the Marquess possessed.

And what announces wealth more than gold and glittering jewels?

"The pineapple looks ravishing in the midst of so much fresh fruit," remarked Papa with a note of pride.

"I thought it was a nice addition to tonight's dinner. Do you care for pineapple, Lord Fairfield?" Everleigh questioned with a teasing tone.

"I must confess that on occasion I have absolutely delighted in a ripe pineapple," Gideon answered good-naturedly.

"That is very good as I have it on excellent authority that Papa dislikes those who put on airs and decline his favorite treat." Everleigh imparted this tidbit in the guise of teasing; perhaps letting Gideon know that eating the pineapple would spare them all her father's rantings later.

Quirking a brow, Gideon replied, "I will remember to be thrilled when dessert is served." Gideon winked at her.

Everleigh felt herself blush, so she quickly turned her attention to the soup in front of her and brought the spoon to her mouth. After she had taken a bite, she looked up to find that Gideon was still looking at her. She raised her eyebrows in question, and he shook his head, as if to clear it. Then he directed his attention to the meal and began to eat his soup.

Do I affect him as he does me?

The thought brought her joy.

Everleigh had moved heaven and earth to locate a fresh pineapple. It was not always an easy feat. It was a current trend to dress the table with one in a prime place of honor. There were those who rented the fruit just for dinner parties, but even those prices were quite high. And only the very wealthy actually served the treat. Her father always ate them heartily. She had not had to locate one before as she had never hosted a dinner party, but she wanted to make her father proud.

The soup was quickly consumed and then the next course of mutton was presented to the table, which the Marquess stood to carve. When both Miss Owens's and Everleigh's plates were full, he served Gideon who thanked him. Once his plate had been seen to, he re-took his seat. They had skipped any fish course entirely.

"Regale us of your former practice, Fairfield. What tales do you have to tell us?" asked her father.

Setting his fork down, Gideon answered him. "My prior practice serves all of Bramley. During my time there I have treated bee stings, animal bites, influenza, scarlatina, and all manner of complaints. I have an assistant, Delaney, who has been training under my tutelage, but will soon be up to managing a practice of his own. He is caring for the town until Lord Bramley chooses a replacement. I have offered my recommendations for his consideration."

"And did you find a country practice more refined than, say, that of London?"

"Physicians here in Town treat all manner of ailments, particularly in poorer parts. As Bramley differs vastly from Town, I tended to see fewer life-threatening conditions. 'Tis easier to treat in the smaller towns than in the city, since the populace is more spread out. It helps prevent disease from spreading," Gideon stated with confidence.

"You will miss your life there no doubt?"

"I do not pretend that I shouldn't; in fact, I know I will as I have made lasting friendships there. The community is close-knit and kind. But, I am gaining much more than I am giving up, and that contents my heart." Gideon looked over at Everleigh and grinned at her.

"For how long I wonder…" mused the Marquess as he twirled the white wine in his glass.

"Pardon?" Gideon turned his head toward the man again.

"Will you not come to regret giving up your life? And will you not grow tired of the life of a titled peer when you have lived as one who earns wages?" The Marquess raised his gray eyebrows.

"I shall find new ways to aid those who practice. I may give lectures; that would not be too tedious. I may use my wealth to establish a hospital or fund for cures. There is no end to what I can be part of from this side of things. I am excited to discover the ways I can still help people." The earnestness of Gideon's vice spoke to her heart.

Here is a man that a woman would be proud to stand beside. I cannot wait to support him in whatever ventures he undertakes. My heart continually discovers new ways to fall more and more under his spell.

17

A GIFT OF HIS HEART

*D*inner was another of the Marquess's tests and Gideon felt like he had done splendidly. He meant every word that he had said and he would have had to have been blind to miss the tender expressions dancing across Everleigh's beautiful face. In the low light of the candles, she was magnificent. Her skin held an otherworldly glow that was difficult to look away from. When the time came for dessert, which was both the honored pineapple and a pudding, he chose the former and caught the Marquess's smirk. He didn't actually mind the fruit as it was far less sweet than other desserts he felt duty-bound to consume.

Besides, I would happily eat a million pineapples if it raised the man's opinion of me.

Everleigh had hidden her soft smile behind her delicate bites. He had rather disturbing thoughts coursing through his mind every time he had seen a bite pass through her luscious lips. 'Twas not the time for errant thoughts. He would soon be wed to the enchantress, and he would then be able to follow through on the dreams that consumed his sleeping hours.

Now that their party was settled in the drawing room, he felt like the time for making a declaration to his lady was at hand. He would not depart the home this evening without having paid her the proper respect due to her. She deserved a showy display, and he would gladly bend upon his knees to honor her.

Looking around, he frowned. He had yet to view his estate and new manor home but hoped that they did not lack the opulence to which Everleigh seemed accustomed. He hoped that she would not be upset or displeased by the state of any of their residences. If anything displeased her, he would just insist that she redecorate until her heart was content. So much gold nearly blinded him, but so be it, if his wife was happy.

It would take her a lifetime of shopping to drain the family coffers.

He had been astounded when his solicitor had given him the sum total of his new wealth and holdings.

"Well, 'tis time for me to be off to my club. Horace awaits my presence. We have business to discuss, and I shouldn't like to keep him waiting." The Marquess looked expectantly at him.

He means for me to see my way out.

"We will miss your brilliant conversation skills, my lord. Shall I meet with you on the morrow to draw up a new marriage contract?" Gideon stood when the older man did.

The Marquess narrowed his eyes. "Why the rush?"

"One would suspect you would be thrilled to see at least one pressing matter behind us," Gideon told him.

"*Bah!* It can wait! Let us wait and see what the Queen decides first."

Gideon felt his heart sink thinking of all the many ways the situation could go terribly wrong. That he could lose his lady made him want to cast up his accounts. If the former marriage contract was dissolved and a new one signed he would have no fear of losing Everleigh.

"I am most comfortable and you are an excellent hostess, my lady." Gideon pointedly ignored the Marquess and turned to Everleigh instead, addressing her as though a question had been asked.

"See that you take your leave soon, *Lord Fairfield*. My daughter needs her beauty rest." The Marquess nodded to his daughter, then to Miss Owens, and left the room.

"I apologize for his... Him," Everleigh said with a sigh.

Gideon gave her a smile and with sincerity assured her. "You can no more be at fault for his poor behavior than I can be for my brother's." He noted the amusement shining in her eyes and knew he had not caused offense. She understood his humor and that boded well for their future.

"Agreed. Shall we speak of more pleasant topics?"

"An excellent idea. I wonder, Miss Owens, if perhaps you would be so kind as to inquire whether your chef has any cucumber sandwiches?"

With a knowing look twinkling in her eyes, Miss Owens nodded her head. "I think that's an excellent idea. I shall return directly. Oh, I think ten minutes should be sufficient time?"

"That sounds very reasonable to me," he beamed at her appreciatively, grateful that she understood his intentions.

Miss Owens stood with the help of his offered hand and made her way from the drawing room. He watched her leave, then turned his attention back to Everleigh, who was gazing up at him.

Gideon knelt on the carpet in front of her. Everleigh's eyes widened at his action, and he reached for her left hand. He brought it up to his mouth and held it to him before he pressed his lips to her skin. This time she didn't even attempt to repress the gasp that escaped. He felt male satisfaction flow through him that he could elicit such a sensuous sound from her. She was just as affected by him as he was by her.

How glorious!

He lowered her hand and cleared his throat. He carefully peeled the glove from her elbow to her wrist, to the end of her fingertips. The entire time he held her gaze. Neither blinked as the air between them became electrifying.

"My darling Everleigh," he began. "I have been remiss in not offering a token of my affection and I intend to remedy that now with a gift that I hope pleases you. However, I should not offer any gift without an official understanding between us. Will you allow me to pay my address to you?"

Everleigh's face was solemn as she nodded once. Her eyes were locked with his and he didn't want to break the spell that was drawing them closer.

Could I actually drown in the depth of her gaze? Time to let my heart speak to hers.

"Will you become my wife? Before you answer, you should know that *I adore you.* I have thought of nothing but *you* since the moment we first met. I *hunger* for you, I *burn* for you. I promise to be faithful to you in both mind and body; you consume me. Together we can make a life that will be filled with moments of bliss and joy, even during times that may not be perfectly smooth. Will you entrust your dreams, your forever, with me?" Gideon swallowed with the heaviness of the moment. As long as he lived, he would never forget the look on her face as he uttered each word, or the tears of happiness that gathered in her eyes. She was a radiant beam of light, a source of unending joy.

"Yes. If you ask me a thousand times, I will give you the same answer!" Everleigh laughed in jubilation as the tears streamed down her exquisite face.

Gideon felt his heartbeat quicken as he reached into his waistcoat for the small blue velvet ring box he had carried around all day. "I searched for the right token as I wanted it to be the perfect expression of my admiration, my devotion to you." He opened the box to ensure that all was well with the ring, as he had done every hour since procuring it from the jeweler. He slowly turned it toward her, taking in every expression that passed along her face. There was surprise and a furrowing of her delicate brows before she again burst into tears. Everleigh flung herself from the settee and against his chest. He fumbled as he caught her and wrapped his arms around her. He sat back on the Aubusson carpet with her in his lap.

Is this how it feels when everything is exactly as it should be?

"I take this to mean you approve of the ring?" he asked as he rested his chin on the crown of her head amidst the tiny pearls threaded through her golden tresses.

From his chest, Everleigh nodded before she mumbled, "It's perfect! You are perfect. The ring is perfect. I feel so ridiculous to be blubbering when you have expressed such tender wishes and sentiments. But I fear that I cannot help myself."

"I rather appreciate your reaction. A man always worries about how his declaration will be received. I take it that I did well?" He deeply inhaled her scent of rosewater and lily. He closed his eyes, savoring the moment.

"Of course. Is there anything that you do not do very well? *You are perfect,*" came more mumbled words.

"Perfect? No, if anything at all I am perfectly *flawed*. But I am happy that for now, at least, you find me to be charming," he chuckled.

Now she on the other hand is sheer perfection…

"Would you be so kind as to place the ring on my finger?"

He set the box in front of them and carefully withdrew the ring. He gently lifted her left hand and slid it onto her third finger where it fit like a glove. She gasped, and they both watched as the rubies sparkled in the firelight. The setting was unique with a heart-shaped ruby surrounded by tiny golden roses in the middle, flanked by two larger roses surrounded by smaller rubies; a truly unique setting for his truly unique lady.

He had known as soon as he had seen it that, with a few enhancements, it would be the perfect token of his affection for her. A gift of his heart.

"'Tis exquisite! Thank you," she raised her face up to his.

Such kissable lips nearly tempt me beyond all of my control.

"You are exquisite," he countered as his lips descended to hers, and he was met again with the sweet taste of her mouth. The scent of her drove him mad. He changed her position on his lap so that he could better ravish her mouth. Her tongue followed his until she brought the tip of hers to his top lip. She tasted him and moaned.

"I must stop this," was his last coherent thought as he let his mouth and tongue dance with hers in flawless harmony. Time no longer meant anything to them, so lost in each other as they were. Discoveries were being made, hearts were being woven together, and love unfurling like roses in spring; tender, new, and beautiful to behold.

"Oh my heavens!" came a voice that immediately had Gideon drawing away from Everleigh. He leaned forward with her still enfolded in his arms, as he assisted her to her feet so she could assume her seat on the settee. When she was secure, he took a few deep breaths, willing his body to cool itself lest his ardor be discovered and he embarrass himself. From the innocence of his beloved, he doubted if she would understand her effect on him and he wouldn't welcome questions about such things in the presence of her companion.

Think of Gibbons… In a dress. Hair in nearly every place. Or the horrible case of gangrene festering in the cut that marred the Matthews' lad some weeks ago. Picture the snow in winter and how the cold emasculates a man when he's forced to use the out of doors to see to his bladder's needs. Beestings... bunions... Ah, yes that will do the trick.

Feeling as if he was fine to rise, he did so.

He looked toward the door and smiled lazily. "Ten minutes does not seem to be quite as long as I remember."

From her place behind him, Everleigh delightedly called out, "Look! Is this not the most exquisite ring you have ever laid eyes on?" He looked over his shoulder to see Everleigh looking at Miss Owens with her left hand held aloft. The rubies caught the light from the fireplace and seemed to catch fire themselves.

"Ohhh!" Miss Owens squealed as she rushed over to examine the gemstones. She flew right by him.

Gideon watched the women with the same male satisfaction. He had won his lady and she was elated with his gift. He had never known such happiness or contentment before. This was bliss and he couldn't wait to create more moments with her that were just as precious. The future was bright and beautiful for both his lady and himself.

18

CONCERNING CONVERSATIONS

The next morning, Everleigh and her companion returned to Bond Street for another fitting of her Court dress at the modiste's fashionable salon, and decided to visit a more prominent tearoom afterwards. They were greeted by a cheery woman dressed in lavender and smelling of French perfume. She sat them at a small round table against a wall. Miss Owens commented that the seating was perfect, as it would allow them to see all, but not draw unwanted attention to themselves. They were surrounded by polished members of *the ton* who were engaged in various conversations.

Gossip at its finest.

Lace drapes covered the bay windows, allowing only a small amount of sunlight through as tiny dust motes floated along the air. A small candle in a globe sat on each table to provide more light as patrons gossiped over their tea. Small floral arrangements rested upon each lace tablecloth which varied in colors throughout the room. There was a profusion of smells and Everleigh wondered how those who lingered did not come away with a headache.

Once their tea and sandwiches had been placed upon their table, Everleigh and Miss Owens began to eat as they enthused over the beautiful imported fabrics they had been shown by Madame Genevive, as well as how lovely Everleigh would look in her dress. She was relieved to have found it coming along nicely given the time frame. Of course, having the funds to pay for the expedited order aided in the progress.

"Oh no. Pray, do not turn your head, but I see that horrid Lady Michaelton coming up behind you. We should leave at once." Miss Owens could not keep the annoyance from her voice as she narrowed her brown eyes suspiciously.

The two rose but a voice put a stop to their escape. "Why, is that not little Lady Everleigh Winslow? My, but what a beauty you have become. I can discern much of your dear mother in your features." Lady Michaelton approached their table and faced them. She was dressed in the height of fashion and her blonde hair was arranged in the current mode with two single feathers trailing behind the mass of curls atop her head. The three ladies lightly shook hands.

"We did not know you were in attendance today," Everleigh began.

"I am not usually a patron of this particular establishment, but today I found myself with an invitation. Tell me, have you been introduced to Lady Burbury? Her balls are always such a crush, but I never miss one." Lady Michaelton smiled brightly at Everleigh.

"We were just taking our leave, my lady," said Miss Owens with determination.

"Oh, what a pity! Lady Everleigh really should meet Lady Burbury since she will be coming out soon. I shall be delighted to make the introduction." Lady Michaelton insisted with an impatient gesture toward a table set in the middle of the room.

Everleigh saw Miss Owens' resolve was wavering, so she agreed. "We do have another engagement soon, but I will be happy to join you for a short time."

"Excellent!" Lady Michaelton clapped her hands together. "I have already requested that more chairs be brought out and they are being set up now. Follow me?"

Miss Owens nodded to Everleigh, and they trailed after the other woman. In a few steps, they stood before a larger round table. A white lace tablecloth was barely visible under an assortment of confections and sandwiches.

"My dear Lady Burbury, I am pleased to introduce Lady Everleigh and her companion to you. And this most beautiful dear here is Lady

Burbury, and a more ready wit and better company I have never known." Lady Michaelton beamed at the trio who quickly exchanged pleasantries before taking their seats.

"Now, Lady Everleigh, when you attend your first ball at my residence, I shall direct you to all the proper young gentlemen; should the circulating rumors about *a certain marquess* and you not be true. Now, you will want to choose your friends wisely, and with that in mind, I shall also endeavor to keep you away from the more unsavory ladies and their equally unsavory daughters. There will be some this season that I wish we could altogether avoid, but such is the life of the most sought-after hostess in London," Lady Burbury sighed.

"In London? No, all of England, at least!" Lady Michaelton enthused over her teacup with her hazel eyes twinkling.

"If you say so," Lady Burbury smiled with artificial humility. She looked to be in her early fifties, although she was still quite beautiful, despite the lines around her eyes and mouth when she smiled so. She wore a mint-colored day dress embroidered with tiny flowers. Her silver hair was elegantly piled atop her head with several curls cascading youthfully down her neck and over one shoulder. Two ostrich feathers waved just along the back of her head, and as she spoke it was impossible not to stare at them.

"Would either of you care for refreshments?" offered Lady Michaelton.

"Tea is always a refreshing treat," answered Everleigh even though she was not at all thirsty. The idea of more tea, when she had just had her fill, made her want to retch. But manners were manners and she could hardly refuse after having accepted the lady's original invitation for company, so she took a sip.

"Now, what sort of news is there to discuss?" Lady Michaelton asked Lady Burbury before turning to Everleigh. "I do hope you had a governess who was quite skilled in the art of communication," she tittered. "It's so very important to know all the latest *on dits* so that one does not appear ignorant at any time." She ignored the cutting look Miss Owens directed at her. "But don't worry about it too much, dear. Lady Burbury and I will be more than pleased to take you under our wings and ensure you do not embarrass yourself. Although, I'm sure one or two mistakes at first can be forgiven. After all, who even knows what happened after your dear Mama…" She patted Everleigh's hand, again ignoring Miss Owens.

"Thank you," Everleigh said graciously, more than ready to be away from the woman.

"Where was I? Oh, I have a very newsy tidbit to share!" she announced with glee.

"Do tell," Lady Burbury encouraged as she leaned in closer.

"Well, now I hesitate to speak when 'tis of such a sensitive nature." Lady Michaelton seemed unsure as she directed her gaze to Everleigh.

Everleigh tilted her head to the side and wondered what this delicate topic could possibly be. Lady Michaleton's face held a calculating look. Dread began to pool in her stomach.

Surely she's not implying that the news is about me! What could I have done?

Lady Burbury looked from one lady to another with silent interest.

"Well, my dear Lady Everleigh, if your dear Mama were still with us, I am sure she would tell you this herself, but you will find that men do not honor their marriage vows whatsoever. They make them lightly. I am in no doubt that, sheltered as you may be, that you too have heard the rumors at Court or perchance, even read them in the newsprint about the Marquess of Netherfield." Lady Michaelton paused to await her answer. Her gaze fixed onto the lavish ruby ring gracing Everleigh's finger that was shining within the room's light.

"I have," Everleigh said, directing her gaze to the lace tablecloth.

"Though it is highly improper and we risk censure even discussing these things, I feel it my duty to forewarn you of the dangers that can befall those of a certain social set. It seems the opera singer the Marquess is so enamored of is with child. I have heard it reported that every morning this week she has cast up her accounts. In the afternoons she is right as rain, so it can only be a babe that ails her." The smug look on Lady Michaelton's face detracted from her beauty. Everleigh had thought her very pretty before, but her obvious delight in the misfortune of others had Everleigh finding her quite ugly now.

Everleigh expected such news was supposed to shock her, and indeed it did, but not in the way Lady Michaelton obviously expected. If she were expecting hysterics or tears, she would be sorely disappointed. That an unmarried lady was with child momentarily stunned her, for how was such a thing possible? Certainly, such news was not meant for her ears but she would not show her confusion. Lady Michaelton's revelation was badly done. Setting her wonderings aside, she adopted a concerned look and mused, "Oh, one wonders how this tragic affair will affect her career. I have heard she is quite talented."

"Indeed," Lady Burbury nodded her head, picking her teacup up and taking a delicate sip.

"Oh dear me!" Lady Michaelton's hands flew up to her cheeks. "Oh, what am I thinking?" She looked at Everleigh with feigned pity. "I have only just remembered that you are betrothed to the Marquess, Lady Everleigh. How shocked you must be!" She turned to Lady Burbury. "It is so difficult to keep up with all the news related to those who are out. When arrangements are made between those who have not been presented, they quite slip one's mind, do they not?" She shook her head and tutted. "Oh, I shall never be able to forgive myself for being the one to break your poor heart." She patted the back of Everleigh's hand. Everleigh felt Miss Owens stir softly beside her.

"Fear not, dear Lady Michaelton. My upcoming nuptials are only a business arrangement, as most of these affairs are," Everleigh commented with a wave of her hand. "I assure you my heart is in no way in danger and I am certain that despite my motherlessness, I will have no trouble in learning to look the other way." She looked directly at Lady Michaelton as the comment hit its mark; the gossips were also all astir with tales involving Lord Michaelton and his various paramours.

Take that, you vile creature!

Lady Michaelton's nostrils flared with her anger.

"Oh, my! Look at the time! We shall be late meeting your father if we dally any longer," interrupted Miss Owens. She stood and waited for Everleigh to join her.

Without delay, Everleigh rose and said, "It has been a pleasure visiting with you lovely ladies. I look forward to spending an afternoon in your company soon. After I am out, of course." She smiled at Lady Michaelton, who did not return the gesture.

"That would be most excellent. I shall send an invitation." Lady Burbury shrewdly appraised her with a slight curve of her lips.

Everleigh nodded at Lady Michaelton, who returned the parting, and then took Miss Owens' arm in hers. The two walked from the table with their heads held high. Once they were out of earshot, Miss Owens spoke.

"That woman desires all to be as miserable as she is. I commend you on not showing how her cruel taunts made you feel."

"In truth, her words mean very little when I shall *not* be wed to the Marquess. Now there's an *on dit* only I am aware of." Everleigh sighed before she and Miss Owens burst into laughter. She immediately felt the tension leave her body and became aware of how taut it had been.

How shall Miss O'Brady's current circumstances affect this complicated situation which Gideon and I are in the midst of?

When they exited the teahouse they located the carriage in the waiting line and were helped inside by a groom. After taking her seat, Everleigh allowed her thoughts to dwell upon other, more pleasing things-namely a certain pair of gray eyes. She was an engaged woman, free from fear of the wagging tongues of the gossips where Gideon was concerned. All was right in her world.

19

THE EARLS ARRIVE AND A CONFESSION

Gideon swirled the brandy around in his glass and stared into the fire. He was grieving the fact that the Marquess had insisted that he not call on Everleigh for another day or two. He was cantankerous and irate and just wanted to catch a glimpse of her face.

Is she missing me?

His thoughts were not being kind to him; telling him that she hardly noticed his absence one bit. He had taken a walk in Hyde Park. He had taken care of procuring suitable attire befitting his new rank. He had organized the gun cabinet that the last Earl of Fairfield had constructed and wondered why one so large was needed in Town. He made a mental note to have it carted off to his country estate. He didn't see the sense in so large a collection in the townhouse as the hunts generally took place in the country.

While Gideon was considering pouring himself a third glass, he heard a rap on the front door. He curiously waited to see who was calling. Since he had been residing in his own townhouse, he had received the errant visitor or two, and not all were male. He had promptly sent them all on their way and wondered what sort of a bounder the last earl had been. He chuckled when he wondered what inconvenience it would cause his brother, if any, were he to give them

125

directions to his townhouse. He and Francis had not spoken since their visit with the Duke in Sutton which was a few days ago.

His mind returned to that morning when he knew for certain that there would be no swaying Francis from his path.

I am still slightly embarrassed to have witnessed such open affection that was not for my eyes, not to mention all of the flesh that was on display. Dear Lord, scrub it from my mind.

The study door was opened by the butler, who regally announced, "The Earls Bramley and Hathwell have called. Shall I send them in?" Grant was so unlike Murdock in both manner and physique. Gideon often felt like an unruly schoolboy when he gave a directive and Grant took a moment to act. Did the man think he wasn't quite up to snuff?

Gideon quickly dismissed the thought as he felt happiness overtake him. He smiled wide and nodded to Grant. He attempted to straighten his cravat, but it was wrinkled beyond repair. Instead, he stood up straighter and hoped no one would notice.

Lord Bramley entered the room with a smile lighting up his kind face. Lord Hathwell followed with a grin of equal pleasure. Gideon rose and closed the distance between them. He approached Lord Bramley and the pair shook hands. He greeted Lord Hathwell and exchanged pleasantries as they, too, shook hands. Gideon offered them drinks, which they readily accepted, then inquired if they would like to play a game of billiards, to which both men answered in the affirmative.

Gideon led the way to the billiard room and set his brandy down. He noted that Lord Hathwell had not touched his drink, and thought perhaps 'twas not to his taste. Before he could offer an alternative, the man walked to the wall where the billiard sticks were hung and retrieved three. He then retraced his steps and handed each of the men a stick.

Lord Bramley nodded his gratitude and stated, "I never thought we would get here before midnight fell."

"'Tis true," agreed Lord Hathwell. "We were both loath to leave our wives. And they did not seem eager to send us off. Of course, with the twins in need of constant redirection, I can understand my wife's reserve. We're currently without a governess as the last one left us to marry."

"At least Mariah and Isabelle are together at Bramley Hall. It is not too far from here; should the need arise, we can return in no time at all."

"How is Her Ladyship's health?" Gideon asked as he watched Lord Bramley make the first move. The ball hit its mark and the other balls scattered in different directions along the table. One even made a pocket.

"She is in good health. We miss your visits. But I suppose I must seriously put effort into choosing a physician. I appreciate the recommendations that you sent." Lord Bramley took another shot and his ball missed.

Lord Hathwell approached the table and studied the balls before him. He was content to let the other two gentlemen converse. When he took his turn, he managed to sink three balls.

"I am delighted to soon be welcoming you into our fold, Fairfield," Lord Bramley raised a glass in a toast to him.

"Yes, we need more men with whom to share our consternation with the women known as 'wives'. More insight is always welcome, plus we can guide you through your missteps into marital bliss," offered Lord Hathwell.

"I thank you. Surely the path to maintaining wedded bliss cannot be as perilous a journey as you make it out to be?" Gideon quirked a brow at each man in turn.

Lord Hathwell threw his head back as his rich laughter filled the room. When Lord Bramley joined in, Gideon frowned.

"Just you wait and see… there will come a day when you royally step in it and you will seek us out for aid," smirked Lord Hathwell.

The first game concluded with laughter and a camaraderie that did Gideon a world of good. He had missed being a part of a group and with the easy manner of both men, he felt free to be himself. There was no judgment or desire to one-up the other; they simply enjoyed themselves and conversed with effortless ease.

When the second game was underway, Gideon rang for sandwiches and lemonade, which he learned Lord Hathwell had a fondness for. He suspected that perhaps Hathwell did not partake of stronger drink because he had once been too fond of it. Well, he resolved from that moment on to abstain from alcohol in solidarity when in his friend's presence.

They finished the fourth game as the sandwiches quickly disappeared. Then they removed themselves to the study and settled in comfortably. The topic of horse breeding arose and Gideon became intrigued by the idea of improving the stable at Fairfield.

"Of course, now the cows need grazing land and all manner of care. I have decided to hire an expert in the field of animal husbandry," Lord Bramley informed them, changing the topic.

"What really do they need? They are cows? Can you not simply set them out to do what they please?" questioned Lord Hathwell with a sparkle in his eye.

"One would think that. But Thayer has taken up an interest in the raising and breeding of cattle and is adamant that his cows are treated with respect." Lord Bramley quirked a dark eyebrow at them.

"Respect?" guffawed Lord Hathwell.

"Just so," smirked Lord Bramley. "What else am I to do? While I am here in Town, I will try to find someone to hire who can please both my nephew and his cows. His interest has not waned since he first laid eyes on Mervin."

Shaking his head, Lord Hathwell stated, "You could have just served the original two at the table and been done with the business."

"No, that I could not do. I gave three very precocious children my word that it would never happen." Lord Bramley replied.

"Well, then. Here is to forevermore raising cows for company and not for food!" laughed Lord Hathwell. "How udderly amazing."

Lord Bramley raised his glass of lemonade and chuckled at the jest. "Huzzah!"

It was late when the two lords departed, each headed to his own townhouse. Gideon thought he was very blessed to have two wonderful friends in his life as he climbed the stairs and rang for Gibbons.

Gideon was dreaming of his lady love when he was roused from his slumber by a rough hand shoving his shoulder. He awoke quickly, thinking a patient must need his attention at once. He rubbed his hand over his eyes and saw that it was Francis who hovered over him.

"What has happened? Is grandfather-"

"No, the old goat is fine, as far as I know. 'Tis my Shannon. She returned home ill this afternoon and she seems to be worsening. Will you please come see her?" His face was etched with worry. He looked as if the weight of the world was pressing heavy boulders down upon his shoulders.

Nodding his head and tossing his coverlet aside, Gideon rose from the bed and walked to the dressing area to don his clothing. He forwent his cravat and was pulling on his fitted tailcoat as he followed Francis down the staircase. He remembered to grab his medical bag despite their haste. Without words, the two climbed into the awaiting carriage and made their way to Miss O'Brady's residence. He had never seen his brother in such a state of panic before. Gideon wondered how ill the woman could be.

When the carriage stopped, Francis leapt from his seat and opened the door. He jumped down and ran up the steps to the front door. Gideon followed behind him at a more sedate pace. The moon was hidden behind clouds, leaving the walkway cast in menacing shadows. He would be of no use should he fall and injure himself, so he took care with his steps.

Gideon found his way to the master bedchamber and entered through the open door. He took the few steps needed to reach the side of the massive four-poster bed. Francis was sitting on the bed next to Miss O'Brady, who moaned in pain as she regarded him wearily. She was sweating and shivering, which indicated to Gideon that she was fevered.

"You can see she is ill. Please do what you can to aid her," Francis pleaded, rubbing a hand through his tousled hair.

Nodding and carefully approaching the other side of the bed, Gideon set his black medical bag down. He removed the candle from the bedside table and raised it to examine her eyes. He could see anxiety in them, and her pain was evident. He had questioned Francis on the ride over, and his brother had advised him that Miss O'Brady was not given to fits or bouts of poor health. He wanted to question her, but his brother's presence made the task more complicated.

She licked her dry lips and struggled to speak. "My love, please wake Mrs. Addams to fetch tea. But not with the bell. There is no point in waking the entire household," panted Miss O'Brady.

"They are servants. It's their job to serve, even if that means being woken at any hour!" fumed Francis incredulously.

"Please, darling. For me?"

Looking toward the door, then at Gideon, he slowly nodded and rose from the bed. Once he had left, Miss O'Brady turned back to Gideon.

"Please," she panted. "Please, you cannot divulge what I am about to tell you." She winced. "If you treat me, you will answer only to me, not to him. We are not wed, and my health is my own."

Gideon began to protest. "I cannot keep secrets from my brother–"

"Then you may go, if your conscience allows it." She turned her head away from him.

He knew he must choose, to adhere to her wishes or to go against his every instinct as a healer and leave her to possibly die. Even if he was no longer treating patients, he could not walk away from her. "That is the only way?"

"Yes."

Gideon sighed and nodded his agreement as he lifted her wrist and began to count her heartbeats.

She winced and swallowed a cry.

"Take your time," he encouraged her as he let her hand go and leaned closer to better hear her whispered words.

"I haven't time before he returns," she reminded him through gritted teeth. "I was with child," she began as she swallowed back her emotions. "I was referred to a clinic in Cheapside that specializes in abortion. I was hoping for a brew to end it, but it was too late. I was told I was too far and must undergo a procedure, and I agreed." She winced again. "I did not fully understand the scope of suffering, nor the copious amounts of blood it would entail. I fear that something has gone wrong."

Horror and disgust filled his being. "You could have died there! You still may!"

"If that is to be my fate, then I will embrace it. I made my decision," she replied with steel lacing her voice.

Gideon rubbed a tired hand over his face. The chop shops were a bane of any healer's existence. The sort of "medicine" they practiced was nothing but crude villainy. Many women died just from the consumption of the special brew Miss O'Brady referred to; the actual procedure to abort a babe was even more dangerous. One of the things that had impelled him to leave for the countryside in the first place was a dislike for tending to the messes made by those so-called doctors and midwives.

"There are herbs that can be mixed. I will have them located and procured. Your maid can brew them. I will prescribe some laudanum for the pain. There is not much else to be done other than to wait. You must keep to your bed. We will keep your lower half elevated and hope that gravity will aid your recovery." He began positioning her pillows under her feet. As he did so, he checked the damage done to her and shook his head.

They were butchers!

Francis returned with her maid in tow. Gideon motioned for the maid to join him on the other side of the room and gave her a list of herbs to procure from the apothecary, along with instructions on how they were to be prepared.

"Where are you sending her?" demanded Francis.

"To the apothecary for the herbs needed," Gideon replied, not meeting his eyes.

How am I to keep this from my brother? My heart is being rent in two. I owe him my loyalty, but I also owe it to my profession to treat his lady.

He was also consumed with grief for the child his brother knew nothing about.

The very idea of a babe being torn from the safety of its mother's womb made him ill. He had chosen to become a doctor to save lives; the idea of taking them was unthinkable.

Gideon understood that there were those who could not afford to increase their brood or feed another child. He knew there were far too many starving children running dirty-faced and hungry in the slums. The idea of a member of his family having to endure such a thing made his blood run cold. He knew also that it was not always sought by those who were the poor; many women of *the ton* feared childbirth, especially those with failing health. He tried to remain nonjudgmental; it was not his place to cast stones, but it did not ease the hurt in his heart. Gideon had bore witness to the heartache felt by those who wished desperately to bring a child of their own into the world; that there were those who threw them away made his pain more acute. He wished there was an easier remedy but, aside from abstaining, there was nothing he knew that could be done which was an absolute.

And my brother has certainly taken his share of pleasure outside the bonds of marriage and now he would pay the price; the life of an innocent child in exchange for the careless indiscretion of a selfish man.

His regard for his brother and his lack of care cut through him like a knife. Sharp and deep.

And his penance may not end there. Francis may lose the one woman he values above all others. Dear Lord, keep her safe and heal her. This wound is beyond my hands and skillset. Heal my heart as well and let nothing taint my view of this terrible situation that could have been prevented.

Had Francis not learned from his unsavory friends that there were ways to prevent such a thing from happening? Of course, they were not foolproof. He knew Francis's selfishness now and suspected that applying the methods had been tossed aside. Many men had taken to using the French letters in order to avoid a by-blow. But not Francis, he would not see the reason in practicing care when he meant to wed the woman.

Gideon ran a hand over his aching chest. He was hurting for the woman lying prone on the bed, for his unsuspecting brother, and for the child they created who would never be born. Sometimes being a doctor frustrated him, and this was one of the times when he would carry a wound from the ordeal. This was entirely of his brother's making, and Gideon felt his heart harden toward him.

Dear Lord, give me strength and forbearance, for no good can come of what has happened.

20

MISSING THE ONE

The next two days passed dismally for Everleigh. Gideon had not called upon her even once. He did send her extravagant floral arrangements, and she often found herself gazing lovingly at them. Their scent filled the drawing room as well as her bedchamber. He knew she favored roses, so each bouquet was made of roses in various colors with greenery and baby's breath. If she still had harbored any doubt as to his affection for her, this was enough to allay any fear.

Everleigh was giving the housekeeper directions when Ashburn informed her that the Earl of Fairfield and two other gentlemen were there to pay a call on her. He had placed them in the drawing room and taken the liberty of ordering tea. Everleigh set her menu planning aside and rose from her desk. Quickly she dismissed the housekeeper and sought the full-length mirror in her bedchamber. She had dressed in a pale peach morning gown with ribbons and lace burgundy accents. Her hair was styled in her usual manner, and she tugged the tendrils hanging on either side of her face and wound her index fingers through them. When she was satisfied that she was as perfect as she could be, she rushed from her chamber and descended the staircase. In a few more steps, Everleigh stood still before the drawing room door as Ashburn opened it.

Peering into the room, she spied her intended with two gentlemen that she had never been introduced to before. Both men were handsome and regal in bearing. The slightly bigger of the men had his hair styled just a tad longer than was fashionable. His chin sported the hint of a beard and he had just said something to the other two which caused the men to laugh. The other man was dressed impeccably and had coal-black hair. He held an air of quiet dignity and reserve in his manner. Everleigh's interest was piqued and, wishing to be introduced, she glided into the room and came to a halt beside Gideon. The men directed their attention to her.

Smiling brightly and curtseying at the trio, Everleigh received bows in exchange. When she rose, Gideon clasped her hand in his and brought it to his lips. She didn't bother to wonder what he had done with his gloves. With alarm, Everleigh took in the tiredness of his face and dark smudges under his eyes; that he was losing sleep made her heart sore.

She ignored the thrill of their bare hands clasped together and smiled hesitantly up at him.

Oh dear, I do hope that all is well.

Gideon must have sensed her agitation as he smiled at her with such brilliance, her worries scattered away. "Darling, may I present to you Earls Bramley and Hathwell." He pointed out each gentleman as he spoke their name. "My friends, I am pleased to present Lady Everleigh Winslow."

Lord Bramley addressed her first. "I am certainly glad to make your introduction." His Lordship's kind teal eyes were alight with good humor as he took a step back.

"'Tis a pleasure to meet you," Lord Hathwell remarked with a straightforward ease of manner.

To say that Everleigh took an immediate liking to them was an understatement. They were both exceptionally kind and well-mannered. They didn't leer at her, nor try to see down her dress as the friends of Prinny's were wont to do the few times she had crossed paths with them at St. James's; these gentlemen made eye contact and treated her as an equal. There were too many men who held titles that were far from refined, and elegant, and wouldn't think twice about taking liberties. She felt safe in their company.

"Would you care to sit? Ashburn has sent for tea," she informed them. She directed them to the wingback chairs that were set a few feet from the settee. The Earls made their way to the chairs, then turned to face her. Once Everleigh had taken her place on the settee, they sat. Gideon took the space beside her. The heat of his body sent a delicious thrill through her as memories of their kisses passed through her mind.

If I do not want to appear as some silly gel, I need to tuck these thoughts away and be the proper hostess that I am.

Everleigh blinked and gave her attention to the other gentleman as she cast them a small smile.

"Fairfield has requested we join your party when he puts his request before the Queen. I do not envy you the task ahead, but know that you have my unwavering support," spoke Lord Bramley, beginning the conversation.

"I sincerely thank you. I must admit I do not believe it will go smoothly," she replied.

"I believe it will come down to the wording," mused Lord Hathwell.

"You must have Her Majesty thinking it's her idea and her way of solving the issue." Lord Bramley nodded in agreement.

"I agree," Gideon added. "We have discussed the matter at length and attacked it from every direction. You need not worry." His gray eyes held hers.

"It is a great asset to us that you are her relation," Lord Hathwell spoke, gaining their attention. "I owe my happiness to Gideon and his skill as a physician. Were it not for him, I might not be here."

"Oh?" questioned Everleigh, arching a pale brow at Gideon.

Gideon shrugged and said, "I attended to Hathwell after an accident. We feared that the injury would take his life. He was a difficult patient, but did as instructed, for the most part."

In reply, Lord Hathwell chuckled.

"If we are to keep score, I believe he has saved my own life more than once. Tell me, Lady Everleigh, have you ever been stung by a colony of bees?" Lord Bramley inquired.

"Good heavens, no! I take it then you were beset by them?" Everleigh felt her eyes widen.

"I was. As was my brother-in-law. We had to jump into the fountain to fool them into thinking we had disappeared." Lord Bramley grinned.

"Dear me! I cannot imagine the terror. Bees are quite common in the garden. I wonder… Did you come in contact with a hive?"

"Yes, and it must be stated that 'twas only because the twins had knocked it from the eaves in my stables," replied Lord Bramley.

Everleigh turned to Gideon and questioned, "Who are the twins?"

"Ah, they are the parson of Bramley's brothers-in-law. They were quite… curious and given to mischief in their younger years," Gideon replied as his lips curved.

"Those twins are always into some scrap or another. 'Tis a wonder we are all still alive to tell their tales," Lord Hathwell remarked as his chocolate gaze met hers.

"I must meet them!" she declared.

"No rush though," chuckled Lord Hathwell.

"Despite my brother-in-law's best attempts in correcting their behavior, and believe me, he has worked diligently with them, there are still instances where they act beyond the pale. Generally, though, I find them to both be good lads with very active interests," Lord Bramley expounded further.

Ashburn came into the drawing room with the tea cart and cucumber sandwiches. He stopped the cart before Everleigh who immediately began preparing the refreshments to serve her guests. Once the Earls were busy with their tea and sandwiches they began a conversation between themselves, allowing Gideon to inquire where Miss Owens was. Everleigh told him that she was off visiting with her boarding school friends who met once a month to discuss their literary pursuits.

"Why do you not join them?" He cocked his head to the side, studying her as she prepared his tea. Once she handed him the teacup, she picked up her own and carefully took a sip.

"They are a group of spinsters who have not a titled lady among them. And that is just the way they prefer to be. I have never wished to intrude. Miss Owens is free to spend her time where she desires and to keep the company of those she wishes to. Besides, we were not expecting callers. I seem to have been deprived here as of late." She fluttered her lashes at him.

Unfortunately for Gideon, he had just taken a sip of his tea when she flirted with him. He spluttered for a moment signaling to the others that he was well. Everleigh smiled demurely at the other two gentlemen who grinned in response.

"I realize I have been remiss in my attention," began Gideon. "A certain marquess requested that I stay away, while another requested that I visit." Gideon gave her a lop-sided smile.

"Oh. I hope all is well?" Everleigh longed to clasp his hand in hers and give it a gentle squeeze, but such was not the actions of a proper young lady; Gideon's friends would believe her to be quite ill-bred.

When he looked up at her, his eyes seemed to possess a secret sadness and Everleigh didn't know what to say next. Her thoughts flew to the gossip surrounding Miss O'Brady. When she had broached the subject to Miss Owens, her companion had insisted that they allow the matter to drop from their minds. It was all an unseemly business and better left for the entertainment of others, should those others desire to gossip about such an unfortunate occurrence.

Does he know? Has something happened? Does this change any of the plans we have made? What else could make him display such sorrow?

Everleigh wanted to discuss it with him, but how did one go about broaching such an indelicate topic?

When the tea and sandwiches were finished, the men rose to take their leave. They expressed their joy in the coming union between Gideon and herself. Everleigh rose as well, and when the two Earls walked toward the door, she laid a hand upon Gideon's arm. He looked down at her and frowned.

"Something the matter, Darling?" his gaze met hers.

Everleigh hesitated, then decided to just blurt it out. "I've heard a rumor regarding Miss O'Brady."

"Go on," he peered intently down at her.

"They are saying that she is with child…"

"I see." Gideon swallowed. "I am not at liberty to discuss these matters with you. There is a side of humanity that you will not yet be acquainted with. Were it up to me, I would keep you in ignorance if only to spare your heart unhappiness." Gideon rubbed his thumb along the back of her hand in soothing circles. Everleigh could not suppress the shiver that assaulted her. She knew he felt her movement when the seriousness in his eyes darkened to passion. His gaze lingered on her lips and then he looked away.

"I will not press you further," she replied as her eyes searched his, wishing that the situation made more sense to her. The last thing she desired was to earn his ire for her questions. Though she suspected that were it information directly relating to her, he would have told her more.

He nodded and looked at the men who were in quiet conversation by the door. She studied his handsome face which still looked drawn, despite the refreshments that she had hoped would perk him up.

"But what has kept you from your slumber?" She could not help but ask. "Are you regretting your choice of bride?" Everleigh directed her gaze at the carpet, not wanting to see what truths his eyes would reveal, especially should they tell her that she was no longer his desire.

Gideon tilted her chin up with his index finger. "I will never come to regret my choice of bride." He leaned his head down to hers and placed a gentle kiss on the end of her nose. Everleigh's lashes fluttered in response. He released her, then offered her his arm.

They made their way to the gentlemen. Everleigh walked with them to the foyer and watched on as Ashburn handed over their outerwear. After bidding their farewells until the next evening, the two men exited the townhouse.

Everleigh rose to her tiptoes and placed a delicate kiss upon Gideon's cheek. His smile made her heart skip.

"Until tomorrow, my lady," Gideon bowed before her and took his leave.

My heart has left my chest and taken its leave along with him.

21

MEASURING HIS STEPS

fter parting ways with his friends along the street, Gideon traveled the short distance to Miss O'Brady's townhouse. He had spent a good deal of time there, attempting his best to ignore his brother. He hated keeping such a heartbreaking secret from Francis, but 'twas not his place to divulge the source of her illness.

His conscience would have regretted taking liberties in revealing more to Everleigh. But he could summon neither regret nor contrition on not having told her more.

The worried look in her gaze pinched my heart but I would not burden her with the woes of this world when the chances of her joy being robbed were high. It was better to remain silent. She is such a bright light in my life; an unending source of goodness and joy.

Gideon was careful in his interactions with Francis; measuring each step, feeling as if eggshells littered the ground beneath his feet. He knew that keeping this secret only widened the chasm that had grown between them. He was torn in two. He felt grief at the loss of such an innocent life, but he was also suffering from a case of acute anger directed squarely at his brother.

When the townhouse came into view, he stopped and watched the busy street. It was a hive of activity with members of *the ton* paying calls upon their friends and relations. The sidewalks were a riot of colors with the trees, shrubs, flowers, and the fashionable clothing of those who dressed to be seen. Finally, he turned from the traffic and climbed the townhouse steps. The butler answered his knock and escorted him in. After handing over his greatcoat and topper, Gideon took the staircase steps two at a time. He was anxious to check on his patient and leave. He hoped to miss his brother entirely, but since the doting man had not been far away from his paramour, Gideon held little hope that his wish would come true.

The maid was exiting the master bedchamber and stopped once she saw him walking toward her. She pushed the door open behind her and curtsied. Gideon nodded to her as she passed by and then directed his attention to the sunlit chamber. Tiny particles of dust floated along in the streaming sunlight. The room was bright and he easily found his patient lounging on the chaise. She was propped up on the curving head of the chaise, and while her color was looking better, the shadows still clung to her eyes and mouth, stealing her vibrant beauty. He would be hard pressed at the moment to call her lovely. She was the complete opposite of Everleigh.

Where one is dark, the other is light.

Gideon rubbed a hand over his chest when recollecting the look that had overtaken Everleigh's face when she had voiced her fears of his rethinking his choice of her as his bride. He was blessed beyond measure, and hoped to show her the true depths of his feelings once they were wed. His affection was endless and plumbed the deepest waters. He could not measure it were he to scale the highest mountain. The poets were all fools; nothing they could have ever written could come close to what his feelings were. He was made stronger by his emotions, he was saved by her very existence. She was his bright beacon and his reason for all he would do from this moment forward.

Am I in love?

Instead of the thought felling him to his knees, it filled his chest with warmth.

"What is that expression for?" Miss O'Brady inquired in a tired voice.

He cleared his throat and regarded her.

It seems she is still in pain.

"I am here to discuss you and your health," he told her, completely ignoring her question.

"But I would much rather not, for even the walls have ears. I am improving thanks to your expert knowledge."

Gideon knelt by her side and picked up her wrist to check her pulse, then peered into her eyes. "I am glad to be of service."

"Are you? When you revile me so?" The look on her face was part mocking and part insecurity. 'Twas not a becoming look.

"My feelings for you are not that strong," he told her. "I know that you can be kind, but I am grieved that you are keeping my brother ignorant of what you have done. He should know the truth. You owe him that much." He set her hand back to rest at her side.

"I owe him? He has taken his pleasure of me, repeatedly."

"You have offered yourself up to him. Certainly, you understand how these things work. If my brother weren't your protector, another would be in his place. I know that you have no wish to wed him, but he is hopelessly in love with you. And now not only have you deceived him, but you have dragged me into it as well." He blew out a frustrated breath. He had not allowed his thoughts to dwell on this long enough before to acknowledge her blame in the conception of the babe. In truth, she, too, bore some of the blame.

Mayhap that means there is still some good in my brother; for he was not entirely responsible for this situation.

"I have done nothing to you. 'Twas he that insisted you come." She huffed.

"Because you mean the world to him. Because of the choices each of you have made, I now face the responsibility of keeping your secret which further serves to drive a rift between my brother and me. I am set to take the responsibility while you both cavort as you desire."

"I cannot change what is done. I do feel an ache within my heart, but it will pass. I can never tell him." She looked at him with tears rimming her lashes.

"I apologize for berating you. It is not the place of a physician; a brother perhaps, in a gentler manner. I am beyond frustrated with all of this." He waved his hand around.

"I think you are by far the better brother. Lady Everleigh is one very fortunate young woman. I hope in time she comes to know it."

"I believe that she does. I have made no secret of my regard for her." Gideon looked toward the window, though he could only view the sky.

"Good. Never leave her in doubt."

Gideon nodded, then rose to his feet. He looked down at her. "I shan't come around again unless you worsen. You will heal, given enough time."

"I understand. But… Do not cut Francis off completely. He needs you. He needs your kindness and goodness." She smiled at him sadly.

With a dip of his head, he left the bedchamber and descended the staircase. He would endeavor to never step foot in this townhouse again, if he could at all help it. He found himself in his outerwear and out on the street. His gaze turned back to the window overlooking the street and felt nothing but remorse and sorrow. This was a place of secrets and illicit desires.

PLANS HAD BEEN MADE EARLIER IN THE DAY TO MEET BRAMLEY AND Hathwell at White's for dinner. While they did not plan to gamble, they were to dine. It was as good a place to meet as any other. When he entered the St. James's Street establishment, he caught sight of his friends waving him over. They shook hands, then found their table for the evening. The masculine decor made for a relaxed atmosphere. None needed to fear the odd bit of liquor spilling as the colors were dark.

"Lo, my friend, I must say, Lady Everleigh is a perfect match for you." Bramley beamed over his brandy at him.

"I could not agree more. She is a graceful beauty, and I am excited for both Isabelle and Mariah to make her acquaintance," stated Hathwell with a salute of his flask.

"I am glad to know that you approve. She is delightfully perfect and I am looking forward to our future."

The liveried waiter came forward, and after apologizing for the interruption, took their dinner orders. When he left, Gideon watched as Hathwell took another sip from his silver flask. Seeing that he was being inspected, Hathwell spoke.

"'Tis nothing more than lemonade. Rest easy."

Feeling chagrin, Gideon nodded in reply.

"I promised my wife years ago that I would never imbibe, and while we have celebrated with a toast here and there, I no longer make it a habit," Hathwell added.

"We should always keep our word, especially to our wives," agreed Bramley. "However fine a house is, it's never a home without the love of a wife to make it such."

Truthfully, Gideon had never given the topic much consideration. Lakewood House was perfectly adequate. But the thought of returning there or even to his Fairfield estate without Everleigh was not a welcomed concept. As for peppering their life with untruths, he wasn't adept at lying and had no wish to do so to his wife. One horrible secret was one too many.

The conversation soon took a turn to stables, he engaged in a lively discussion of the best methods of caring for a stable and which other titled gentlemen had the best sires. Possibilities were revealing themselves for what life in his country seat might entail.

In the company of my two best friends, I can breathe easier. While I may have lost my connection with Francis, I have a wealth of friendship at my side. I need not worry if I happen to blunder, because I have these honorable gentlemen to support me. And with the prettiest bride by my side, what could I possibly want for? Yes, I am blessed beyond measure.

22

TODAY IS THE DAY

Rhinoceroses were rampaging within Everleigh's stomach, and she felt in very real danger of tossing up her tea onto the ornate carpets of St. James's Palace. The carriage ride had been much too short. Her nerves had only worsened as she watched her father anxiously twist his gloves in his grasp. Miss Owens was perched upon the cream-colored bench seat beside her. When her companion tried to engage her in conversation the air seemed to disappear.

Are my stays laced too tightly? My skirts are voluminous and ridiculous, and I feel frumpy, not regal. Certainly not beautiful.

Her nerves had been plaguing her all morning, and she felt only Gideon's presence would truly allay her fears. The thoughts of his charming grin and perfect white teeth caused her to smile softly.

Dressing this afternoon had been tedious. There were so many layers. She feared tripping and begged Papa repeatedly to ensure that she did not end up on her face. While the idea of her coming out had not caused her anxiety, this task was seeing her fare far differently. Her whole happiness depended on the kindness of the Queen.

When she thought about what her future could have entailed if she were wedded to Francis, she felt chilled to her bones. He was so very unlike his brother. Before, she had been prepared to do her duty and take her vows regardless of his fidelity. Now that Gideon was in her world, she could not imagine a life without him.

His gentle words, addictive touches, and passionate looks at me fill me with wonder and make me want to defy decorum and fly to his side to bask in his warmth.

Her lips tingled when she thought about his lips upon hers.

When the carriage entered the gates of St. James's Palace, she leaned forward to look from the carriage's window. The imposing stone facade loomed before her. Royal Guards were stationed every few paces, resplendent in their scarlet uniforms. Everleigh's heart rate accelerated, and she had to take careful measured breaths. 'Twould not do to appear anything other than serene and calm.

"Ladies don't feel panic or much of anything. We just are mere decorations to a room." The words of her mother echoed in her mind.

But I could be so much more… And I believe that beside Gideon, I could accomplish any feat we could dream of.

When the young tiger leapt from the back of the carriage to open the door for them, she watched as he let the wooden steps fall to the ground. Everleigh stood and held out her hand for assistance in alighting the conveyance. Holding the liveried groom's hand in a firm grip, she took measured steps down. Her billowy gown floated in her wake.

Once she was standing on the ground she gazed at the imposing palace. It was created in the shape of an L. The building's Tudor-style had once been the height of architecture. There had been a terrible fire a few years ago and parts of the Palace had since been rebuilt. In certain places, one could glimpse the red brick it had once been constructed of. 'Twas still magnificent.

The Marquess came to stand beside her. He offered her his arm and she accepted it. He was dressed in an eggplant-colored fitted tailcoat and cream satin knee breeches to match. The white silk stockings clung to his legs and made them resemble sticks. The buckles of his black slippers gleamed in the afternoon sunlight. His white cravat was tied very prettily, and the lace was very detailed and fine.

Everleigh turned her head to look at Miss Owens, who was to remain in the carriage and await their return. Her companion nodded to her and smiled. Everleigh returned the gesture and then allowed her father to lead her into the Palace. She attempted to calm her breathing and let her gaze roam over the gilded opulence surrounding her as the slippers on her feet made whispered footfalls.

Gold dripped from every corner and crevice. Suits of armor and oil paintings lined the walls. Potted palms, various statues, and vases were in every direction one looked. The scene had never daunted Everleigh before; she had always felt welcomed and a part of the events and entertainments while in attendance. She had created beautiful memories by her mother's side in these hallways and drawing rooms.

I hope today I may add another joyous memory to tuck away and cherish.

They were greeted by the under-butler who took their outerwear and then escorted them to one of the Queen's private Drawing Rooms. Once they had been left to themselves, Everleigh stood anxiously. The rest of their party had not yet arrived. Extra chairs had been brought in and placed around the red settee. Landscapes and portraits in ornate gold frames hung along the walls. A pianoforte stood in a corner. Her gaze took in the moldings that melded the walls to the ceiling. It was all so regal and beautiful. She was fixated upon the ceiling when the door opened and the Earls Bramley and Hathwell were shown into the drawing room. No introduction was needed between her father and the newcomers as they were already acquainted. The gentlemen greeted her father even though the Marquess seemed distant and cold.

"My, you look stunning, Lady Everleigh," commented Lord Hathwell as he took her gloved hand in his, bowing over it. He looked elegant in his cobalt fitted tailcoat and cream knee-breeches. His waistcoat was cream silk with swirls in a light blue.

When Everleigh rose from her curtsey, humor filled her eyes as she replied, "Why my lord, I am not entirely sure you mean that as a compliment at all." Everleigh's eyes saw the mirth shining from his gaze.

"On my honor, I do. You are quite a vision," he replied as he grinned at her.

He is teasing me! I look positively dreadful.

"*Pah!*" she said merrily, turning her attention to Lord Bramley. The kind man smiled at her and shook his head at his friend. His fitted coat was cobalt as well, and he had also donned cream knee-breeches. His waistcoat was cream-colored and he looked very regal. The colors of his attire accentuated his eyes, which were the color of the sea.

"He is ever the charming fellow. I think we must be early? I expected Fairfield would be in attendance with you by now," said Lord Bramley as a wrinkle marred his forehead.

"I do hope all is well." Everleigh was much too anxious to consider what could possibly be keeping him. At any moment the Queen and her retinue would be entering the room and how were they to justify taking up her time if the subject of their discourse was not present?

"Do not fear. I do not imagine that anything would keep the besotted man from your side, today of all days." Lord Bramley joined his peers in taking a seat. Everleigh was left standing, and she much preferred that to sitting in the monstrosity she was garbed in. No disrespect was taken that the gentlemen had sat while she had not.

"I am not impressed at all. The man should be here by now. This entire affair rests on his character and as of now, I find it wanting," the Marquess droned in displeasure.

"Papa, one incident does not make a full sketch of one's character," she spoke as she took to pacing the confines of the drawing room.

"Today is the day we have been anticipating all along. The pup should be here!" Her father's fisted hand landed atop his thigh in indignation.

What was she to say to that? He was not here, and he really should have been by now.

Dear Heavens! Where could he be?

When the door next opened, the Duke of Sutton ambled in, leaning heavily on the golden globe of his walking cane. Everleigh ceased her pacing and made quick work of presenting him with a curtsey. She heard fabrics rustling behind her and knew that the men within the room had risen to greet the Duke as well. When she rose, he closed the distance between them and addressed her.

"How wonderful to meet with you this afternoon, Lady Everleigh. I trust you are in excellent health?" He peered at her face.

Everleigh felt herself blush at his intense scrutiny. "I am well, Your Grace. I do hope that you are in good health as well?" He nodded once and then took her hand and patted the back of it. When he did not relinquish it, she simply measured her steps to his as he pulled her further into the room.

"Thornwhistle, Bramley, Hathwell, each of you look impressively put together today," the Duke praised as he directed his gaze to each of them.

Feeling the older man teetering on his feet, Everleigh spoke, "Your Grace, mayhap you would care to sit? The armchair nearest the fireplace looks quite inviting." She would have expressed her concern for his well-being no matter who he was to her, but as he was soon to be her relation and he was in need of care, she took it upon herself to see to his comfort.

The Duke gazed at the chair. "Indeed it does." He let her lead him to the seat. When he stood before it waiting for Everleigh to take her seat before siting himself, she informed him that at present she had no wish to sit. Understanding dawned in his gray eyes and he gratefully sat. He ran a gloved hand down the front of his forest green fitted tailcoat and observed the men who were busily retaking their own seats.

"Terrible business this is." The Duke shook his head.

Everleigh felt sadness for the man. He looked as if the weight of the world rested upon his stooping shoulders.

Does he feel responsible for his eldest grandson's misdeeds? How tragic. He is no more to blame for that than Gideon. Gideon... where are you?

Dread began to fill her.

Perchance he changed his mind despite all his protestations and reassurances? I know that he is a sensitive man, and he would not have let us arrive today if he had no intention of coming himself. What if something terrible has happened? Could fate bring us this far just to let us both falter now?

23

CRUSHING DESPAIR

He was almost there. The intervening hours had been torture for Gideon. He had longed to be in Everleigh's company, if not expressly fixed to her side. When the carriage finally pulled up before St. James's Palace, he let his rigid shoulders relax. He was soon to have an answer and a way forward no matter the Queen's decision. This air of indecision was making him moody and fidgety, which was so unlike him that he was beginning to find his own company tiresome and vexing.

Steady on, old boy. This all shall soon be settled.

After alighting from the newly purchased carriage, he straightened his periwinkle tailcoat. Gideon had not bothered with a greatcoat; he felt stifling enough without its weight. He did not look around as his sole focus was on reaching Everleigh. Once Gideon was within the Palace, he handed over his topper to the under-butler. The liveried man escorted him to the Queen's Private Drawing Rooms, and he halted a moment to calm his racing heart.

"A moment if you please, dearest brother," came Francis's voice from off to the side. Gideon turned his head and saw his brother approaching him. When Francis reached his side, he grabbed Gideon's arm and tugged him as he walked away from the door. Furrowing his brows, Gideon allowed the rough treatment and walked beside his brother. Francis stopped before another door and opened it. Once they had both entered the room, he closed the door and released Gideon's arm.

Francis walked to stand in the middle of the room with his back to Gideon. Gideon paused and took in his brother's posture. Francis sniffed, then turned to face Gideon.

"We are brothers, are we not? We share a bond and are steadfast in our loyalty, keeping no secrets from each other?" Francis's face radiated rage. His skin was flushed red, and his eyes were furious.

Gideon swallowed and bowed his head. "We are."

"Yet you did not honor our relationship; did not seek to confide in me. I am disappointed in you, brother." Francis awaited his reply, but Gideon did not know what to say. He felt as if all of his new hopes and dreams were about to be crushed into nothing more than dust beneath his brother's shoe.

"Even now, you choose silence. What have you to say, Gideon? I truly wish to know how you can remain so calm, when my whole world has been ripped from under me?"

Gideon looked up at him. He knew without a doubt that Francis knew of his deception. His heart squeezed painfully.

This is not what I wanted. This is not how I wanted to face him.

"I am not your enemy." Gideon took a step forward when his brother spoke.

"If I were you, I would tread very carefully now. I am not myself at present, and all I want is to beat you to a pulp. So 'tis in your best interest, *dear brother,* to stay where you are." Francis glared at him hatefully.

"I will not feign ignorance about what you are so upset about-"

"Upset? *Upset!* Upset is when your maid breaks a family heirloom while dusting. Upset is what happens when you lose a bet. When your carriage wheel breaks in the middle of nowhere. I am not *upset.* I am *furious,* and all of my rage is burning in the direction of you and that vile woman who dared to deceive me." Francis began to pace the room, his arms swinging at his sides.

"I understand-"

"Understand? How could you possibly understand? Has the woman you love betrayed you? Has the one man you thought held you in regard and high esteem lied to you? *No?* Well, then you have not an inkling how I feel."

Gideon's eyes searched his brother's face. He felt loathing fill him for his part in this betrayal. He had hurt his brother and he knew the truth would be the fatal crack in the bond they had once shared. "You are right, I cannot understand. That was a poor choice of words. But when you brought me to her, she vowed she would refuse treatment if I did not keep her secret. I felt I had no choice; she would have died without attention. I did not keep this from you willingly, Francis. I argued with her; I *begged* her to tell you!" Gideon ran a hand through his hair, mussing it.

"And why could you not tell me after you treated her? Of all the people on this earth, Gideon, I should have known! You should have disregarded her wishes and confided in me!" Francis's voice was lowered with an edge that cut Gideon to the core.

"I had to decide whether to betray you or let her die. As a doctor, I had to save her."

"And what of my say in this matter? What of my well-being?" Francis began to pace again.

"I knew this would crush you. I did not want to deliver such news to you." Gideon heard the waver in his voice, but could not control it.

"News?" Francis laughed. "It was news that the woman I was giving up everything for had cut my child from her womb? That she had cast my child to the rubbish bin like an old glove. Of no more importance than an *old glove*." Francis put a fisted hand to his mouth.

"What of your role, Francis? You played with fire, and this is what you got. Do you not bear some of the blame?" Gideon began to feel anger that Francis felt he bore no responsibility for the wellbeing of the woman he claimed to have loved.

"My role? So, I am to have a role now? As the father, you mean?"

"If you were not so irresponsible in your pursuit of carnal pleasures, this never would have happened. You planted the babe." Gideon shifted his stance.

"Yes, I did do that. Indeed, I did. Tell me, Gideon, what is it like?"

"What is what like?" Gideon felt confusion and despair clouding his mind.

"To be such a paragon of virtue and good deeds? To never falter in your path? To always be right."

"I am no such things. I am-"

"You are late, or about to be, for your meeting with Her Majesty. We should not keep her waiting. You would not want to disappoint your lady love; of that I am certain." Francis turned to stride over to the mirror that hung to his right, just over a long, polished table. He smoothed his hair and adjusted his clothing. "Come, Gideon, we have matters to settle. And *you* may depend upon me to do the right thing and act just as *I* should."

Gideon balked at his brother's sudden change in mood and a sense of foreboding overcame him.

Francis walked toward him, then passed him by. Without another look. Gideon turned and followed him.

What choice do I have?

He felt crushing despair settle over him.

What plans does Francis have for me now? Does he seek to punish me? Dear Lord, do not let him take his anger out on Everleigh. That I could neither abide nor bear.

24

FAINTING AWAY

There was not much time to greet Gideon once he did finally make his entrance. To Everleigh's surprise, his brother, Francis, was at his side. Francis wore the same mask of cruel indifference he had greeted her with the night at the theater. Gideon looked pale and discomforted; his golden hair was mussed, and it was so unlike him as he was always groomed to perfection. She felt her anxiety increase.

"My lady, how fetching you look," Francis addressed her, coming to stand before her and bowing over her hand. Everleigh was too stunned to curtsey.

Why is he being so cordial?

Once again, the double doors opened and in glided the Queen. An air of elegance floated in her wake. Her gray hair was piled high atop her head, and decorated with white feathers that waved and bowed from their perch. Her periwinkle dress was decorated with embroidered flowers of white and gold. Her dark eyes held intelligence and kindness. The men were bowing to her elegantly. When she spied Everleigh, she moved to stand before her.

Everleigh sank into a low curtsey and waited for Her Majesty to speak. When she felt fingers lifting her chin, she met the Queen's gaze and slowly rose to place a kiss on her great-aunt's cheek.

155

"My, how lovely are you, my dear. I am pleased to see you today." The Queen said, then directed her attention to the Duke. "And how dashing you look this afternoon, Sutton," she said as she nodded regally.

The Duke, who was stooped over, rose and made his way to her and bowed over her hand. "You are a vision of loveliness as always, My Queen." He let her hand go and stepped back.

Beside her, Francis firmly stood in place.

The Queen turned to greet the Earls, and they exchanged pleasantries. The Earl of Hathwell said something that made the Queen laugh.

Gideon was standing to the side of Francis and Queen Charlotte stopped before him. While they exchanged no words, the Queen did nod her head at him, and Gideon grinned in response.

When Her Majesty circled back to Everleigh, she looked Francis up and down with a small frown and pursed her lips.

"You are quite the industrious fellow, young man. My Court hears much pertaining to you." She gave him a taut smile before she turned her back and softly padded over to take her seat. Once she sat, the two ladies accompanying her stood behind her chair as their skirts skimmed the wall behind them.

Francis did not look chastened, and Everleigh wondered if there was anyone capable of shaming him.

I cannot wait to be away from him. I find his presence greatly irritating. Why must he stand so close to me? Why is he even here? What game is it he is playing?

Everleigh made her way over to the settee that was situated before the Queen and sat. Her father took the space beside her. Her posture was ramrod straight as she perched on the very edge of the cushion. Gideon sat in the chair nearest to her. When he noticed her stare, he gave her a tight-lipped smile.

"Now, what brings you to my Drawing Rooms today?" Queen Charlotte inquired.

"Shall I attend to this matter?" Francis spoke to the room at large. When no one objected, he continued. "Your Majesty, we wanted to seek your blessing officially in the union between our two families."

From the corner of her eye, Everleigh caught sight of the way Gideon startled. He half rose then sat back down.

"Indeed?" The Queen looked directly at Everleigh. "And how do you feel about such a union?"

"I am thrilled, Your Majesty." Everleigh attempted to curve her lips into a smile but feared she had failed, and hoped that she had not grimaced instead.

"Hmmm. I do believe the young man could benefit from the influence of a sweet person such as yourself. It may even reform his rakish ways. That is why I had previously given my consent to the match. I am pleased to know that you, too, desire for it to take place." The Queen nodded at them.

Everleigh felt the blood drain from her face. This was not what she had meant at all. Not a union between her and Francis, but between her and Gideon. They were supposed to have addressed the matter of dissolving the marriage contract forever tying her to the Marquess. Before she could voice her protest, the Duke's frail voice rang out.

"Your Majesty-"

"Your Majesty, I vow to reform myself and be the perfect doting husband. As you can see, my friends are here to lend their support; even my brother, the newly conferred Earl of Fairfield, congratulates me on this auspicious occasion." Francis's voice was firm as he cut a glare at his brother. Everleigh watched his face change to a look of pure delight at the discomfiture of everyone else in the room.

He is demented, his wits have gone begging and now what is to be done?

The room went utterly silent. Was no one going to dispute him? This could not be happening. This was not how things were to be. He had never even wanted her hand.

"Your Majesty," began Lord Bramley. "I think there has been a-"

"No need to prattle on, *my friend,*" Francis smiled coolly at him. "There is no need to take up any more of Her Majesty's time."

Lord Bramley blanched, but remained silent. The Marquess outranked him.

The Queen rose and everyone followed suit. The men bowed and Everleigh lowered herself to the floor in a curtsey.

"There is one more thing, Your Majesty." Francis's voice filled the room.

"Yes?"

"I should like to present my bride to you once we are wed. There is no need to see her come out before then." Francis spoke blithely, waving a gloved hand through the air.

"As you wish. I will, of course, be sending an invitation to tea in the coming days. 'Tis my wish to see to the wedding arrangements; Everleigh is motherless, and as she is my niece, I take her situation to heart." Queen Charlotte's desire shook what little composure Everleigh had left.

The Queen and her retinue left, and the doors were closed behind them. Everleigh could not catch her breath and black began to fill the edges of her vision. She felt herself tumbling forward and was helpless to catch herself.

25

WITH A BROKEN HEART

Gideon saw Everleigh begin to fall, but was too far away to catch her before she fainted completely. She had never risen from her curtsey, and now she lay in a heap beside his brother. Francis was kneeling over her when Gideon reached her.

"Look what your actions have wrought!" the Duke's harsh voice carried around the room.

Gideon took her gloved hand in his and removed her glove, checking her pulse. He suspected that she had simply fainted, but he needed to be holding onto some part of her, no matter how small. He needed to assure himself that she was still here before him, and not some mirage forever from his reach.

Dear Lord! How could Francis do this?

He seethed internally. He could not bring himself to look at his brother. He had been betrayed, but how could he say his betrayal of his brother's trust was worse than what Francis had just done to him and Everleigh?

Mayhap this is my due.

"Calm yourself, Grandfather. Was this not what you wanted? For me to come to my senses and do my duty?" Francis met the Duke's gaze over Everleigh's prone body.

159

"Not once this had progressed thusly. You have gone too far." The Duke shook his head.

"*I* am the titled heir. *I* am fulfilling my obligations," Francis stated coldly.

Everleigh moaned as her free hand twitched by her side.

"Ah, another task taken care of, I see. Thank you, Gideon, for procuring a token of our family's high esteem for *our dear Everleigh*." Francis commented as the light hit the jewel upon her finger.

Gideon laid Everleigh's hand atop her stomach. He was simmering with impatient rage. That was his ring, his symbol, and his promise to the woman his heart was screaming at him to flee with.

But how can I do so? She does not belong to me... and never truly did. How I have blundered, inviting her heart to care for me, when this is the result.

"We must take our leave," stated the Marquess of Thornwhistle. "Will she be well enough to make it to the carriage?"

"I daresay she has suffered nothing more than a case of the stays she is wrapped in being laced too tightly," Francis spoke as he rose to his feet.

"Everleigh," Gideon rubbed the back of her bare hand with the tips of his fingers. "Everleigh, you must wake up." Gideon leaned over her.

With a fluttering of lashes, Everleigh awoke. Her gaze went from Gideon to his brother. Her face crumpled before she closed her eyes again. Taking as deep a breath as she could, she exhaled slowly, then said, "Please help me rise."

Gideon slowly pulled her to her feet and held onto her arm while he wrapped his free arm around her middle to steady her. Everleigh gave him a nod, then stepped away. He felt the loss of her greatly and wanted to cry out for her to never let him go. She tugged her glove from his grasp and pulled it back on.

His lady turned to his brother and calmly said, "Will we expect you for dinner this evening, my lord?"

Francis smirked at her, then bowed at the waist. "Of course, my dear. We should become accustomed to each other, and the sooner the better. I am sure my brother will wish to accompany me as well, if that is acceptable to you."

"But of course, my lord." Everleigh strode to the Earls. "Thank you for coming to Town to assist in this delicate matter. I trust your travels home will be safe." She curtsied to them both. They both bowed to her, but she would not meet their eyes. Neither gentleman spoke, but the dark looks they were directing at Francis didn't seem to bother him one bit.

Next Everleigh reached the Duke, stepped up on her tiptoes, and pressed a kiss on his cheek. "I shall see you again very soon, Your Grace." Her voice was a mere whisper. The Duke nodded to her with sorrow clearly present in his gaze. He patted her hand.

"I am your servant, my lady," the Duke replied gravely.

With as much grace as she could muster, she turned for the double doors and held out her arm to her father to take. He quickly made his way to her side.

"No parting words for my dear brother?" Francis taunted from behind her.

Everleigh halted her steps and let her father's arm go. She turned around to face the brothers.

"'Tis time for us to depart," Bramley told them. Hathwell agreed and the two hastily quit the drawing room.

"Because I am feeling magnanimous, I, too, will take my leave. Will you follow me out, Grandfather?" Francis awaited the Duke's answer. The Duke nodded his assent and let his grandson lead him from the room.

The Marquess of Thornwhistle took a few steps to the side of the room, and waited. Everleigh would not look up at Gideon, even when he closed the distance between them.

"You must know, I had no prior knowledge of my brother's schemes. I had no hand in what occurred today." Gideon's voice held tenderness. His heart was breaking, and he wanted to grab her hand and flee with her to any place they could be together.

"I saw your face. I knew it surprised you as much as it did me. I do not blame you in the least. I am only sorry that I let myself believe in… more." Everleigh cleared her throat, blocking what he suspected were tears. He had never felt lower in his entire life. He wanted to hang his head in shame, but then he would miss her face as they had this aching parting. He would withstand her sorrow; he could not miss her loveliness for anything.

"I misled you terribly. It was badly done of me."

"No, no…" she insisted. "You were all that was honorable and just and kindness itself. I will treasure what time we did have." She stepped closer toward him and removed the ring from her finger. "Return this, or gift it to another. I have no wish for your brother to lay claim to it. It makes no difference if he replaces it or not." Everleigh held the ring out to him.

Gideon opened his hand, and she gently placed the ring into his gloved palm. Everleigh smiled beautifully at him, and it ate at his soul. Unshed tears were swirling in her magnificent eyes; how she was keeping them at bay was a marvel. He desired nothing more than to hold her to him and assure them both that all would be well. But that would be foolish and would do neither of them any good.

He could not bring himself to return her smile. His hand fisted over the ring, allowing its sharp edges to dig into his gloved hand.

"Until tonight, Earl of Fairfield," she fleetingly met his gaze. Turning toward her father, she waited for the man to reach her side again. The Marquess held out his arm, and she wrapped her arm around it. Without looking back at Gideon, they left the room.

Gideon ran both of his hands through his hair. He wanted to land a facer to his brother for causing this anguish to Everleigh. He had never been a violent man, but just now, he felt as if he could impart real damage to his brother's body. How had this failed? How had everything been within his reach? Now he was to be forever separated from her. Francis expected him to witness his wooing of Everleigh. His brother could be charming when the situation called for it, and Gideon had no doubt that he would employ all his experience and expertise when courting Everleigh. He wished him well; Everleigh was not some stupid chit, and she deserved true devotion, but true devotion was not in him.

How am I to stand by and allow this to happen? My heart is hers. Every last broken piece of it.

26

HOLDING THE BROKEN PIECES TOGETHER

The carriage ride home was taken in complete silence. Miss Owens took a long look at Everleigh and must have been sensible to the fact that all was not well. Her eyes widened as she scooted over on the bench seat to accommodate Everleigh's cumbersome dress. The Marquess stared out the window, giving Everleigh leave to gather herself. He had never been unjustly cruel to her; he had been stern, but never diabolical. She felt that he must be suffering an attack of his own conscience for the role he played in today's drama. They were all now just chess pieces being moved along the board by the will of one man. She was holding herself together until she was alone in her bedchamber. There she could let her bleeding heart release its anguish.

Everleigh would gather these broken pieces of her heart and carefully tuck them away to keep them safe until perhaps one day she could piece them back together. She tried in vain not to direct her anger at Francis, though it was his indecisiveness and his inaction that had placed them all on this path to begin with. He was set on correcting his flaws, and that began with taking her to wife.

How am I to wed him now when I know I cannot love him? I could have easily done so before I came to know Gideon as I have. Before he kissed me with such passion. If I had never had a taste of what could be, this would be such a simple task. It would be so easy to just do my duty and pledge myself to him. I will still do my duty, but how will I ever bear to be in Gideon's presence and not wish for the things that I will now never have? How do I make my heart forget him?

She was glad that she had returned his ring. Her finger felt bare, but she had done the correct thing. It was but a small thing to lose when Gideon would never be hers. His face had imprinted itself onto her mind and wrapped itself around her heart.

I may never be truly free of him, but I will make this work somehow. I will allow myself time to grieve first. I cannot go forward until I have at least released the heartbreak that is even now threatening to break free.

When the carriage stopped in front of their home, she was the first to depart. She took the stairs rigidly, as if dreaming, to her bedchamber. Her heart thumped erratically in her chest, making her heave with the need to release her pent-up tears. But she would not yet do so. Quickly, she opened the door to her room and entered, letting the door snap closed.

Avril met her in the dressing area to help remove the Court dress. It took a few minutes to remove the heavy material and underthings. Everleigh remained silent and stoic through the entire affair. She found herself seated before the dressing table as the many pins were removed from her coiffure. She allowed her maid to attend to her as usual, and then when her golden tresses were falling to her waist, she climbed into her bed. When the servant left, she curled into herself and let the tears flow. They coursed down her cheeks and neck to land amongst her curls. When her sobs became louder, she turned onto her stomach and buried her face into her pillow to muffle the sound. The last thing she desired was for someone to discover her thusly in a torrent of tears. Her shoulders shook as every wound came to the surface and she grieved for a life, a dream, that she was never to claim. She had been so certain that a life with Gideon was possible, so ready to be by his side as their future unfolded, and now... now they were to be forever parted. How was she to endure another man's kisses and share another man's bed, especially when he was so vile?

It hurts all the more that they are brothers, and that I must endure all of my days knowing that I am wed to the wrong one.

She cried until she could cry no more, then fell into an exhausted sleep. Hours passed and the dim light of evening greeted Everleigh when she finally peeled her eyes open. Her eyes were sore and felt puffy. She thought she must look frightful and, no matter how she felt, there was still the dinner to prepare for. Gideon and Francis would both be in attendance as their only guests and it would never do for her to look as if she were either unwell or unhappy. 'Twas one thing for others to suspect that she was affected by the days' events, but quite another for them to view the evidence on her face. Though she was in agony, and it hurt to breathe because her heart had bled itself dry, she would put on a brave front. She would not show any weakness to Gideon, the man her heart still wanted above all others. Nor would she show her disgust to Francis when she suspected such a thing would only give him perverse pleasure.

Everleigh threw her coverlet to the side and sat up. Swinging her legs from the massive four-poster bed and searching with her toes, she located her slippers and donned them. She slowly made her way to the bellpull and summoned her abigail. She would request some hot compresses for her eyes, and some lavender and rose water would also aid in her recovery. Her nerves were overwrought, but she forced herself to the mirror, taking small steps until she stood before it.

As she gazed into the full-length mirror, her haggard reflection stared back. Everleigh vowed to herself that she would remain calm and graceful no matter how the evening unfolded. She could fall apart again once their guests had departed, and she was once more alone in her bedchamber.

No one needs to ever know the folly of my heart as I tumbled into dreams of a future by the side of the one who ignites my entire being. This longing will cease… one day… it must…

When Avril entered her bedchamber, she quietly went about the task of preparing Everleigh for the evening. A cool compress was placed on her face, soothing her tired skin and lessening the visible signs of her sorrows. When she could delay no longer and it was time to dress, Everleigh allowed her maid to choose which dinner dress she would wear. The abigail styled Everleigh's hair in the Greek fashion Everleigh was fond of, threading sweet peas through the heavy masses of curls. The pink and purple of the flower petals matched the violet shade of her dress and slippers. There was a wide orchid-colored ribbon just under her bosom.

Rising and thanking her maid, Everleigh took in her appearance. The light dusting of powder had done wonders for her complexion, and she looked every inch the image of a composed lady. She was ready to don a mask of indifference and thought it would be practical as she could envision many days and nights hiding her true self.

Though I am not the master of my own destiny, I will steer ahead as I must with cool indifference.

There was a quiet rap on the chamber door, and before she could bid them to enter, Miss Owens was peeking her head around the door to peer into the room.

"You look lovely," she gushed.

Everleigh gazed at her through the mirror and gave her a tight smile. Her face felt brittle with the movement.

"Thank you." She turned from the mirror and took a few steps. Everleigh took stock of her companion's appearance. "You, too, look marvelous. Shall we go down to wait for our visitors?" Miss Owens was attired in a pale pink that offset the highlights in her upswept hair.

"If we must. Dearest, are you ready to confide in me?" Miss Owens' large eyes studied her.

"Not now. Perhaps never. Just know that I am now to be wed to the elder brother and the particulars do not matter." Everleigh forced the words from her mouth, and they left a horrible taste on her tongue.

Bitter, like ashes fresh from the fireplace grate.

Miss Owens gaped at her before collecting herself and holding out her arm for Everleigh to take. The two friends clung to each other as they made their way from the bedchamber, through the hallway, and down the grand mahogany staircase. They were soon seated upon the silk-covered settee in the drawing room while the fire crackled loudly into the silence. Each lady was lost in her own thoughts.

Everleigh smoothed her skirts and stared at her now ringless finger, wondering how long it would be until another ring replaced the one she had given back. She suspected that if the Marquess were to gift her with such a token, the new one would feel like a weight that would draw her low, no matter its true size.

I will never love him. I will never love anyone again. I will never allow another to turn my head, and when I am aged and no longer a beauty, I will go gratefully to my grave.

How many lonely nights was she to sustain before then?

27

UNCONTROLLABLE RAGE

Uncontrollable rage flowed through Gideon's entire body as he battled his grief and despair. Witnessing the havoc and evil that his brother was capable of wreaking had thrown him. Losing Everleigh was something he would never be able to recover from. His heart would never heal from this severing, and though he bore some of the blame for what had transpired, he was unable to rectify matters one wit. His wishes and desires had been thrown to the wayside as surely as Everleigh's had been. He had known his brother was vengeful, but he had never been the recipient of his rage; he had never had cause to be. When Francis had announced his betrothal to Everleigh, his whole world had ceased to function. Gideon's very body seemed to have momentarily shut down, and now he wondered if, in those moments, he might have gathered himself more swiftly and put an end to Francis's machination.

Francis had forever lost something precious to him, and so he was taking away the one thing Gideon cherished most. But how had he known? How had he deduced that Everleigh was his entire focus? He ridiculed himself and poured more brandy into his glass. Gideon watched the flames from the marble fireplace dance across his glass as he twirled it in his fingers. He had never wanted to enact his own revenge before. Would that he could whisk his Everleigh away right out from under the noses of his brother and her overbearing father. But what life could he truly give her? Such an action could ensure that his title was stripped, and they would never be free from vicious rumors. He knew that Lord Bramley would welcome him back in the role of town physician of Bramley. But would the life of a country lady truly suit his bride? He certainly couldn't clothe her in the finest fashions on a doctor's wages, and without the aid of the allowance bestowed by his brother, he would lose Lakewood House.

His home would be modest but comfortable. Would she feel confined and uncomfortable there?

What does any of it matter when she will never be mine?

He took another large gulp of brandy, savoring the burn as it slid down his throat and settled in his stomach, causing warmth to flow through him.

I can never take her away from her home anyway; I would not bring a scandal down around her for anything. The only way I can protect her now is to support my brother in this. Though it will only serve to further fracture my heart, I will not show her undue attention, nor stare at her exquisite face, or desire to taste her delicious lips or mold them to mine. I do not know if one can conquer love; that will be my mission henceforth. For how can I possibly watch Francis kiss her, wed her, and know he is taking her to bed while I stand blithely by? But who else will take him to task when he missteps? He will likely only come to despise me further for attempting it.

Gibbons strode purposefully into the study and stopped short as he observed the scene before him. Gideon was reclined in his brown leather chair, more than slightly in his cups, with his booted feet flung over the desk, one ankle crossed over the other.

I have never overindulged like this before. I have never had my heart so expertly crushed before, either. 'Twould seem that today is a day of firsts.

His vision swam while he gazed up at the plaster ceiling.

Such a curious thing alcohol was. It seemed to be both friend and foe, offering both comfort and doom.

"My lord, 'tis time to ready for the evening. You are still attending the dinner party?" Gibbons inquired as he came to stand before the other side of the desk.

"Just so." Gideon swung his feet from the desk and onto the floor.

The rug swayed before him as he tried to steady himself. His stomach gave an unwelcoming lurch.

"Whoa there," said Gibbons as he rounded the desk and took hold of Gideon. He swung one of Gideon's arms over his shoulder and clasped him around the waist.

"I am a lost cause, I fear," Gideon commented as he matched his steps with his valets. The act took every bit of his concentration. They traversed the study and the hallway until the staircase loomed before them. Gideon groaned. He did not want to climb the steps. He wasn't even certain he could, even with the aid of his loyal manservant.

"You are a good man and a good friend, Gibbons. I have been remiss in fully appreciating you. Fully… That's such an odd word. I don't reckon it gets used very much. Poor lonely word." Gideon stumbled, and it took Gibbons a long moment to steady him.

"I believe a cure would do you much good. You are in no state to visit with anyone, most especially young ladies." Gibbons spoke as he tugged Gideon up the first few steps.

"They do not work. Cures, that is." Gideon faulted on the next step, then clung to the banister with his free hand. He began to use his upper body strength to pull himself forward.

Hmm… It seems at least rowing was good for something.

"My father swore by them. I will get you situated in the tub and go concoct one." Gibbons peered at him. "That is, if you think you will not drown in the tub?"

Gideon was concentrating on making his limbs work properly, so he only nodded in reply. He didn't clarify whether he thought he would or wouldn't drown, and felt grateful that his kind valet didn't press him further.

When they reached the last stair, Gideon blew out a breath. He wanted to throw his fist into the air in victory, but very much doubted he would remain upright if he did so. So, instead, he grinned triumphantly.

One must celebrate the small wins.

"Huzzah," Gibbons deadpanned, then rolled his eyes. "You are as heavy as you look. Solid mass." Then he continued lugging his master down the corridor until they reached his bedchamber.

Gibbons let Gideon fall into the chair in the dressing area and began to help him undress. It was a difficult task as Gideon was uncooperative. He would easily become distracted in his quest to examine the buttons along his waistcoat.

Have I ever seen them shine so brightly before? Ah, poor buttons. I have taken them for granted too. Well, no more.

Gideon patted his buttons. "Clever little things, keeping me orderly. Gibbons, have you ever wondered about how marvelous buttons are?"

Gibbons made no reply and, before Gideon could focus on something else, directed him into the copper tub. Gideon sighed with pleasure, forgetting all about buttons as the warm water slid over his skin. Water was his friend. He loved water. And the more he considered his love for it, the more he mourned over the lake that he liked to row across. He had planned to take Everleigh to it, even if they were residing elsewhere.

She would have looked ethereal with the sun shining behind her, covering her in a soft glow. Everleigh is lovely, so she must love water too.

He felt a sharp pain strike his heart when he realized he was no longer free to sit by her side and freely converse with her. A day would never dawn when they would sit in silence as they had run out of things to talk about. They would never again be as they once were; or be something so much more.

He felt Gibbons begin to scrub his back and when the man reached around to cleanse his chest, Gideon took the washing cloth from him. He was man enough to bathe himself and grumbled so to his valet.

"Very well. I shall see to the restorative." Gibbons rose from behind the head of the tub and soundlessly left.

ONCE HE WAS IMPECCABLY ATTIRED IN A CHARCOAL TAILCOAT, TAN trousers, a gray waistcoat whose sole decoration was its brass buttons, and neatly tied neckcloth, Gideon deemed himself ready to endure the evening's events.

Or as close to ready as I'll ever be.

Gideon had cleaned his teeth twice due to the disgusting cure Gibbons had foisted on him, which had literally caused him to toss up his accounts. He was feeling much improved. Purging the alcoholic poison from his body had done him much good. He was clear-headed and steadier on his feet.

When he descended the staircase, Francis was there awaiting him.

"'Tis not like you to be late," Francis remarked as his eyes roved over Gideon. Francis looked the perfect part of the titled gentlemen. His fitted superfine tailcoat was in a cobalt color. His trousers were a shade of charcoal. The cream silk waistcoat had tiny golden flowers embroidered along it, with gold buttons that shone brightly. His hair was tamed, and his eyes were clear.

"An off day, it would seem." Gideon would sooner stick his spoon into the wall than apologize to his brother.

"Well, let us be on our way. I do not wish to keep my future relations waiting." Francis pursed his lips, then turned on his heel to make his way through the foyer and out of the townhouse. He was wearing his cloak and topper, and swung his walking cane in a circular motion as he walked.

When Gideon reached the front door, the butler stepped forward and handed Gideon his own cloak and top hat. He donned them quickly and strode forth.

The ornate filigree carriage with its four matching grays sat stationary along the curb. There were roses and cherubs carved into the side of the carriage that he could see. The door had elegant scrolling along its edges. Gold was affixed in various decorative grooves. The horses boasted black feathers twined into their braided manes.

Gideon shook his head as he followed in his brother's wake. This extravagance was almost too much to bear.

It seems as if Francis is set on making a statement to one and all. It would not be long until the entire kingdom knew the description of this conveyance. Well, the thieves and highwaymen will certainly delight in seeing this pass them by. What a ridiculous waste of coin.

Once the brothers took their places on the black velvet-padded bench seat, the carriage set off.

"I will be reclaiming my townhouse. As the second townhouse was only leased, I have given it up and severed all ties from those under its roof. I have directed my valet to remove my things and set them up in my own residence. I do hope you stay on in Town for a few more days, at the very least. You must have valuable insight into Lady Everleigh's character, and as I am certain you wish to see her attain at least a modicum of contentment, I am sure I can rely on your expertise in handling her."

"The lady is not some servant that you can charm and make biddable. She knows what has transpired between you and Miss O'Brady." Gideon informed him.

"Ah, well that is unfortunate. Very well, I shall take each situation as it arises. Pity, though, I had hoped she was to be easily managed."

Gideon kept silent. He did not think it was the time to knock his brother a sound one. They traveled the short distance in silence. He doubted blackening his brother's eye, or both of his brother's eyes, would do his own head much good at all.

When the carriage came to a stop, he quickly opened the door and alighted. The servant gawked at his behavior until he gave the lad a dark stare. If his steps faltered a bit, 'twas of no importance to anyone except himself. Francis exited the conveyance and took the few steps to reach the townhouse's front door.

The door swung open, and the butler greeted Francis with a bow and waved him in. Gideon hurried his steps. He wanted to escape his brother's presence, even if only for a few seconds. Though what he truly desired, what his heart begged him to do, was to find Everleigh and abscond with her into the night. But he would never sully her reputation in such a dishonorable manner.

She deserves more than rash actions upon my part.

Ashburn awaited Gideon's cloak and topper, which he resolutely handed over. It was not long before Francis's sure footsteps echoed on the tiled floor of the foyer behind him. The butler took his outerwear next, then directed the pair to follow him to the drawing room. When Gideon caught sight of Everleigh waiting for them next to Miss Owens on the settee, his heart stalled. She seemed to have grown even more lovely since that afternoon. But he would have been blind to not notice the dark shadows staining the area under her lashes. It was barely noticeable at all, and yet it pained him. He wanted to offer her solace in any way that was acceptable, but his mind was completely blank.

How does one comfort the love of his life, when unable to reach out to her? She is now and will forever remain just that—my forever lost-love.

Francis sauntered into the large room and halted his stride before Everleigh. He bowed before her, and as she was rising from her curtsey, he kissed the back of her gloved knuckles.

Was that aversion in her eyes? She is every inch the perfect hostess to not flinch or show any other outward sign of her revulsion and dismay. But where had she learned such a talent? Was that a task for a governess to teach, or did it come from dealing with her tyrant father?

"You look beautiful, darling," purred Francis. There was no mistaking that his gaze lingered on the swell of her bosom displayed by the cut of the gown. Gideon wanted to cast up his accounts again.

"Thank you, my lord." Everleigh extracted her hand and let it fall to her side. She motioned to her companion, and Miss Owens and Francis exchanged greetings while Gideon's mind wandered. He watched Everleigh as her unwavering gaze rested on the other two in the room. He silently willed her to look at him, to know that she didn't outright hate and loathe him for allowing Francis to manipulate the situation.

Gideon finally met her eyes across the drawing room, but could not make his legs obey the command to close the distance between them.

Even were I to reach her, there is an entire ocean of proprietary separating us now; invisible waves are pushing and pulling us apart, and I can never again reach her.

Everleigh continued to look over at him, and he saw her eyes slowly take him in. He had never felt so discombobulated before.

How must I appear to her?

He met her gaze once again and nodded at her. She returned his gesture with her face a mask of indifference.

Beautiful and yet as hard as stone.

"Shall we sit and wait for my father to join us?" inquired Everleigh. Motioning to the set of armchairs facing the settee, she waited for the gentlemen to find their seats.

Together, Everleigh and Miss Owens sat down, and Francis took his chair. Gideon knew he was acting foolish, and he calmly walked to the empty armchair and sat. He knew he was providing Francis with endless entertainment, as evident by the knowing smirk cast his way.

"I expect to receive correspondence from the Queen on the morrow," Everleigh commented.

"Indeed, we will defer to Her Majesty with all of the details," agreed Francis. Everleigh nodded at him and then shifted her eyes to her folded hands resting in her lap.

The door opened to reveal Thornwhistle. The gentlemen rose to greet him.

"Shall we adjourn to our dinner?" the Marquess asked as he stood before them, not bothering to step into the room.

The ladies rose, and while Francis held out his arm to Everleigh, the Marquess allowed Miss Owens to accompany him. Gideon brought up the rear of the party as they exited the drawing room and made their way through the corridor to reach the dining room.

Once the ladies had been seated and the gentlemen had taken their seats, Everleigh gave the signal for the butler to begin dinner.

"I think tomorrow would be lovely for an outing to Vauxhall Gardens in the early evening. Would you care to accompany me, Lady Everleigh?" Francis began the conversation.

"Oh," Everleigh looked at her father, who nodded his assent. "I would be honored."

"Excellent. After all, we need to correct the idea that my brother has been sniffing at your skirts. It would not do to let the gossips and their imaginations run wild." Francis ladled soup onto his spoon and took a sip.

Gideon had just taken a sip from his goblet and choked at the crudeness of his brother's language. He hoped the icy glare that he directed at his brother was sharp enough to cut glass.

"Are you so concerned for your reputation?" Everleigh's brow furrowed.

"Yours, my dear. A tarnished reputation for a man is easy to overcome. However, a woman fresh from the schoolroom must take her cues from the men in her life and do as bid. I will require more from the mother of my children; total devotion and obedience must be shown." Francis swirled the wine in his glass.

"And what of you, my lord? Are devotion and loyalty to be expected from you in return for my... obedience?" Everleigh held her head high. She had yet to pay her meal any attention.

Francis chuckled darkly before replying, "What a sharp tongue you have, darling. We will work ardently to dull it so it is no longer a blight on your otherwise so charming personality."

The Marquess of Thornwhistle cleared his throat and looked at his daughter with a censorious look. Everleigh fixed her gaze upon her soup bowl, and a blush infused her pale complexion.

"Perhaps what you seek is not a wife, but a canine. They are easier to train-"

"That is quite enough!" Her father bellowed, causing Miss Owens to startle. His face was flushed in indignation. "I do beg your pardon for my daughter's ill behavior. I hardly know what has gotten into her."

Gideon could take no more. He drew his napkin from his lap and slapped it onto the table. "I think no one could be in doubt that what has occurred today has greatly impacted not only Lady Everleigh, but me as well. I beg forgiveness in advance for my early departure, but I will not sit here and take part in this conversation, nor ill-treatment of the lady. I realize well, brother, that we are mere pawns in your game, but do attempt to remember that there were sincere feelings that had taken root. I will do my part and not meet with the lady, in public or private, again. I will take my leave and beg you, Francis, to consider that your soon-to-be bride does not deserve your contempt, your censure, your degradation, or any other vile attention you would bestow on her. Most importantly, she has done nothing to deserve you. If it is your wish to witness my ire or my heartbreak, it need not be done in her presence." Gideon rose from his chair and took a long look at Everleigh. Tears rimmed her lashes. He wanted to commit every feature of her face to memory, as it would be memories of her that would accompany him into his dotage; he would never let his heart attach itself to another. The vows to her had never been said, but he would honor them nonetheless.

Thornwhistle and Francis sat back in their chairs and regarded him. Thornwhistle's face held a look of surprise and mild aversion. Francis was glaring at him with thinly veiled contempt and rage. He was certain he had made enemies of them both, but he could not bring himself to care.

Gideon nodded to himself; he was doing the right thing by his beloved and by himself. They could not continue to meet each other and experience the heartbreak that each encounter was certain to bring. He had taken a few steps away from the table when Everleigh's distraught voice stopped him.

"Gideon. Please do not leave, not like this." Everleigh rose from the table.

"You will resume your seat at once, Daughter!" Thornwhistle commanded.

Gideon turned to look at her. He quickly rounded the table and reached her side. He took her ungloved hand in his and gazed into her eyes as he reverently kissed her knuckles. He leaned his forehead against hers and whispered, "You have been my greatest happiness, but if I stay, you will be my greatest ruination. I *must* leave. You will forget me, in time, I am sure."

Everleigh shook her head against his. "Never."

Gideon dropped her hand and leaned away from her. "Be well and find happiness. I wish you joy, my lady."

This time when he turned away from the table, no one tried to stop him. Ashburn followed him, and once they reached the foyer, he located Gideon's outerwear and handed the items over. Gideon did not bother donning either his cloak or his top hat. He walked through the door the butler held open and heard it close behind him. How he was to have the fortitude to keep his words, he knew not. It was time to go home, but whether that meant back to Bramley or his Fairfield estate, he wasn't certain.

How can I ever just let her go? It is torture to be so near to her and yet still so far away. Dear Lord, let Francis's lust for revenge die away so that Everleigh might be spared further indignation and heartbreak. That is the only way either of us will ever know peace again.

28

HEARTBREAK & TEARS

After Gideon's abrupt departure, Everleigh struggled to keep her emotions at bay. She felt adrift on a sea of emotions where waves of sorrow sought to pull her under their cumbersome weight and drown her. How could she bear to never see him again?

From his seat at the head of the table, Everleigh's father bade her to sit and finish her meal. With resolution to never show her broken heart again to either man, she complied.

What is done is done, and there is not one thing I can do to change my current situation. One day I will be in Gideon's presence again, and then I'll let my eyes feast upon him just to have another memory to tuck away and treasure. I will wed the Marquess and let him take me to the marriage bed where I shall do my duty. One day, perhaps I will even raise children that will remind me of Gideon, of kindness and goodness and his loving heart. And I will despise myself for being obedient when all I long to do is make a fuss and run after him.

The conversation between her father and Francis was stilted and related to estate matters. Everleigh let their voices drone on while she remained lost in her own thoughts. She neither noticed, nor tasted, what she put into her mouth; it was as if everything turned to cinders upon her tongue. She willed herself to hold together until she could once more fall apart in private.

The gentlemen took their port while she and Miss Owens repaired to the drawing room. Her companion remained silent, though she clung to her hand in compassion. Words had not been needed between them. Miss Owens knew her heart and silently mourned with her.

When the gentlemen came into the room, Papa commanded Everleigh to play a selection of music on the pianoforte. Miss Owens accompanied Everleigh to the instrument and selected the sheet music. As Everleigh's fingers flew over the ebony and ivory keys, Miss Owens stood behind her to turn the pages. Neither woman could meet the eyes of the men as they watched.

The last notes of the music echoed in the room as Everleigh brought her hands to rest in her lap.

"Bravo!" enthused her father. "You see what a fine wife you will have."

"Yes, the finest to be had. Well, the hour grows late, and it is time I took my leave," replied her betrothed as he rose from his chair. Everleigh felt his gaze lingering on her. She closed her eyes and somehow discovered the fortitude to rise from the pianoforte and move to stand before him.

Just a few more minutes, then I will be free to retire for the evening and let my battered heart freely bleed.

"Until tomorrow, for our outing," he said, but did not touch her, much to her great relief. She neither desired to feel his touch, nor wished to be in his presence. He bowed before her and Miss Owens, and they, in turn, curtsied to him.

Ashburn was summoned by Everleigh's father, and upon seeing that Francis was ready to take his leave, escorted him from the room and quietly closed the door behind them.

"I know that in time, you will come to understand this is for the best," began her father. He turned to look at Everleigh. "The heart is fickle, and young women are known for easily falling into and out of love. The infatuation you hold for the Earl will come to its end, especially now that he has vowed to stay away. All will be well."

Was this his attempt to make peace? Can my heart forgive him for arranging this marriage? For neither seeing nor caring how miserable it makes me? He only wants prestige and a title for me; I only desire to follow my heart. Every beat of my heart echoes with Gideon's name; every beat takes him forever further away.

Everleigh realized that she needed to say something in reply to her father. "As you wish it, Father," she heard herself say.

When her father nodded to her, she held out her arm for Miss Owens, who quickly entwined her arm with Everleigh's. Together they soundlessly left the drawing room and sought out the safety of their bedchambers. Once they ascended the staircase, they came to Everleigh's chamber first.

"Shall I stay with you tonight?" Miss Owens untangled their arms and awaited Everleigh's answer.

"No, I wish to be alone. You are my dearest friend, and I know you only wish to comfort me, but I cannot hold myself together much longer. Tomorrow, I will endeavor to do better, but just now, I need to let myself grieve for a future and the life and the babes I will never have."

"But in time, you will have children with the Marquess-" Miss Owens readily spoke to reassure her, but Everleigh cut her off with a wave of her hand.

"They will never be *Gideon's*, so they will never be the ones my heart longs for. And I know that the brothers bear a resemblance to one another, and the smiles my little ones cast at me may only serve to remind me of what might have been. In time, perhaps I will conquer my errant heart, but I shall never be able to do so if I do not set all such musings aside and purge them from my soul. Good night, my sweet friend." Everleigh placed a gentle kiss upon Miss Owens' cheek, then pushed the knob to her chamber door. She entered and closed the door behind her without looking back.

In the safety of her bedchamber, Everleigh let her tears fall unchecked. She was an utter disaster, and how she had made it through the last few hours was a complete mystery. She slowly padded over to the fireplace and fell to her knees before it. The sobs tearing through her quickly soaked the bodice of her dinner dress. Her body listed back and forth as her breaths became labored. Darkness clung to her vision, and she wished it would carry her away.

Oblivion is preferable to this ache inside of me. Dearest Gideon, do you feel how my heart calls for you?

29

PUTTING DISTANCE BETWEEN US

It was the early hours of daylight, and Gideon was still riding Perseus home. He was set to reach the town of Bramley within a few minutes time. He thought if he could just reach his country home, he could begin to forget, and so he had ridden hard as if the hounds of hell were chasing after him. He was in a hellish nightmare and he did not know how to awaken from it. How had he fallen for her so swiftly and so thoroughly that he felt as if he had lost an essential part of his own body?

When his home came into view, he allowed his horse to slow its pace. He had expected to feel some measure of contentment at seeing his home, but thoughts of Everleigh would not leave him alone. He had planned to show her the lake and introduce her to his former life, his friends, and even mayhap persuade her to come to love the quiet countryside that he was so fond of.

Gideon put a halt to his errant thoughts and directed Perseus to the stables. Tobias, the young stable lad, rushed forward to care for the horse. It was not a large stable, only big enough for his horse and the gig he used to pay calls on his patients. Tobias was a willing and apt lad of five and ten and readily took the post assigned to him. His wages helped to support his large family, and Gideon was pleased to offer aid to the residents of Bramley in whatever manner he could.

"It is a might early for you to come down from Town, my lord," Tobias commented as he removed the horse's bridle.

"Nothing like a brisk ride to clear your head and give you a new perspective." Gideon turned on his heel and strode back to Lakewood House. Gideon had felt he could not put distance between himself and Town quickly enough, so he had left with instructions for Gibbons to pack their things and follow at his leisure.

Before he could rap on his front door, it was opened by Murdock, who ushered him in. "'Tis quite the chill in the air this morning, my lord."

"Indeed, I find it rather refreshing." Gideon removed his outerwear and handed it over.

"I trust your business in Town went well?"

"Not quite, but things are as they were meant to be. I will see to freshening up, and then I will meet with Delaney and see how things have fared here." Gideon walked up the staircase to his bedchamber and began to remove his dusty clothing.

A knock sounded on his chamber door, and he called out for the servant to enter. A basin of warm water was brought into his dressing area by one of the lads he employed. When he was once again left to himself, he began to clean the dust from his body with the water and a cloth. A bath would have been better, but he was in no mood to delay his day any longer, no matter how tired his body told him that it was. He would not allow his mind to rest as it would only turn to thoughts of Everleigh. And so he had resolved to press forward, and only when he could no longer stand or think a coherent thought, would he allow himself to fall into his bed and slumber.

Then and only then.

When he was dressed in clean attire and his hair was brushed, he descended the staircase and proceeded to his study to seek out Delaney. He found him there, shelving books. The younger man observed him curiously. Gideon raised his brows at him and advanced to the chair behind the desk.

"What have you to report?" Gideon motioned to the chair before the desk for his assistant to take.

Delaney compiled, and sat. "Nothing too involved. A few colds. I treated Lady Bramley for a pain in her left side. She seems well enough now."

"I will pay her a call first, then. Anything else of note?"

"No. It has been relatively quiet. Not even a complaint of gout to be had. Of course, the weather has not yet turned to bring the freeze." Delaney cocked his head and studied Gideon. "You look terrible."

"Thank you," Gideon let out a huffy chuckle.

"Perhaps a good nap and some hot food are in order."

"Is that your professional opinion?" Gideon smirked at the young man.

"Without knowing more, it's the best thing I can prescribe."

Gideon grunted and gathered up his correspondence, and leafed through the missives. There was nothing of importance there. He was restless and it was still too early to make calls on the residents of Bramley. He needed to be busy, and while the idea of rowing on the lake was never far from his thoughts, he could not bring himself to do it today.

"In that case, perhaps I should quiz you on illnesses you can diagnose and treatments other than naps and food? See what new information you have gleaned from the medical texts?" Gideon quirked his brow at Delaney.

Shrugging his shoulders, Delaney just looked at him.

Gideon drilled his fingers upon the desk and fired off his first question.

Gideon had yet to burn off his excess energy when he was escorted to the drawing room to await Lady Bramley. Instead of sitting, he paced the room without even setting down his medical bag. Soon the door opened and the lady came in with her husband steadfastly by her side. She came to a stop before him as he bowed before her. With a slight curtsey, she straightened as a sympathetic look passed over her features.

"Dear Lord Fairfield, I have heard about what has occurred in Town, and I am appalled that you could be so mistreated by your own blood." Her sapphire gaze locked onto his. The morning dress she wore was the same shade as her eyes and made her pale skin look ethereal. Her pregnancy looked to be progressing well, and he could breathe a little easier now that he had seen her.

If I can't secure my own happiness, at least I can ensure that my friends are well cared for.

"Yes, well I should have done things differently. But that is not why I have called today. I am making my rounds as the town has no official doctor yet, and I wanted to begin with you since Delaney informed me of the pain you suffered." Gideon gestured to her side.

"Oh, yes, well I am perfectly well now," she commented as she waved a hand in the air, dismissing his concern as unnecessary.

Bramley spoke next. "We are convinced she overdid it while taking a walk. So, she has agreed to forgo exercise for the next few days."

Gideon nodded his head and stated his agreement.

"Would you care to be seated?" the Lady offered.

"No, I cannot stay. May I check your pulse?" Gideon perked a brow in question.

"You may, my lord. Your new address will take some time to adjust to, I daresay. But I do wish you would be seated. There is another pressing matter that we would care to discuss with you." Lady Bramley waddled gracefully over to the settee and perched on its edge.

Gideon trailed after her and took the space next to her. He reached for her hand and counted her heartbeats. In his peripheral vision, he saw Bramley seat himself across from them in an armchair. After he released Lady Bramley's hand, he said, "All seems well. You are the model of maternal health."

"As I tried to assure you," beamed the Lady.

"You can't blame us fellows for wanting to secure your comfort and well-being. 'Tis one of the only things a gentleman can do for an expectant mother." He grinned at her and waited for the topic they wished to discuss to be set forth. It was Bramley that spoke.

"When Hathwell and I were in Town, we noticed more children prowling the streets. It had never struck me so much before, but my heart was greatly grieved by their plight. I would like to establish a house here in Bramley for those willing to venture here and those who have not yet begun their lives of crime. I would like to help them before they are forced to steal or do even more unsavory things. It does not sit well with me, now that I have my own little ones, that so many are helpless when I have the means to aid them." Bramley took a breath and then directed his gaze at his wife. Gideon noted the look of total devotion and love flowing between the Earl and his wife. He felt as though a small vise had gripped his heart.

I shall never have what they do…

When Gideon turned back to the Lady, she was a touch more pale, and a frown marred her beautiful face. He concluded that it was the topic that had affected her so. He brought his thoughts back to the matter at hand and ruminated on it for a few moments. He, too, had noticed the plight of the children in London. They were such a blessing and the only hope for the future. They deserved a safe environment in which to flourish, somewhere they could benefit from charity and goodwill. He immediately knew that he would like to see this to fruition.

"I wholeheartedly approve of your plan," he announced.

"'Twould not just be here in Bramley, but in Hathwell, as well. Hathwell readily took to the idea, and he has a plot of land in mind. We would need to hire teachers and nurses. It would be a huge undertaking, and now that you are in a position to offer your aid financially, we could use an additional investor. I am relieved to know that these children will benefit from your expert care, should the need arise." Bramley smiled sadly at him.

"I would gladly agree to give references and travel back and forth between here and Hathwell to help in any way-until a doctor is in residence." The more Gideon thought about it, the more eager he became to be useful.

Lord, is this your new purpose for me?

"I should like to establish a committee to oversee matters and vote on them. I know it could muddle things, but we would screen committee members carefully first. I believe that Matthew and Grace would be a welcomed addition. We would have the Lord and Lady Hathwell, the parson and his wife, and now our esteemed former doctor to begin with." Bramley tilted his head to the side in thought.

"This sounds like a solid way forward. How will you choose who to bring? How will you identify the ones most in need?" inquired Gideon.

"I know of several charity matrons in Town, and we will begin with them," Lady Bramley informed him.

"Excellent." Gideon sat back on the settee and rested his folded hands atop his stomach. If this was now the path God wanted him to walk, he would take it. He would trust in the Lord and wait to see what miracles He performed.

I will endeavor to cling to this new purpose, and perhaps one day soon, thoughts of missing Everleigh will not cause me so much heartache. As it is your will, Lord.

30

PROMENADING WITH THE PEACOCK

For the second time in the span of five minutes, Everleigh struggled to keep her face a mask of indifference. Francis had brought her to Vauxhall Garden, which was located on the south bank of the Thames near Lambeth, and she could not feel more wretched. Their party of three, as Miss Owens had accompanied them to chaperone, had been transported via boat over the Thames, and the ride had made Everleigh feel nauseated. Not only had the company of her intended strained her nerves, but the water's buoyancy had made her feel disconcerted. Everleigh wanted to fall to her knees in thanksgiving once she was on solid land again. The idea of the return trip made her anxious. She tried to push the dread away into a corner of her mind, as she wished to keep her wits about her so she didn't appear mulish or simple-minded to those who gawked at the sight of her and Francis. Since the Queen herself had given her blessing to the union, the news had spread through the gossip sheets; her being out with Francis wasn't a scandal since they were betrothed.

Her betrothed was striding by her side with her arm linked with his and his head held at a haughty angle. He was as proud as a peacock, and this exercise of promenading was trying her nerves.

How much longer must I endure this? I am not certain I can withstand a lifetime of this endless performance. Is there nothing of substance to this man at all? How can he and Gideon be so different?

When another couple halted their progress, Everleigh inwardly groaned. She didn't recognize either the gentleman or the lady, but that was hardly surprising, as there were a great many of the peerage she was unacquainted with.

Not to mention that with his reputation, I cannot be certain that all of the people he speaks to are even of the peerage.

"I say, chap, you have one pretty lady upon your arm. Take care that no other squires her away," boomed the gentleman.

Francis gave a guffaw and replied, "Indeed, 'tis too late for any other. I have secured her hand." He looked down at her with insincere affection.

"Well, congratulations, man!" The older man shook hands with him, then began to saunter away, leading the lady with him.

Everleigh did not feel slighted in the least for not being introduced. In fact, she was happy that her status of "not out" saved her from what she feared would be many unsavory introductions. She suspected the gossip sheets would be rife with speculation on the purpose of their outing.

At least, they are familiar with Marquess's bad behavior. I suppose, in time, I will become accustomed to being fodder for the masses as well. What a ridiculous couple we will be.

Everleigh studied the gravel walkway they were traveling. High hedges and carefully spaced trees surrounded them. Here and there were statues easily identifiable as Greek gods and goddesses. Pillars rose to stand sentry, inviting spectators to take notice. The picturesque scene before her boasted temples, rotundas, lodges, fountains with gurgling streams of water, and other delights. Strains of music from the orchestra teased her ears from another path. There was something beautiful and ornate to behold, no matter what direction her gaze landed. It was bemusing and enchanting and caused her heart great sorrow. She had no desire to be there with Francis. While the beauty was undeniable, their true purpose for visiting the pleasure garden was so she would be seen on his arm.

I am but another ornament in the midst of all the other decorations.

They were to take dinner in one of the hired supper-boxes that easily accommodated a party of eight guests. Then they would bask under the glass lamps threaded throughout the trees that lined the walk. Fireworks were set to begin shortly, once evening had set in.

With Gideon beside me, this would all be so wondrous. But instead I must remain at his brother's side and simper and coo to all he says and does. Though I have been doing a very poor job of that thus far. The very idea is enough to make me quite ill.

Looking over her shoulder, Everleigh made sure Miss Owens was still behind them. Her companion was keeping up with them, which offered Everleigh a small measure of reassurance. The pace they kept was not enough to leave her friend winded.

"You will miss her, I daresay," Francis remarked dryly.

"Who, my lord?"

"Your Miss Owens. Such a sad existence for one of her station to always be ousted from their position. It must make for a very disagreeable life." Francis smiled at a passing couple.

Everleigh nodded her head to another passing couple and then addressed what he had said. "I had intended to keep her on."

"That is quite impossible. You are no longer in need of a governess, and I will be your companion. We would only be expected to entertain her, and that would hardly do for a newly wedded couple."

"Miss Owens is perfectly capable of occupying herself," Everleigh stated frostily.

"I am glad to hear that. It will surely help her in securing a new post quickly." His tone brooked no further argument.

With ice in her veins and ire heating her face, Everleigh disentangled her arm from his. She turned back to approach her friend, linking arms with her instead. They walked along the path together.

I may not be able to openly oppose him for much longer, but I will not fall under his thumb quite as easily as he wishes.

Miss Owens shot her a look of warning as she narrowed her eyes, but Everleigh pretended to take no notice.

Francis shortened his stride until he was once again at Everleigh's side. He didn't rebuke her, or even look in her direction. In fact, he paid her no attention whatsoever. He simply walked by her side and exchanged greetings with those they passed.

I will gladly accept any reprimand and tongue lashing my father may wish to give me later to not be hanging on to his arm now.

When the darkening sky made its approach, and the birds began flying overhead to settle in for the night, Everleigh could no longer avoid her intended. With one last look at the dim purples and blues marking the sky, she sighed and let him lead her into dinner.

Once their party was seated and had placed their orders for the chicken dish, Everleigh let her eyes wander to the paintings decorating the small space. She could not make out the artist's signature on each painting, but she had learned that William Hogarth and Francis Hayman were the resident artists whose work was currently on display. The light in the box did not allow for a proper view, but from what she could see, they were quite lovely.

Once the footmen began to serve them, Francis deigned to address her again. "My darling, I trust you received a missive from your aunt?"

"I have, and she wishes for me to come to tea the day after tomorrow to begin our wedding arrangements." Everleigh looked off across at a table into the box nearest to theirs. Other courting couples were entranced by their partners, whispering together and exchanging loving looks.

This should have been me and Gideon.

Everleigh could not stop her lamentations. She listened in part to the conversation Francis held with a retired navy sea captain situated at a table across from them. She was thankful that she need not participate in their conversation. She was silent and sullen and knew she would hear about it from her father on the morrow. Neither the chicken nor the salad she had been served were appetizing, and she pushed the food around on her plate to give the appearance of showing at least a modicum of interest in it.

When the sound of the fireworks exploding filled the evening air, Francis stood and came to assist her in rising. He settled her palm on his forearm and led her from the tent with Miss Owens trailing after them. The jubilant sounds of the onlookers drowned out her inner musings, and Everleigh was forced to admit the shower of sparks that lit the sky were beautiful. She didn't want to enjoy anything about the evening, but her mood was tiring even for herself. She was not designed to be sad and withdrawn. Was it betraying Gideon to allow some degree of pleasure in?

Oh, Gideon, are you looking up at the same sky as I am right now? Are the stars shining down upon you? Are you now wooing another? As much as that thought fills me with dread and horror, I hope that you find a lady to love who will fill your heart with joy and your mind with peace. At least one of us should be happy.

31

ONE STEP AT A TIME

Gideon pried his tired eyes open as the early morning light crept through the minuscule space between the window and the heavy drapes. The tiny amount of light should not have been enough to stir him from the deep slumber that had finally overtaken him. It had only been a few hours ago that his tumbling thoughts had ceased and allowed his mind to quiet. Instead of turning on his side and attempting to fall back to sleep, Gideon gave a weary yawn.

He had missed the lake while in Town. Now was as good a time as any to row his boat across the water. There was enough light, and he would be able to fully enjoy the start of the day as the brilliant shades of sunrise continued to creep across the blue sky. He would enjoy birdsong to welcome the adventures of the day.

Tossing the dark blue coverlet aside, he sat up, then swung his legs to the outer edges of the massive four-poster bed. With minimal wiggling, he reached the edge, felt for his slippers, and slipped into them once they were found. He rose with the reminder that he needed to take one step at a time. Little by little, he would get through another day without his beloved by his side. He brought a hand up to rub against his aching chest. He supposed he could have tried to ask the Lord to take away the anguish he felt at losing Everleigh, but in truth, the ache was a reminder she was still in the world. He could still grieve for her, and for that, he was grateful.

In her father's townhouse she still breathes and, for that, I give you unending thanks, Lord.

Gibbons entered Gideon's bedchamber with *The Times* held under his arm. He set about pulling attire from Gideon's wardrobe. Gideon didn't wish to dress formally, as the idea of a cravat strangling him as he tried to row would be aggravating, to say the least. He quickly donned trousers and a white linen shirt. Paired with his black leather boots, he was the very picture of a country gentleman at his leisure. When Gibbons turned to offer him the broadsheet, Gideon requested that it be set on the terrace with his breakfast in an hour's time. Gibbons nodded his assent and left to let the cook know when Gideon would break his fast.

Striding from his chamber, Gideon took in a lungful of air as he descended the staircase. Though he was still indoors, he took joy in the fact that even the air in his home was fresh. The horrid air of Town had been oppressive, and he had felt as if he had been unable to take a deep breath the entire length of his stay.

Murdock greeted him in the small foyer. "Will you be requiring your hat or greatcoat, my lord?"

"Not yet. The lake is calling out to me, and I intend to heed its call."

When Murdock opened the door for Gideon to pass through, Gideon looked up at the clear blue sky. Not even the hint of a cloud met his eye, and that further brightened his mood.

Small blessings add up.

It was only a brisk walk to the lake. The water was calm today. No wind was active in making ripples across its shining surface. He pushed the rowboat into the water and gingerly stepped into it. After he had seated himself, Gideon took up the oars and began his exercise. The muscles in his arms and back strained, but it was a good feeling. He relished the fresh air, the task before him, and even the fish that leapt from the depths. This was a balm to his soul, and he enjoyed every moment of it. When he had rowed the entirety of the lake back and forth twice, he let the oars go and leaned his head back to let the sunshine caress his face. Beads of sweat clung to his hairline and face, and he used his sleeve to wipe it away.

This, this is what I needed. No matter what ails my heart, there is peace here.

Feeling invigorated, he reached for the oars again and pushed himself toward the land. When he was even with the shore, he rose and stepped from the rowboat. Gideon was busy dragging the conveyance to its permanent spot when a voice called out to him.

"Lo, there my friend!" Mr. Morten greeted as he reached Gideon's side.

Gideon straightened and shook hands with the man. Over the passing years, Matthew Morton had come to be a good friend. As well as a source of wisdom and entertainment whenever Gideon took to flirting with the man's wife, Grace. Gideon had been put to the task of wooing Grace Buchanan by none other than Mr. Morten's own mother, Mrs. Morten. The older lady had been playing matchmaker between her son and her companion; it had worked out splendidly for all involved. Gideon's heart had not been in the wooing; he liked the woman well enough, but he could tell that she was not for him. Matthew and Grace were a striking pair, and as the spiritual leaders of Bramley, they set an example of grace and forgiveness.

"Hello to you, Mr. Morten." Gideon returned.

"I have heard various tales regarding you. I came to suss out which ones are fact from fiction. Might you have a few minutes to spare for your friend?" Morten looked at him with his chocolate-colored eyes holding warmth and sincerity in them. His brown greatcoat was a striking contrast with his forest green trousers. His black leather boots were well-worn, and the topper on his head just cleared the low-lying branches. His walking cane was held aloft in his hand.

"Ah, yes, well I have been up to quite a lot. Walk with me?" Gideon motioned toward his house. The two took their time ascending the small incline leading up to the house and continued to converse.

"I had heard from Harrison that he and Hathwell were to attend an audience with the Queen on your behalf, and I can only surmise all did not go well for you."

"It did not. My brother intervened, so I have retired to where I belong while I attempt to figure things out." Gideon spoke as he stretched his neck from side to side.

"How did the Lady fare in the matter?" Morten inquired as he tilted his head to the side to examine the leaves hanging over their heads. The colors were beginning to turn to shades of amber, goldenrod, and mulberry purple.

"So, you do know a lot of it," Gideon confirmed.

"But I would much rather hear it from you. You seem to be carrying around a great deal of sorrow. Perhaps, I can give you insight or direction? Are you in need of any?" Morten turned his head to meet Gideon's gaze.

"Thank you for your offer, but I don't believe either of those things would be of help at present."

"I will not press you further then. But I will say this: if God is in the midst of working out the details, then all shall be done by His Will in His perfect timing." Morten smiled softly at him.

"I do not feel that God is currently concerned with my feelings on this matter. I let myself be carried away by a pair of beautiful jade eyes and I bear the brunt of injuring the Lady, as I led her to believe that we were possible." Gideon felt himself beginning to feel unburdened, and thought mayhap it was cathartic to share what was in his heart with another.

"And you feel guilty for having given her hope?"

"Would your conscience not plague you if you gave hope to the one your heart longed for, only for it all to come crashing down around your ears?" Gideon ran a frustrated hand through his hair.

"Of a certainty. But did you ever have trickery in your actions or your heart when you sought to rescue her from a marriage that paired her with your unworthy brother?"

"Of course not. I meant to give her another way, another future. She does not deserve the unhappiness that my brother is sure to give her. I kissed her, I bought a ring as a sign of my unending affection for her, and I even went so far as to ask if she'd have my hand. I saw our lives together almost as if we had already lived it. I would have given up doctoring for her! I would have done anything to secure her happiness." Gideon felt raw and exposed. 'Twas not a pleasant feeling.

Am I now turned inside out?

"Be patient, my lord. This is not over until they have exchanged their vows before God. Return to Town and be there. Watch and pray, as I will be in prayer for you both here. The Lord has led me to you today, and I feel compelled to encourage you. Return, and even though it might cause you pain, be there for her. Our Father is still at work; I feel this to be true. Whatever lessons He is teaching may not be yet visible to the eye."

"I fear that were I to return, Francis would only torment us both all the more. He is set to punish me for my part in a deception that was not of my own making." They had reached the house, but neither made a move to enter it.

"I am sorry he has taken to mete out the Lord's vengeance on you both." Morten rubbed a hand over his stubbled jaw.

"I do not know if I can witness his cruelty toward her and not enact my own brand of punishment. I would normally never seek to harm my brother, or anyone, but I distinctly saw red fill my vision as he was belittling her. No, my friend, we are all better off with me being here." Gideon nodded at the parson, then strode to his front door.

He could feel his friend's gaze bore into his back, he knew he had behaved rudely, but he could not stand to listen to any more advice that would only lead to more heartbreak.

I can only take so much! I was just beginning to gather brief respites of peace. No, I will stay here, where my presence can best serve those that I can aid, until I feel led to visit my estate.

32

MEETING WITH THE MONARCH & THE
RABBLE

$\mathcal{E}$verleigh felt her shoulders drawing up and her neck tightening. In just a few moments, Queen Charlotte would enter the drawing room. Everleigh had not slept well since the last time she visited the Queen. Her appetite was nonexistent, and while her temper had fallen into a meeker demeanor, there was no doubt that she was unhappy. Her abigail had begun fussing at her because even with powder or applying warm compresses, she could not mask away the dark circles staining the delicate skin beneath Everleigh's eyes. The lavender sachet the ladies' maid had put under her pillow would not lull her peacefully to slumber. Everleigh could not bring herself to care about how drawn she looked. Inside she was a bundle of nerves and dread, and she desperately hoped acceptance of her fate would soon eclipse all other emotions inside her. There was nothing she could do to alter her course. She was of no more importance than chattel, and much less of use. If only acceptance didn't make her feel as if she were being discarded.

Miss Owens gripped her hand and gave it a squeeze. Her companion had been invaluable these last few days. She had constantly kept herself at Everleigh's side and took to overseeing the smaller household tasks. Everleigh had needed another Court dress for today, and Miss Owens had met with Madame Genevive to create one.

As this was to be a private affair, Everleigh's companion had been allowed to accompany her inside the palace today.

The side door was opened, and that was their cue to rise to greet Her Majesty. When the Queen came into the drawing room, she smiled until she caught sight of Everleigh, then a frown overtook her face. The Queen's retinue filed into the room after her and stood along the back wall, observing quietly. Everleigh and Miss Owens dropped into perfect curtsies before the Queen. When they rose, Queen Charlotte latched onto Everleigh's hand and pulled her toward the settee where they both sat.

Feeling the intense scrutiny of her aunt's eyes on her, Everleigh wriggled atop the settee. Miss Owens took to one of the armchairs when the Queen indicated it with a wave of her hand.

Pursing her lips together, Queen Charlotte addressed her, "You look horrid, my dear. I have never seen you so pale, nor have I ever seen your very countenance so wanting. What has happened to bring you to this lowly state?"

"I am well, Your Majesty," Everleigh was quick to assure her.

"Lying to your Queen?" she arched a graying brow at her niece.

"'Tis simply all the excitement of the upcoming nuptials that have unsettled me."

"Are you certain that *all* is well?" Queen Charlotte's dark gaze never left her face.

"I am engaged and I shall be a marchioness. What more could I possibly ask for?" Everleigh fixed her gaze on her gloved hands, which were tightly clasped together in her lap.

"I am not oblivious to the rumors, you know. And I am quite certain that you are not either. Were you some simpering ninny, I think the pairing might be good enough. But you are so very intelligent, and kindness itself. I worry this might not be in your best interest, my dear."

"Please, Your Majesty, do not fret over me. All will be well. I am resolved to do my duty and, given time, I shall find happiness." She meant the words that she had just said. All hopes were dashed. Her eyes flitted to Miss Owen. "I do wonder if you can help me in securing a new post for my companion. As you are aware, Miss Owens was my governess and like my own sister. Her character and bearing are incomparable, and she is a treasure. I know that this is not your responsibility, but there are none I would ask and feel comfortable doing so. But perhaps you will think such a task is beneath you."

Queen Charlotte turned her head to observe the lady in question. "I am the Queen. There is nothing to worry yourself about where I am concerned. When the time comes to wed, send Miss Owens to me, and I shall find a suitable position for her."

"Thank you, Your Majesty. I am forever in your debt."

"Pish posh. Think no more of it," the Queen gave a deep sigh. "Allow me to question you one last time; then I will remain ever silent on the subject. You are agreeable to wed the Marquess?"

"I am. I will do my duty and find purpose in that." Everleigh demurely smiled at the Queen.

"If you are absolutely certain, then I can have no further objections myself. So let us plan for the nuptials! I have cleared my schedule for a week from Thursday. 'Tis not enough time for most to have everything seen to on such short notice, but am I not the Queen? I can see my wishes are followed with haste. Does the date suit you?" Queen Charlotte smoothed a hand down her voluminous skirts.

"Of course, Your Majesty." Everleigh's stomach wanted to revolt, but she managed to rein in her feelings and drew her figurative Court mask securely into place.

'Tis better to be done with this entire affair than to continue to draw it out. With luck, my new husband will soon tire of me, and I will be left to pursue my own interests.

"Splendid!" The Monarch clapped her hands together, and one of her ladies' maids rushed to her side to hand over several cream sheets of stationery. She nodded her gratitude, then began leafing through the pages. "Ah, so I had a few thoughts. Goddess knows, I have had much practice in the planning of weddings, with so many children. And this brings me joy, to know I may step in, in place of your dear Mama."

"I could think of no other that I would value more than you, Your Majesty. I cannot express my thankfulness enough."

"You need not worry. We will soon be surrounded by vast amounts of Brussels lace, rosebuds, and satin. Oh! And you shall wear my pearls! I know weddings should be an immediate family affair, but I think we need something to celebrate. If you would not mind, I, too, will be present at your nuptials. And remember this, as this is the very last I will ever utter on the subject; with the right connections, you can weather any scandal your husband creates." The Queen took a breath and softly smiled at her.

"Good heavens, what a list!" exclaimed Everleigh when Queen Charlotte handed her the stationery. There were lists of decorations for the ceremony, a menu for the wedding breakfast, music to be played, and every detail pertaining to the gown she would wear. Every detail would be seen to, and Everleigh felt contentment settle over herself. There would not be a thing she would need to plan, and she would have nothing to vacillate between.

"As you can see, I have left nothing to chance. Are you pleased?"

Everleigh slowly nodded her head. "Oh, my Queen, this is superb."

"Naturally. I have had a hand in it." The Monarch arched a graying brow, then dissolved into laughter that Everleigh joined. Everleigh suddenly felt tired and listless and knew that once she returned to the townhouse, she could finally find slumber. A great burden that she didn't want to even consider had just been seen to for her.

THE NEXT AFTERNOON WHEN THE CLOCK CHIMED THE HOUR OF FIVE, Everleigh was awaiting Francis's arrival as they were to take a ride in His Lordship's phaeton. Since it only sat two, Miss Owens was to remain at the townhouse. Courting couples had the luxury of escaping their chaperones when their behavior could be observed by one and all. The open carriage was the current mode of fashion, and Francis had been adamant about showing off the conveyance and his bride-to-be. They were to ride through Rotten Row in Hyde Park. The Serpentine River flowed nearby, and with its green lawn and shady groves of trees, it was a lovely place to promenade. But they would not be leaving the confines of the phaeton.

Nonetheless, Everleigh was dressed in a promenade dress of a striking cobalt blue. The ribbons attached to her bonnet matched its shade. She would be the height of elegance.

When she heard the rap on the front door, she bid Miss Owen goodbye and padded toward the foyer. Francis was just walking through the front door. He was resplendent in a greatcoat that matched her ruby red pelisse. He gave her a bow, which she returned with a curtsey, then she took the bonnet Ashburn handed her. Everleigh turned to look into the golden-framed mirror hanging from the papered wall to tie the ribbons properly. When she was satisfied, she stepped to Francis and took his proffered arm. He then led her from the townhouse to the curb, where a matching pair of gray horses stood affixed to the phaeton.

"You look marvelous today, my dear," Francis crooned to her as he assisted her into the carriage.

"Thank you," Everleigh replied as she looked forward. She could have complimented him in return, but didn't find it necessary. He needed no one else's opinion about himself.

Francis climbed into the phaeton and directed the horses to walk on. Everleigh reminded herself that she must be poised and allow the actions and words of her intended fall to the wayside. She meant to do better and endeavored to be pleasant company. She could not always be unhappy; it was far too tiring.

When Francis neglected to steer them in the direction of Piccadilly, Everleigh's thoughts became troubled again. "Are we not to see Hyde Park today, my lord?"

"No, for I have a surprise! I have a few friends that are quite excited to make your acquaintance. We are to head to a private club and meet them there for refreshments." Francis flashed her an unsettling smile that reminded her of the sneer he had directed at Gideon on more than one occasion.

Everleigh didn't bother to voice an objection. What was she to do? It was not as if her protestations would be met with a kind and receptive ear. She had to trust that Francis would not lead her to total ruin and humiliation. He was tasked with seeing to her welfare, and though he wore the villain hat well enough in her story, surely even he wouldn't act beyond the pale.

Within minutes they were in a secluded part of Town that Everleigh had never been to before. There were storefronts advertising the varieties of wares they sold or services they rendered. A nondescript building loomed on the left, and it was there that Francis directed the horse to stop. The attendant standing at the back of the phaeton leapt down and took the reins that Francis handed off. Francis then rose and climbed down, then turned back to assist with Everleigh's descent. Timidly, she placed her gloved hand in his. Within seconds she was standing beside him. Francis linked their arms and then strode to the brick building. The door opened, and a gentleman in worn clothing stepped aside to let them enter. When the heavy door clicked shut behind her, Everleigh felt chills dance along her spine.

I should not be here.

Francis pulled her along a corridor. When the space opened to a large room, Everleigh tried to avert her eyes. Scantily clad bodies were in every corner and crevice. She heard unfamiliar noises that set her nerves on edge. Everleigh felt her cheeks heat, then she paled.

Ruined. I will be ruined, no matter that we are engaged. He truly is a monster to bring me to this place.

Her betrothed chuckled at her, tugging her further into the room. A hand came to rest along her shoulders. French perfume met her nose as her eyes listed to the side and were met by a large bosom clothed only in some sort of lace corset. Repulsion filled her. Everleigh neither wanted to smell nor to see what was before her. Disgust roiled through her in crashing waves.

"We will take the private room for the evening, Polly. See to it that my friends are ushered in," Francis commanded as he began to walk again. He still held onto Everleigh's arm, so she continued by his side, keeping her eyes downcast. Her thoughts were racing, wondering how she could weather this disgrace.

How can he care so little for me, for my reputation? Am I not to be his wife? Does that not garner some respect?

When they arrived at another door with peeling red paint, Francis opened it. He guided her inside and closed the door with his foot. There was no one else in the room. It was filled with lounges, chairs, and pillows. The distinct odor of alcohol greeted her. The air was stale with the scent of old cigar fumes. He let her arm go, and she walked to the center of the windowless room. It was everything she imagined a house of ill repute would be, based on the whispered words she had overheard from the servants.

Am I standing in a brothel? How can this be? What does he mean to do with me? To me?

"You need not look so frightened. I will not ravish you *tonight*. 'Tis as I said, my friends would like to meet you. The townhouse we used to meet at is no longer in my reach." Francis sauntered over to one of the lounges and sat. He patted the spot next to him. When she didn't move, he groaned. "I give you my word that no harm will come to you. I have it on good authority your Papa is away from home and won't return until the early hours, and you, *my pet*, will be tucked safely into your bed by then."

Swallowing in an attempt to moisten her dry mouth, Everleigh crept to the spot his hand was resting on. At her approach, he lifted it; keeping her posture ramrod straight, she sat gingerly on the edge.

He chuckled at her again. Everleigh wanted to please him so he would not become tired of her and toss her from the room. How could she make her way home without him? It was true her pin money would be enough to hire a hackney, but could she convince one to even stop for her?

"There's a good girl," he droned as he leered at her. "Do not make yourself uneasy. These are no mere rabble; they're my friends. They'll treat you just as I tell them to, and as you are every inch the *lady*, they will be tamer than usual in your presence; there will be no need to spend the entire time gifting the room with your cold disdain."

Everleigh felt rebuked by his harsh words. Yes, she was genteel and refined. He had his chance to be done with her, but he had chosen differently. She was just a possession to him, something to be owned and shown off. Just an object of no more importance than a jewel or the winning card in whist.

The door opened, and a trio of gentlemen, who looked as if they were already three sheets to the wind, sauntered in. The distinct odor of alcohol again met her nose, and combined with the cigar smoke-heavy room, Everleigh felt a headache forming. She rose when Francis did, and after the brief introductions were made, he swatted her on the bottom, making her flinch forward into the chest of the heavy-set man whose name was simply Blinkley. She tried to push herself away from him, but he only tightened his hold on her.

"There now, sweetheart, you needn't throw yourself at me. I am always up to entertaining you; you need only ask." Blinkley smirked at her and brought his lips down toward hers.

Everleigh stomped on his boot, which didn't so much as harm him as it did surprise him. He let her go to the guffaws of the other men in the small room. Everleigh kept her composure and backed away until the back of her legs met the lounge, then she sat. To keep the shaking of her hands hidden away, she tucked them in the folds of her skirts.

Oh, to be a man who can wield a sword to cut him down! To cut them all down, right where they stand. Dear Lord, show me a way out of this horrible mess. I cannot stand a lifetime of this degradation.

"She's a peach, lucky man, I say!" boomed the slender man with oily hair and beady eyes.

"Ripe for the picking, she is!" agreed Blinkley, who licked his lips. A new level of repulsion slithered into Everleigh's bones.

"After you've sired your heir, what will you do with her then? Share?" inquired the third man, a Mr. Pickering, as he leered down at her.

"Gentlemen, *tsk*! I gave the lady my word that you all would mind yourselves in her presence. You have wanted to meet her, and I have granted your request. Let us move on from these lascivious comments and enjoy the evening. Polly is to send in some entertainment soon, and I promise you'll have quite the rousing good time." Francis smirked at his cronies, then made his way back to sit at her side.

The trio of men located their own seats, and when Polly re-entered the room, a young boy trailed behind her with a rounded table. He placed it down amongst the chairs, and before he could back away, Blinkley was at the table throwing down a set of well-worn cards. The other two men joined him as Polly and the lad quit the room.

When they began to play cards, Francis leaned toward her ear. "Worry not, my pretty one. 'Tis for me and me alone to strip the veil of your innocence away. That is something that I will never share with another; *you belong to me.*"

Polly threw the door wide as another scantily clad woman came in with a tray of glasses and a decanter. She set the tray down on a side table and poured the amber liquid into the glasses. Once they were filled, she walked over to the men, hips swinging. Mr. Pickering grabbed onto her hips and pulled her into his lap with a wink at Everleigh. The drinks were passed around to those at the table who were vigorously throwing down large sums of money for their bets.

Francis rose, collected the two remaining glasses, and took them back with him to the lounge. He tried to hand one to Everleigh, and when she refused to take hers, his nostrils flared. "You will take the glass; you will *never* refuse my gifts. Whether you take a sip or not, I do not care, but you will not refuse my kindness."

Everleigh reached out for the glass, then cast her gaze to the dingy carpet. She gasped when his large hand closed over her chin and drew her face up toward his. His fingers cruelly dug into her flesh.

"You will obey me in the future, will you not, *darling*?" he crooned to her.

She attempted to nod, but his grasp did not allow her to move. "As you wish, my lord."

How dare he harm me? How worse will his violence grow?

"Good girl."

"That'll teach her! 'Course nothing like a good hit to knock sense into the mind of a useless female," remarked Blinkley.

"You attend to your wife how you wish, and I shall do the same. She's much too pretty to bruise," Francis replied. He withdrew a cigar from his waistcoat and located a match to light it. The smoke overwhelmed Everleigh, and she coughed as she waved a gloved hand in front of her face. Francis enjoyed his vice, much to her dismay.

He blew out a perfect ring. "Are you famished yet?"

"No, thank you. I am perfectly at ease," she remarked with a stony face. She wanted to massage her flesh where his strong fingers had dug in.

I would not give him the satisfaction.

"Too bad, I had reserved a table at Wilton's oyster room. However, if you would rather stay here, I am happy to oblige."

"I find that I am famished after all. May we depart?" Everleigh waited with bated breath to hear his reply.

Francis rose and rubbed the lit end of his cigar into a crystal tray and left the stub there. He turned to Everleigh and held out his arm to help her rise. She practically flew from the lounge in her eagerness to be gone from the establishment. He chuckled at her, and Everleigh felt her face flush.

"We're off to dinner, chaps. Do mind your manners. Polly has the room reserved until midnight, so be sure to leave by then," Francis addressed his friends.

"A right pleasure to meet you, my lady." Blinkley bowed his head at her.

Everleigh inclined her head to him and the others seated at the table as well.

I cannot wait to wash the stink of this entire evening from my body. If I have any skin left after I scrub it, thrice over, I will consider it a miracle. At least Wilton's is a place where I can feel comfortable again. I will never forget this foray into his world. What atrocities await me next, I cannot even begin to imagine.

Francis escorted her from the room. Everleigh thought they had remained for the span of two hours. The room which they came out into was swamped with ladies plying their trade and eager gentlemen who were standing much too close to said *ladies.* Leering and flirting were taking place in every direction her eyes moved.

A man approached them, still wearing his greatcoat and topper. He carried a walking cane topped with the golden head of a lion. When Everleigh lifted her gaze, her eyes grew round as she recognized the man in front of her and Francis. He quickly grabbed Francis's free arm and drew them toward yet another room. When they entered, and the door was closed behind them, Everleigh felt relieved that the room was unoccupied.

"What are you playing at?" demanded Lord Michaelton as he threw Francis's arm to the side.

"Whatever can you mean?" Francis seethed back at him.

Lord Michaelton pointed at Everleigh and declared. "She does not belong here! How dare you sully her reputation in this disgusting manner?"

"Thank you for your consideration in a matter that does not concern you at all. What I do with my bride-to-be does not need your opinion." Francis let Everleigh's arm go and stepped into the other man's space. They were nearly nose to nose.

Everleigh brought her hands up to her cheeks with dismay. She had been discovered, and now she would bear the brunt of Francis's misdeed.

What will everyone think of me? Will my father send me away? What of Miss Owens, being tainted by my presence?

"You will take her home this instant. You will stop acting the libertine. She is to be your wife! *Your wife!*" Lord Michaelton bellowed. "One does not treat *their wife* as *their mistress*. You will return her safely to her father's house, and never darken another door of ill-repute with her in tow ever again."

"You will not lord over me! What right do you have to even speak to me of such things? You who bandy about your mistress for one and all to view. You should heed your own council and mind your business." Francis shouted as spittle flew onto Lord Michaelton's face.

Lord Michaelton drew himself away from Francis, and pulled a handkerchief from his pocket. He wiped his face as his eyes burned into Francis. When he had completed his task, he spoke again. "You will return her to her father's house at once. If you do not, you will receive a summons to your death at dawn. Decide whether your luck runs better with swords or pistols. The lady does not deserve to be treated in such a low manner. Your behavior toward her is revolting. You've gone too far."

Francis laughed. "You make demands upon *me*?"

"*I make a promise to you*. Return her at once to where she belongs, and nothing more will arise from this unfortunate event. But if you fail to do as instructed, I will hunt you down. I am not some puppy you can kick or a brother you can manipulate. Mark my words, as they are my promise to you. Leave this place and never attempt such folly again." Lord Michaelton stood staunchly in his place.

"Bravo!" clapped Francis. "Well done, your conscience can be at peace now. You have had your say."

"Excuse me, my lady," Lord Michaelton looked at Everleigh and bowed. He took two massive strides and swung his arm back. When he brought it forward, it crashed into Francis's stomach, eliciting a strange whooshing sound from Francis.

Francis doubled over and groaned. "Bloody man!"

"Do you box at Gentleman Jackson's? You should. If you've a mind to be a complete blighter, you really should hone your defensive skills. Now I can strongarm you into compliance, or you can act like a gentleman and do as you are told. I fear for your ego should I lay you out here and now in front of the lady."

Regaining his breath, Francis stood upright and glared at him. "Why does any of this matter to you?"

"Because I have let my marriage wither away until my wife has become a stranger to me. I would not wish that path for anyone. You can make this right. You can take her home and begin again on the morrow. Do not make even bigger mistakes than I ever did."

Everleigh had watched the exchange through her fingers that had moved to shield her eyes when the punch landed on Francis. She feared what would happen next. She had never seen such a display of violence before. She knew men were easily capable of fighting; the heroes in her books proved that, but never had she expected to witness such a thing because of her. The small part of her that lamented over the fact that Gideon had not fought for her settled into place in her heart. She had been pushing those thoughts and feelings away, ignoring them completely. Now, she could be at peace, knowing that such violence between the brothers would have broken them apart forever.

Never will I be the cause of such actions between Francis and Gideon. No blows will be permitted to fall between the brothers who were once each other's world.

"Take her home," whispered Lord Michaelton.

Francis wiped his mouth with his sleeve and looked over at Everleigh. His gray eyes searched her face. What he looked for or what he saw, she didn't know. He looked back over at Lord Michaetlon and nodded his assent.

Lord Michaelton walked to Everleigh. He smiled at her kindly, then removed his greatcoat. He held it out to her. "Place it over your head as this libertine escorts you to the phaeton that awaits you. It's not too late to protect you. I will do whatever I can to stifle the gossips about this." He looked over at Francis. "But only this one occasion will I offer that service." Turning back to face Everleigh, he bowed at her and exited the room. Everleigh was too stunned to curtsey in reply.

"I think it is time I returned you to your residence," Francis said, but did not meet her eyes.

Is he furious at himself or me? Will I earn more of his abuse?

"Very well," she agreed as she settled into the dark greatcoat. When Francis reached her side, she tugged the coat over her bonnet, so that her face was barely visible. Francis cupped her elbow and drew her from the room. Together they traversed the large room and reached the door. When they left the establishment, Everleigh felt flooded with relief.

Almost safe! We will soon reach my home, where I can wash away this entire affair. How glad I am that Gideon was not present to witness this evening. May he never learn of the events of the night; I could not bear to sink in his estimation.

33

EVERY MAN CAN BE AN IDIOT

week had come and gone, and Gideon was no closer to finding peace. He was just as hollowed out and depressed as he had been when he left Town, despite the tranquility he found while on his lake. Although his fit of rage had passed, he found it difficult to get through his daily tasks. On more than one occasion, Gideon had let his mind idly wander, and that was never a good thing, as thoughts of Everleigh pushed themselves to the forefront of his mind. He had attended the town church on Sunday, and though Morten was a very good orator, he could not keep Gideon's attention. While stitching up one of the farmers who had a wound from an errant ax, Gideon had almost sewn his own index finger into the ailing skin. That was when he knew that, for the foreseeable time, Delaney should take over the care. He simply wouldn't be of use until he could master his own mind.

He was on the terrace taking his tea when he picked up the scandal sheets that he had been studiously avoiding. The last thing he wanted to see were more ruinous rumors regarding his brother. With trepidation, he opened the broadsheet and scanned the articles. Not too far down, his eyes landed on what he had been dreading. Accompanying an article was a black and white drawing of a character that very much resembled Everleigh with her hands clutched together over her heart. The expression marring the vile drawing's depiction of her face showed a creature completely overwhelmed. To her right was a preening version of Francis. He was sipping from a tumbler while his other hand held a corset.

What in the blue devil!

Dear Reader,

I have stumbled upon a very juicy piece of news that I could not help but share with you. I know you are the soul of discretion, and so I will leave any wild imagining to you, for the truth is much too salacious to doubt its validity. This author received a tip that the elusive Lady E and her betrothed were spotted in a certain elite boxing den one night and then in a less-than-savory establishment that serves appetites for both drink or flesh on another night. Now, I, being the upstanding member of society that I am, could not simply take the word of a source. So I set out to investigate. And I must say, the happenings between the Marquess of – and Lady E were exactly as described. I witnessed such scenes of depravity with my own eyes that would shock and dismay you, dear reader. Before you go casting Lady E to the winds, I must tell you that she was as unwilling a participant in these festivities as any innocent could be. Indeed, she was the picture of abject misery and sorrow. Her pale complexion continues to grow more drawn, and I must say her seamstresses must be overtaxed with the altering of her entire wardrobe to account for the weight that has fallen from her once fine figure. I do hope her wedding dress will fit. Time will tell as the clock is ticking down to what promises to be one splendid affair, or perchance I should instead say, spectacle of a marriage.

GIDEON WAS GRINDING HIS TEETH TOGETHER WITH SUCH FORCE, HE WAS not at all surprised when his jaw painfully popped. The newspaper was fisted in his shaking hands. There could be no doubt regarding whom the article was written about.

Has Everleigh's physical health been put in jeopardy? And how could Francis take her to those places? What more is she to suffer by his will?

Turning the paper over and searching for the date, he saw that it was printed three days ago. He wondered what other havoc and depravity his brother had wrought upon her. His vision blackened. There was only one thing worse in his mind than Francis taking her to wife and into his bed. What were the chances he would offer her to others for their enjoyment? He had seen the worst of his brother, and this would not surprise him in the least.

What an utter disgrace! To think of what he has subjected her to…

He balled the gossip rag up and threw it across the lawn. He leaned forward and, with a great deal of force, threw his fist down on the table; bare knuckles met the iron surface. The fact that his hand was swelling up was not lost on him, but he could not bring himself to care. What were broken bones when his lady was suffering with no end in sight? Gideon attempted to calm his ragged breaths. His heart was racing, and heaven help him, he had never wanted to blacken an eye and break a few ribs before as he did in these moments. He would not stand idly by for a moment longer. Everleigh would not wed his brother, not now or *ever*, and any person who would take objection could just sod off. There was nothing that would change his mind. Not one more indignity would befall the woman he loved.

Love… Yes, I do love her. Desperately, passionately, with a burning thirst that could never be quenched. How stupid of me to attempt to lock my own feelings away. It's brought nothing but abject misery to us both.

Gideon purposefully strode into his house and searched until he found Delaney in the medical supply room. The young man turned from the shelves and took in the fury radiating from Gideon.

"What has happened?" Delaney inquired as he took a step toward him.

"My life has shifted yet again. Tell me, would you take over here in Bramley for me if I were to suddenly depart?" Gideon stood taller, firm in his resolve and the knowledge that he was finally acting.

"Of course, in a heartbeat-"

"Good. I will be departing presently, and I do not know when, or if, I will return." Gideon unapologetically interrupted the man.

"Will you not tell me what has happened? I might be able to help."

"I have finally decided to behave like a man. I am going to Town and calling my brother out. His dishonor will not stand. I will not stand idly about being stupid when the fate of the woman I love hangs in the wind." Gideon nodded at his pupil and turned on his heel to exit the small closet.

"What if he is a better shot than you? What if you are maimed and cannot function properly? Think about this, Lord Fairfield, I beg of you!" Delaney had followed him from the room, trailing in Gideon's wake.

The pair ascended the staircase and made their way to Gideon's bedchamber. Gideon stomped to the bellpull to summon Gibbons. He would need a saddle bag packed with whatever clothing would fit in it. He would need to visit the safe in his office to withdraw funds. If he didn't die, he would need to flee the continent. Dueling was against the law and was punishable by imprisonment. Who would hire him if they knew he had spent time in Newgate? This was rash and he knew it. But he could slow the pace of his racing thoughts.

When Gibbons entered the bedchamber, his steps came up short. He had a bewildered look on his face as he met Gideon's stare. Before he could speak, Gideon was barking orders to him.

"Have Perseus readied at once with a saddle bag. Pack as many of my things as you can into it. If you should find yourself in need of a new employer, go to Lord Bramley. He will aid you." Gideon walked to the window and looked out.

Gibbons stood in place, earning Gideon's ire when he turned back around. Gibbons cleared his throat and looked at Gideon's assistant.

"Why are you not doing as instructed?" shouted Gideon.

Why are they showing such idiocy when there are things to be seen too? Time is not on our side!

"My lord, you must know what today is?" Delaney stepped forward, then stopped at the menacing look Gideon was casting his way at the interruption.

"Of course! 'Tis Tuesday."

"No, it is Wednesday and late afternoon at that. Your lady is set to wed in less than four and twenty hours. Even should the road be clear, and you ride hard, you would not make it much before the early morning hours and then... Well, how will you gain access to St. James's Palace?" Delaney looked at him with mounting pity.

Horror and dread filled him as a heaviness weighed upon his heart. *So soon?*

She was to be wed on the morrow? In just a few hours, she would be lost to him *forever*. Gideon raked a hand over the contours of his face. Hope, he would have hope that all the variables worked in his favor. If this was the Lord's will, he would make it before vows were exchanged, and He would find a way to smooth the path ahead. Gideon had to believe it, this had to work.

Please, dear God, let it be so! Do not let her pay the price for my playing the fool.

Gibbons slowly approached him as if he were a wounded animal, and the idea made Gideon belt out a stifled chuckle. He must be the perfect picture of the word deranged.

"Sir, what have you done to your hand? It is mangled."

Delaney closed the distance between them and took Gideon's hand in his to inspect. He *tsked*. "We really need to set this bone. Your hand will not work properly without the correct care."

Gideon tried to yank his hand back to his own person, but Delaney was persistent. "Very well, I will acquiesce. But in the meantime, Gibbons, see to your task. I am depending on you." Gideon strode from the chamber and thundered down the staircase. He made his way to the medical area where he saw his patients. Delaney was fast on his heels and Gideon sat to let his student set his hand and bandage it. He didn't give voice to the thought of what a hard ride would do to his hand if it rained; the damage to the bandages would be irreparable. Delaney was most likely wasting both of their time.

And time is proving to be a short commodity.

"Do hurry it up," he barked at Delaney.

Turning around with bandages in hand and a splint of sorts, Delaney replied, "I am trying, *doctor*." He came forward and began to settle the splint in place. He wrapped the bandage in place and secured it, then stepped away from Gideon and nodded his head. "The bandages should hold, though even under ideal conditions, your hand should be rested. Riding pell-mell won't do you any good."

Gideon narrowed his eyes. "I will be of no good to anyone if I do not make it in time. Never mind about my hand. My heart can't continue on this way, knowing that I have failed the one person I should have protected and cherished above all others." He ran his good hand through his hair and huffed out a strained breath. "I do apologize for my shortness. 'Tis not directed at you, or anyone else. I am upset, raging at myself. And at present, I don't know how to handle these feelings of ineptness."

Delaney closed the distance between them and placed a hand on Gideon's shoulder. "You are the most carefully controlled man I know. I hate that this has all happened. If I were you, I imagine I would be quite a fire-breathing dragon too. Take heart, this battle is not lost until the vows are exchanged. I will pray your horse is carried along on swift winds. Good luck, my friend. We are all cheering you on." His teal eyes held compassion and quiet strength, bolstering Gideon's cause.

Nodding at Delaney, Gideon promptly retraced his steps until he found his study. The safe that was hidden behind a stack of books resting atop one of the many bookshelves was his sole focus as he strode through the room. He turned the dial to the correct combination, and the tumblers gave way. He reached into the safe and withdrew banknotes and coin, pocketed it, and then closed the safe, returning the books to their proper place. He turned to the desk and placed some funds on it. He would not shirk his responsibilities; he would leave behind enough to ensure his staff was paid and that Delaney would have no difficulty in keeping things running for a time. It didn't escape his ire that the money he was relying on came from his brother.

Looking up, Gideon gazed around him. He had become attached to his estate. He had made friends and a good life here in Bramley. This study had heard many private conversations between him and the men of the town. He had written his correspondence behind the desk. He had dreamed of introducing his home to Everleigh, because this was not just an estate, or a town; this was home. But then, if things should go in his favor, his home would be wherever he and his bride resided, even if he had to flee to America or some other foreign land. Would Everleigh give up everything for him? To take his name and his heart forevermore? The more he thought about it, the more certain he became. He was headed in the proper direction. Why had he allowed this ordeal to continue? Why hadn't he stepped in and stopped it? He was the one to tuck tail and turn his back on her, on their future happiness.

I just hope that she can forgive me. I will simply have to explain the idiocies of men. We really can be the daftest creature in the world where our hearts are concerned. Please dear Lord, keep her heart open for me. Keep her safe until my arms can hold her, offering all the comfort and love I possess.

34

DREAMING OF THE ONE

Everleigh was roused by the gentle lights of the awakening dawn. There was much to do to make ready for her wedding. The servants bustled about, drawing her a bath and setting her wedding finery on the edge of her quickly-made bed. Everleigh was numb. She felt as if she were a puppet on a string. No hope had been offered, and no aid had been sent. There was no way out of the marriage, and Everleigh's macabre thoughts told her that death was always an option.

A lot of women die in childbirth. But that does not comfort me; I cannot fathom leaving an innocent babe in his care. Perhaps we'll both reach Heaven at the same time. One can only hope…

When a servant steered her into the warm water of the copper tub, Everleigh held her breath and dunked her head under the water. Her lungs soon begged for air, and she rose, spluttering water from her mouth and furiously blinking her eyes.

So drowning was not an option. Mayhap I will trip on the way to cutting the massive cake Her Majesty had made and land badly on the knife. Perhaps a misstep could send me falling and breaking my neck. And even these thoughts do not make me feel better, only worse.

Closing her eyes, Everleigh took a deep breath.

Pretend all is well. Don a mask of such serenity that none can doubt your feelings. Be the blushing bride, and soon this will all be over.

The maid extracted Everleigh from the tub and wrapped her in a plush towel. Next, she was directed to sit before the toasty fireplace to allow the heat to dry her tresses. Everleigh felt disconnected from her body, as if she were outside of it and looking down on herself. This was so surreal and terrifying: the idea of Francis being her husband. She felt shaky and off balance; perhaps it was due to all the weight she had recently lost. Food simply held no interest for her. Every morsel that met her tongue tasted of embers. Her life was a raging inferno, uncontrollable, with no way to keep away from the flames that were certain to destroy her.

An hour passed or perchance two; Everleigh couldn't say, and she truly didn't care. She rose when requested to and padded over to sit upon the cream satin cushion of the bench before the rosewood dressing table. She sat woodenly and took in her bleak face and vacant eyes. Perhaps haunted was a more apt word.

From behind her came the sound of many footsteps, and in the mirror, Everleigh saw the Queen and three of her ladies-in-waiting. They came to stand behind their monarch, who glided just behind her. Queen Charlotte's countenance was severe. She pursed her full lips and narrowed her large expressive eyes as she scanned Everleigh from head to toe. Everleigh took her in as well. Her dress was decorated with shimmering diamonds catching the candlelight and reflecting it around her. Her periwinkle satin dress was cut high at the waist with a modest bustline. Her gray hair had been swept up into an elaborate style with feathers and strung seed pearls threaded throughout her tresses.

"You are not the vision I had expected. No blushing is bride sitting before me," the Queen's stern voice carried all around the bedchamber.

"I am sorry to disappoint you, Your Majesty." Everleigh avoided the Queen's searching gaze as she stared at her folded hands resting in her lap.

"No bride should look so grim. You do not wish for this after all."

"I am content. This is the man my father has chosen, and I must endeavor to abide by his wishes." Everleigh was aware that she could have gotten down on her knees and laid herself prostrate before her great-aunt, begging her to spare her for another fate. That would anger her father, to have his carefully arranged plans come to naught. Such an action, such a request, would tarnish her father's name. Everleigh had been raised since birth to make a well-made match.

Duty before heart, duty before anything.

And she had been content. Perhaps not happy, but she had made peace long ago that a loveless marriage was likely in her future.

Until Gideon.

But dreaming about him would not make him appear to whisk her away. He wouldn't be standing at the front of the chapel to wed her. Dreaming of him brought nothing but heartache. She had contemplated how he had accepted their fate. Gideon had not even made a peep when his brother had shown up to change everything for them. But now… she was loath to recall the event. He had not stood up for her; he had promised to always put her first, but in the end, he had turned his broad back on her. She would have run away with him, even if it meant she was regulated to wearing rags and consuming day-old food; starvation would have been welcomed if only he had made an attempt to choose her above all else. But no, he had acquiesced to his brother's decree and left her.

And if he should return? Blows would come between the brothers, and I could not ever stand to witness abuse where there was once adoration. Things are better as they are…

"You are so very far away. Where have you gone to, my dear?" Queen Charlotte leaned over her shoulder and brought her cheek to rest against Everleigh's.

"To places that are best left behind," she cleared her throat and leaned her head away from the Queen's. Everleigh turned her head and placed a gentle kiss on Queen Charlotte's cheek. She smiled at her and willed her tears not to betray her aching heart.

"You need only say the word and I shall put a stop to this whole thing."

"After you have spent so much time and devotion, I could never do so."

Besides, who would wed me if I were to cry off? Gideon is not here. I am alone in this as I will be in all things henceforth.

"You need not go through with this. Nothing matters but your wishes."

Everleigh nodded her head and then said, "'Tis time to ready for the ceremony. I will not keep my future husband waiting." Though she really wished she could. The past week had been a trial to her nerves and sensibilities. Francis had endeavored to introduce her to the shadier and more unsavory parts of London she had never known existed. As shocked as she had been, she knew that there was still more that she would be made to suffer, the marriage bed being her chief concern.

He has delighted in tormenting and shocking me, and I suspect he will offer no considerations or kindness... I have no doubt... the wedding is only the beginning of the worst.

"You may dress her hair," instructed the Queen as she backed away from Everleigh. Her voice was uneasy. But Everleigh had no more words to offer when she was so very terrified herself.

I will be the quintessential bride and be obedient without complaint. Besides, what do my feelings or desires really matter? In the end, I am just a mere vessel for the illustrious Netherfield name.

35

HEARTBREAK AND HORSES

Gideon was soaked through and shivering, the abject portrait of misery. The Lion and Lamb Inn that he had been forced to stop at was not one of the finest in England. But the ale he quickly downed brought warmth to his body and a tingling to his numb extremities that nothing else could. Perseus had thrown a shoe shortly before midnight, so Gideon had been forced to walk with his animal for miles on the mud-caked roads. His feet were weary, and his spirits low. There was a rather bothersome blister forming on his left heel. His hair was mussed and damp, as were his clothes. The careful work of Delaney's bandaging was an absolute wreck. His hand was even more swollen, but somewhere along the road, it had grown blessedly desensitized from the freezing rain. He still couldn't feel it. He had never been more despondent of body or spirit.

The mantle clock told him that it was close to five in the morning. He *might* make it to Town *today*, if he could purchase a new horse, or simply borrow one. But he would not have much time to change and ready himself enough to step foot into St. James's Palace. They would never grant him entry in this bedraggled state. However, he questioned whether he could manage a necessary shave. Facial hair was not at all the thing. He ran his hand across his stubbled jawline.

The inn's proprietor entered the private room and nodded at

Gideon. His graying hair was plastered to his head with what Gideon could only surmise was sweat and dirt. He had a sallow complexion that gave away his inebriated state.

"The horse has been procured and stands at the ready, Lord Fairfield," the greasy man stated as he reached around to scratch an insistent itch on his backside.

"I thank you," Gideon replied as he set coin on the wooden table and rose. He wanted to offer the sage council that baths were good for one's health, and that he greatly suspected that lice were hatching in the strands of the man's hair. Deciding he would act the gentleman, he refrained from voicing his thoughts, but just barely. He strode from the private sitting room and through the hallway. When he reached the inn's front door, he opened it and stepped through it. The rain has ceased!

Praise the Lord! Now I only have to ride pell to leather and reach Town in time.

Reaching the saddled horse's side, he put one foot in the stirrup and swung his other leg across the beast, taking care with his injured hand. Once he was properly mounted, he squeezed his legs while clucking his tongue to instruct the horse to gallop. The stallion tossed his head, ready to race along the muddy roads. Thoughts of Everleigh flew through his mind. He would do anything, brave any element, to get to her. This was but the first day of his happily ever after. Whether it remained happy was up to God.

The horse sped through the countryside in a flash. Gideon counted himself blessed to have such a charger at his command. The sun shone down on him, and he felt it and the wind drying his hair and clothing. He didn't bother to adjust his seat in the saddle, he was too numb to take note of any discomfort.

Another blessing I shall be happy to note. I am not yet saddle sore.

Sights of civilization met Gideon's weary eyes as elation filled him. He would soon be on the outskirts of Town.

Huzzah!

He made his way to his townhouse unimpeded by heavy traffic. He leapt from the saddle and turned back toward the horse. He untied his saddle bags, thankful that they didn't appear to be waterlogged. A footman came from the direction of the mews. He led his horse to the stables after pocketing the coin that Gideon had given him.

When Gideon rapped on the front door, the butler eased it open, then stood aside as Gideon entered the foyer. With raised brows, the man took in Gideon's ruined state. Gideon attempted to project a regal bearing, but he knew he failed.

I rather resemble a highwayman, no doubt. What Lord carries his own saddlebags?

"We were not expecting you, Lord Fairfield," Grant stated in a disapproving tone. He looked behind Gideon. "Has Gibbons not followed you?"

"He has not. I left quite suddenly." Gideon tried not to flinch under the man's scrutiny.

"I shall see to it that you receive warm water and a footman to assist you in redressing. Perhaps a light repast would not be amiss," Grant commented as he watched Gideon set the saddlebags down and began to remove his outerwear.

"Thank you," Gideon gratefully intoned. After handing his ruined greatcoat and topper off, he turned in the direction of the staircase and quickly ascended it.

No doubt Grant is still staring at the dried mud attached to Gideon's attire in a state of disbelief.

He wanted to chuckle at the thought, but his heart was too laden with anxiety.

Gideon entered the chamber and trod to the dressing area. He quickly sat on the bench that awaited him and began to remove his sodden boots, which was quite an undertaking as they seemed to be unwilling to leave his person. Eventually they freed his feet, and he took a deep breath. He heard a stirring by the fireplace, and then a match struck. The room would take longer to warm than he could afford to wait, but he appreciated the kindness.

Within a few moments, a liveried footman stood before him and aided him in removing his wet clothing. As they were completing the task, another footman came in with a bucket of warm water, which he poured into a navy blue basin. Gideon expressed his thanks and stepped to the table that bore the basin. He reached for the washing cloth and began to scrub his face.

The former footman came to stand behind him. "Looks as if we might need several buckets to thoroughly cleanse you, my lord." He then left the screened-off area.

Gideon spied an oval bar of soap and lathered it between his hands. The scent of rose hips and some elusive spice filled the air. He dunked his head into the basin and proceeded to vigorously cleanse his hair.

The footman returned just as Gideon had rinsed the last bubble from his dripping head.

"'Tis a good thing, it is mopping day. The cook had quite a lot of heated water readied to hand over to the scullery maid." The footman lifted the bucket onto the table next to the basin.

"Mop water, how exceptional," deadpanned Gideon.

"At least it had not been used yet, though, if you'll pardon my saying so, even that water would have been cleaner than what's mucked up the basin," he pointed.

Gideon couldn't reprimand the servant. He wasn't being rude, only stating a very obvious fact. Gideon was filthy. He handed one of the clean cloths to the footman. "Help me, please," he asked.

The footman wet the cloth and scrubbed Gideon's back and arms. The rest Gideon had been capable of seeing to himself. Once he was smelling better and could see his skin tone, he asked the younger man to fetch his saddlebags. He needed to be on his way. There was no time for a shave. The footman began to pull out articles of clothing that, while pristine, were horribly creased. Gideon's shoulders drooped, but what had he expected? The night's events had not been nurturing. Perhaps he should have left some of his new attire here after all, instead of insisting that Gibbons return with it all.

Starting with his small clothes, Gideon began to don his attire. Piece by piece, he was painstakingly put together, and each article lent him more strength and poise. He was a gentleman; he could draw upon his upbringing to get through the next several hours.

But then, gentlemen didn't hie off to palaces to wreck weddings by declaring their love for another man's bride; especially not if that other man was his brother. I hope they let me in. If not, I will shout to the heavens with all of my might. I will not be deterred. Gentlemanly manners be dashed!

36

WEDDING BELLS

This was it. The final still moments before Everleigh walked down the pale blue runner to greet her groom at its end. There were six people awaiting her presence: the Queen, her father, Miss Owens, the bishop, the Duke of Sutton, and Francis. She looked down at her wedding dress. It was made from the softest mint green muslin, and the Brussels lace that made up her sleeves and edged her hemline and bodice was sumptuous. The ribbon that gathered just under her bosom was a darker shade of green with tiny silver flowers embroidered along it. Her slippers matched the shade of her dress. Her hair was curled and pinned in an elegant twist under her bonnet. Everleigh clasped roses and lilies in her trembling hands, the whole bouquet shaking before her. Her father caught her eye and nodded at her. Taking a deep breath, she began to glide down the aisle at her father's side, their arms entwined.

Her steps took Everleigh to her future. Francis stood dressed in a navy fitted tailcoat, cream-colored velvet knee breeches, and white silk stockings. His waistcoat was cream with golden swirl designs on it. His cravat was elegant, and the lace fell prettily against his white shirt. His black leather pumps boasted golden buckles and heels.

What a dandy.

He seemed to be much more alluring in his wedding finery, but still held no sway over her. He was not Gideon.

Everleigh turned to her left and curtsied before Queen Charlotte, who was in a dour mood. Her face was pinched and Everleigh worried that she had displeased her. When Everleigh rose, Francis took her arm. He didn't speak to her or even bother to look at her. Everleigh let him lead her to the bishop as her gaze once again drifted to her father. The Marquess of Thornwhistle's expression was stony and indifferent.

Is he not pleased? Am I not being the dutiful daughter?

The bishop opened the Book of Common Prayer and began to recite from its contents. These were the same words that had been spoken many times before; there was nothing special or sacred about them to Everleigh. Her vows would be a hollow offering, much as she knew her husband's would be as well. The older man droned on, and Everleigh's attention waned. She thought of the rose clippings she had so wanted to take with her to her new home. She had tried to broach the subject with Francis, but he had dismissed her request without knowing the entirety of what it was that she was actually asking. There would be no token of her mother to accompany her into her new role as Marchioness.

'Tis just as well; no false sense of comfort should be strived for. My memories would become just as tainted as my future.

She heard a throat clear, then silence. Everleigh blinked twice and then looked to the aged bishop.

"Will you repeat after me?" he prodded her.

"Oh… Of course," Everleigh cleared her parched throat.

The bishop started to speak, but a commotion was taking place just outside the chamber. Everleigh looked at Francis, who was scowling, then she turned her head toward the entryway. Scuffling and muttered words were being masked by the heavy wooden door.

"Repeat the vows!" demanded Francis. He roughly pulled Everleigh's hands toward him. They had been holding hands since her father had handed her over. She stumbled into his chest. Her muffled sound of alarm could barely be heard. Her bonnet was being crushed by the weight of her against his chest. Everleigh regained her balance and took a step back.

The noise from outside the chamber grew louder.

"What is happening? Are we under siege?" the Queen demanded to know.

"I would hope not!" rasped the Duke from beside Queen Charlotte.

The door was thrown open to reveal Gideon looking disheveled and breathing harshly. He was a magnificent sight, and Everleigh's heart soared.

He has come for me! But we cannot ever be! Oh the futility of this endeavor!

He looked like a crazed man until his gray gaze landed on her. Her heart simultaneously beat up and slowed down. She could no more stop the smile blossoming on her face than she could grow wings and fly to him. Francis tightened his grip on her hands with punishing pressure.

Miss Owens gasped, unable to control her reaction. She cupped her face with her gloved hands.

"My dear boy!" chastened the Duke, who was struggling to rise to his feet from the armchair in which he sat.

"Tell me I am not too late!" Gideon boomed as two guards tried to wrestle him to the stone floor. He had managed to hold them off, but he was flagging before her eyes.

"Young man! What are you about?" Queen Charlotte inquired icily.

"Tell me there is still hope, that all is not lost," he sent an imploring look at Everleigh as the weight of the guards drew him to his knees.

"We were just about to be announced as man and wife. Just a few moments earlier and you might have been in time," Francis curled his lips contemptuously.

"That is a lie, young man!" the Queen scoffed.

"Then no vows have been exchanged! Thank the Lord! I wish to speak with Lady Everleigh," Gideon pleaded with Her Majesty.

"What an odd request at a time such as this!" Queen Charlotte turned her attention to Everleigh. "Do you wish to speak with this man?"

Everleigh nodded; she could not find her voice. Her whole body was engulfed with tremors.

"I think not. You have no place here, *Lord Fairfield*. Be off at once," commanded Francis.

"*I will not!* For despite *your* wishes, *I* must let Everleigh know that I am *hers*. Entirely, if she will have me. I love her most ardently and fervently. I know now I will never conquer this feeling, nor do I desire to. She is my sunrise and my sunset. My cheer on rainy days. She lights up every corner of my heart, and without her, without her smile, her clever mind, her brilliant wit, and her steadfast heart, I am a ruined man forevermore. I cannot exist any longer without *her*." Gideon kept his gaze fixed on Everleigh the entire time the words flowed from his mouth.

"Dear Lord, man! That is quite enough! Will you do your duty, guards, and escort him from the premises?" Francis barked out.

"You do not deserve her," Gideon stated as the guards continued to hold him down.

"That is neither here nor there. *I will have her.*" Francis turned toward the bishop. "If you would, please *continue.*"

Everleigh felt tears fill her eyes. He loved her! And he was here to claim her in body and heart. She tried to tug her hands from Francis's harsh grip, but he would not let them go. Panicked and unwilling to repeat her vows to him, she directed her attention to her great-aunt.

"Daughter, you will do your duty and be wed to the Marquess. You will be a marchioness! The Earl is a step below. Amiable as he is, he is not right for you." Everleigh's father entreated her to see reason.

"We must uphold the marriage contract..." The Duke rubbed a gloved hand down his face in agitation.

"I do not want to be a marchioness! Not when I could stand at Gideon's side. He is who my heart yearns for; he is all of my hopes and dreams. There could never be another I could vow to obey and cherish." Everleigh found the will to straighten her spine and voice her thoughts. Her heartfelt words echoed throughout the chamber. The beaming smile that alighted Gideon's face filled her with joy.

"Impossible, my darling. Contracts have been signed: the license issued. Here we stand before each other, God, the bishop, and the Queen. You can't shy away now. *I will not stand for it,*" Francis seethed venomously.

Queen Charlotte took one look at Everleigh's paling face and rose from the ornate rococo-style chair. Her commanding voice filled the chamber. *"Am I Queen, or am I not?"* When no one dared to answer her question, she continued. "This is not right. A love match for

Everleigh is all her mother and I ever desired for her. I vow she shall have her way this day! You, Marquess of Netherfield, you will cease your claim to her *at once!* And as I am Queen, I shall go a step further. Release him!" She motioned to Gideon. The two guards immediately let him go and backed away. "My dear boy, walk this way."

Gideon rose and tried to right his attire. He quickly gave up, as his cravat was in ruins and his embroidered velvet tailcoat was wrinkled beyond repair. His silk stockings were dirtied from the floor, and one boasted a tiny tear at the ankle where the buckle of his leather pump had snagged it. He did as commanded and closed the distance between them. He gave Her Majesty a courtly bow.

"You were in attendance the day this entire farce was presented to me. Why?" The Queen tilted her head.

"Your Majesty, we were all gathered to beseech your support of dissolving the marriage contract between Lady Everleigh and my brother; since he had made his distaste for society known, as well as his dissatisfaction at being matched with the Lady. My grandfather and Francis were in agreement with this course of action until that day when Francis altered all of our fates." Gideon stated the facts with an unwavering voice.

"I do wonder what could have happened to cause the plan to change so drastically," she mused.

"There was a part I played in another's care that earned my brother's wrath. I felt as if it was justice in a sense; the proceeding events that happened. I was too slow to right the wrongs. That is not a mistake I am willing to let continue." Here Gideon gazed at Everleigh with reverence. "I am willing to do anything, brave anything, in an attempt to earn her regard and respect again."

"And you, Everleigh? I have all but begged you to confide in me." The Queen's stare made Everleigh feel like the worst creature ever.

"I did not want to disappoint you, or my father. I believed love was only one-sided, that I alone bore the feeling. If not wed to Francis, then to whom?" Everleigh shifted her eyes to stare at the runner. "It did not matter to me who I was wed to, if it was not to the Earl of Fairfield."

"Lord Fairfield," Queen Charlotte addressed. "How do you feel about righting that wrong now?"

"I will not be made to stand aside. *The woman is my due!*" Francis's anger made his face flush.

"*Posh!* You will *not* naysay your Queen. *I* will lock *you* in the Tower until such a time as you behave like the Marquess that you are. I suggest you walk away from this chamber at once. Now, this very instance. You are henceforth barred from my Court until you can prove your worth," the Queen commanded as she stared at Francis with distaste.

With a great heaving of his chest, Francis glared at them all and made his way from the room. As he hastily retreated, Everleigh noticed that he bore a limp that he had not had the evening before their parting at her father's townhouse.

Gideon rushed to Everleigh and carefully enfolded her in his arms. He kissed her bonnet in place of her golden hair.

"Am I dreaming?" Everleigh inquired. Her heart was pounding at an alarming pace in her chest.

How can this be happening? How is all I have dreamed of standing here before me, and how has everything been made as it always should have been?

"Not at all," soothed Gideon as he rubbed her back with one of his large hands. Warmth flowed into her in delicious waves.

Miss Owens sighed and wiped a tear from her eye. "Such a better love match I have never known."

"I say, this has been quite a remarkable day. The right grandson is set to wed, and it's a love match! My word, I feel like dancing a jig!" The Duke chuckled as he waved his cane from side to side in a mirthful manner. The action made him falter, but the Queen was there to steady him.

Everleigh could not agree more. This was just the beginning of her happily ever after. She was as light as a feather and giddy with joy. Today was not to be remembered as a stain on her future. It was to mark the grandest adventure she would ever undertake. That of being the wife to the man she compared all others to.

The happiness I feel can hardly be contained. I want to weep with both relief and glee; to shout for all and sundry that he is mine and I am his!

His bandaged hand caught her eye and she drew her brows together. "Gideon, what has happened?" She wanted to inspect his hand, but the idea of causing him pain made her heart ache.

"Nothing to trouble yourself about. It will heal." Gideon leaned down and Everleigh looked up at him.

I could lose myself in his glorious eyes.

"I don't even feel it," Gideon told her with a delighted gleam in his eye.

"Surely, you are satisfied with things as they stand?" Queen Charlotte said as she gained the attention of the room again. She arched her brow at the Marquess of Thornwhistle.

He simply nodded as he looked between the entwined couple's faces.

"There is one more thing, Your Majesty," the bishop piped up.

"Oh?"

"We need a license as the one I have clearly states she is to wed the Marquess of Netherfield. Without approval from the Archbishop, we are in a bind," the bishop swallowed.

"Ah, I came directly from him," Gideon spoke as he withdrew the crumpled license from his waistcoat pocket. He held it aloft, then passed it to the bishop, who examined it.

"Yes, yes. This seems to be in order." the bishop agreed.

"However did you manage that?" The Queen inquired appreciatively.

"Your Majesty, I had a letter of introduction to the Archbishop from the Earl of Bramley. He kindly read the request for aid and drew up a special license. Of course, I now am obligated to join him for tea on a day of his choosing next week." Gideon smiled down at Everleigh. "Shall we proceed?" He waggled his eyebrows at her.

"Ask me a thousand times, and a thousand times I will say yes!" What a twisted turn the morning had taken. Everything her heart desired would come to fruition. She would have the husband of her heart.

I don't know how to contain all of this radiant joy! My dreams are coming true.

"I was happy to envision myself as a doctor's wife. I would have followed you to the ends of the earth and beyond, had you only asked." Everleigh placed a gloved hand against his cheek.

He must never think even for a moment that a title ever held any value to me, where he was concerned.

The bishop cleared his throat. "May we begin? Again?"

Everleigh withdrew her hand, and Gideon nodded his head with a gallant flourish.

Everleigh couldn't pay attention to the words spoken by the bishop. Her gaze was locked with Gideon's. She was lost in the burning passion and blinding love in his gray gaze. The two exchanged their vows, and when it was announced that they were now wed, Gideon grabbed Everleigh to himself and kissed her most ardently.

When they separated, his hand traveled to his waistcoat pocket and withdrew the ruby ring. He carefully slid it onto her finger, then brought her hand up to his mouth and pressed a warm kiss against her finger. "Back where it belongs. This is my promise to you, my lovely lady. This is a symbol that love holds true. No matter what we face in the future, know my love for you is eternal."

Tears fell from Everleigh's eyes as she looked at the ring. It was just a ring, a glittering jewel, but Gideon was correct. It was also a symbol of their love. They burned brightly one for another. And she would ensure she never stopped remembering that love holds true.

Mine for him and his for me. Exactly as it was always meant to be. This is bliss, pure happiness. Thank you Lord, for carrying us through this storm.

37

LOVE HOLDS TRUE

The wine was sweet on his tongue as Gideon took another sip. His bride was seated next to him on the lounge in the master suite of their townhouse, which they had repaired to after the wedding breakfast hosted by the Queen. Not many could claim that not only had Queen Charlotte attended their wedding but had hosted their wedding breakfast as well. Gideon was still reeling from the day's events. While he was tired, he wouldn't dream of denying his bride, or himself, the pleasure of their wedding night.

But I cannot quiet my reservations until I know the full scope of Francis's devilry, and I cannot know unless I ask. I hate to question her on this night of all nights, but I can't take the chance of upsetting my bride if I should do anything that reminds her of his cruelty. Not that I would ever be cruel to Everleigh. Far from it…

"My lady dearest, I hesitate to cause you pain…," he began.

Everleigh turned her head to gaze at him. The firelight cast shadows upon her face and reflected in her jade eyes. "Oh?"

"I fear that we must discuss Francis."

"Oh. Must we?" She turned her gaze away from him and looked toward the fire.

He reached for her and used his index finger to guide her face back to his. "Know that nothing you say could ever sway my total devotion and everlasting love for you. I read some disturbing accounts in *The Times.*"

"My time with your brother will haunt me for a while, I fear. Please be patient with me."

"Was it that horrible? I know I read accounts. I had hoped they had been exaggerated." He felt anger flood him, making his skin grow taut and flushed.

I should hunt him down and give him that bruising that he so richly deserves.

"They were true, but you should know that while he showed me some slight abuses, he never really harmed me. I have suffered a few bruises and indignities, but it was my heart that was wounded most. I have been to parts of Town I never knew existed and witnessed sights that I will never be able to quite expunge from my mind. While I was frightened a good deal, he did ensure no other imposed upon me. His cruel and shocking words harmed my dignity much more than my person." Everleigh turned herself on the lounge so that her front was facing his side.

"And your innocence is intact?"

"I've had some of my world views stripped away, and I have seen some most unsavory sights, but my innocence remains. He never forced himself upon me."

Turning to face her, Gideon spoke. "I suspected as much. He would have flaunted that in my face when I barged into the ceremony. But innocence is so much more than your purity of body." He gently cupped her face with his hand. "He has not corrupted your heart; that is my most cherished possession. For you did promise it to me, did you not?"

"I did. Forever yours, my love. My husband." She leaned forward and gently pressed her warm and luscious lips to his. When Gideon reached for her to prolong the kiss, she pressed against his chest, breaking their contact. "I think he was hurt."

"Francis?"

"Yes. I think something happened between the time I parted from him last evening and when I saw him again this morning. Did you happen to notice his limp as he left?"

Gideon furrowed his brows. "I must confess, once he began to walk away, my sole focus became you. I wonder what sort of calamity he met?"

"Well… I have an idea…"

"Do go on, my darling."

"One of the first nights he took me from home, we encountered Lord Michaelton. Do you know him?" She trailed a finger over her lips in thought.

"I do."

"He punched Francis when Francis refused to do what the lord requested."

Gideon gave her a grin. "And what was that?"

"To take me home. He urged your brother ardently to escort me home and to never risk my reputation again. Francis refused. Lord Michaelton stood his ground. I have never seen him so enraged before; he's always been so polite. And I rather believe it wasn't because of the fact *I* saw him at the brothel, but rather that he saw *me*. He's a curious fellow. I think perhaps he does not deserve a wife like Lady Michaelton after all."

"Not everyone takes their marriage and makes it flourish. I don't know the particulars of their woes nor, I must confess, do I care to." He took her dainty hand in his, marveling yet again at the softness of her skin. He turned her hand over and leaned forward to place a delicate kiss on the pulse point of her wrist. When she shivered, he smiled wolfishly.

The way my kisses affect her is something I will never tire of.

"But that's so sad. I want everyone to be as blissfully happy as we are," Everleigh said with a hitch in her voice.

Her tender heart makes her a credit to her contemporaries.

"If only man was made to experience only joy, and deservedly so. But, alas, man is a flawed creature. But let us put all talk of other men and their miseries aside. I have been awake for much too long. I only want to concern myself with my bride."

"You almost did not reach me in time," she pouted.

"That is not entirely my fault. Blame the rain, or the muddy roads, or even my horse who threw a shoe. Remind me on the morrow to send Gibbons to fetch Perseus from that hovel. I do not desire a lice-infested beast." Gideon shuddered.

"All of that happened to you?" Everleigh asked incredulously.

"Indeed, but it was worth every blister. I am happily ensconced with the love of my life. There is nothing more I could desire." He entwined their fingers together.

"Where shall we go tomorrow?" Everleigh leaned against his chest and sighed.

"Back to Bramley, I think. There are so many friends there that have been wishing us well and lifting us up in prayer. I can't wait to introduce them to you. I hope you come to love Lakewood House, but I am just as anxious to set out for Fairfield House, and the other holdings. I don't wish to become an errant landlord."

To think of all the Queen has blessed me with... It humbles me. I shall endeavor to be worthy.

"I will follow you anywhere, dearest husband, so long as you wish me to."

"There will never be a day that I won't want you or desire you. You have no idea of the depth of my feelings for you, but... I will make it my mission to show you every day and every night. Oh, there is one stop we must make before we begin our journey."

"And where is that?" She pulled away from him and looked at him expectantly.

"To your father's townhouse. You must gather as many rose clippings as you wish and we will spread them at Lakewood House, Fairfield House, and anywhere else that catches your eye."

Everleigh squealed and threw herself at him. He enthusiastically returned the kiss she bestowed upon him. He was not content to let her withdraw from his arms again. He deepened the kiss and swirled his tongue along hers, eliciting a delicious moan from her. She was everything he had never known he wanted, never realized that he needed. Tonight, he would show her how much he loved her and enjoy every second of teaching her how to love him in return. His heart was overflowing, and his arms were brimming with her joyful exuberance. It was time to finally claim her and make a beautiful memory that they both would cherish forever.

EPILOGUE

THE ENDING IS THE BEGINNING

Gideon lounged on the terrace of his estate, Lakewood House, in the town of Bramley, as he perused the newspaper. Everleigh sat beside him, sipping from her floral-patterned teacup. They were enjoying a companionable silence, having just returned from a row across the lake. Spring was an excellent time of year to take to one's rowboat and enjoy the beauty nature presented. They were surrounded by new life as the earth woke from its winter slumber. Daring pinks and fuchsias, along with reds and vibrant shades of blue, would soon be sprouting and Gideon would miss viewing their splendor. In a week's time, his family would be traveling to Fairfield House. They had already visited all the holdings belonging to the Earl of Fairfield, but the House had been a particular favorite of his bride's. She had been overjoyed by the flourishing garden and had immediately begun to instruct the head gardener where she wanted her rose bushes to be situated. They would be seen from the drive up to the House, and the fragrance would waft through the windows when the House needed a good airing out. It had sounded like another bit of Heaven granted to him by Everleigh's hand.

"What have the gossips to rant about now?" questioned Everleigh.

"Oddly enough, my brother. It seems even in America he can cause quite a stir," Gideon mused thoughtfully.

"At least he is by his true love's side," Everleigh cheerfully stated as she collected an errant golden curl and tucked it back into its pin. The shade of pale pink she wore enhanced the rosy hue of her complexion. She still stole the breath from his body when his gaze fixed upon her, and he found that every day his love for her grew. That had been an astounding discovery to make.

How she could remain so calm about Francis's behavior rankled him. His thoughts took him back to the days after their wedding when Everleigh had tearfully confessed all that had transpired between them, imparting more details as time passed. It further proved that Francis was a stranger to him, but time had allowed the hurt to dull. However much forgiveness he could offer would never allow him to view his brother through blind eyes again. Francis's actions and the trauma he inflicted upon Everleigh were inexcusable. Sometimes, Gideon found that he still wanted to pummel Francis. When those times hit him full force, he grew still and silent, begging the Lord for grace. He understood that his brother had been out of control with grief and that rage had turned his heart to stone. But never again would the man be given the opportunity to wound those under Gideon's care.

"Lucky man, indeed," he grumbled.

"You cannot begrudge him and Miss O'Brady their happily ever after." She smiled at him, and he immediately felt his heart warm at the simple action, which aided in his regaining control of the swirling emotions within him. He was thoroughly a ruined man, for he was completely enchanted by his wife.

And I couldn't possibly be happier. Well, at least for now, this summer will present a new joy. I do hope it is a girl just as beautiful as her mother.

"I can and do. We were almost the cost of their machinations," he dully stated.

"But dearest husband, think of all we have gained! A title, several new homes, and a vested interest in both the Bramley House Orphanage and the Hathwell Heritage Academy. And isn't it wonderful that by this autumn both will be operational?" Everleigh was always focusing on the bright side of things.

My eternal sunshine.

"There is that, but something equally as important, but much more dear, is prompting my attention these days. Particularly now." Gideon directed his gaze to her stomach, which was heavily rounded with his child. Her dress was by no means tight; indeed, the style of the high waist hid quite a lot of things, but it could not mask the current antics of their babe. His child was causing her stomach to dance around wildly.

"Seems as if this babe is content to make a fuss. The midwife seems to think there may be more than just one to arrive. I have grown so large!"

Gideon had just taken a sip of his tea, and at her words, he spewed the contents across the tabletop. True, her figure was larger, but hadn't he been spoiling her endlessly and insisting she consume as much as possible now that the sickness had ebbed?

Everleigh's laughter rang in the air. He had a grin as he hastily took the linen napkin from his lap and mopped his mouth and the table, until he gave up his endeavor and rose from his chair. He took three giant steps to reach her side, then he slid to his knees and brought his large hands to either side of her swollen belly, and kissed the center.

"Why am I just now learning this news?" He felt simultaneously elated and lightheaded at the thought of two or more babes-as if he could faint from the added weight of responsibility. But then peace settled over him and he gave his thanksgiving to the Lord.

I am as light as air! The more, the merrier.

"There simply hasn't been an opportunity. You were sequestered away with your solicitor when Mrs. Hawkins arrived. So we met anyway and she confided her thoughts to me. Are you pleased?" Everleigh anxiously fidgeted with her hands.

"I am shocked and elated and excited, and all the other things combined! You constantly manage to surprise and delight me." He reached for her hands and kissed the palm of each one.

"I am only sorry that Miss Owens has agreed to become the matron of Hathwell Heritage. How am I to do this all without her aid?" There was a worried look marring her beautiful face. Gideon was quick to allay her fears.

"She will no doubt visit, and if you were to ask her, I have no doubt she would happily attend to you when the time arrives."

"You are right, of course. But I dislike taking her away from so many that will come to rely on her," Everleigh said as tears rimmed her jade eyes. She was prone to tears now, and they always crushed his heart. He felt like a cad when he was the reason for the waterworks, even if his actions were not in error. She cried when she was happy, when it rained, when she was tired, and when she was filled with sorrow. She cried when he walked into the room sometimes. He offered to let her be until she informed him that it was the joy of his love causing her to weep.

"What is all the fuss about?" came Miss Owens' voice as she came from the House.

"You are set to leave us soon. How shall I make do without you?" wailed Everleigh.

"Oh dearest, have no worry. I shall always be here when needed," Miss Owens soothed as she took the chair beside Everleigh.

Miss Owens had been touring with them off and on as they traveled to the different estates. She told them that she felt led to apply for the position of matron at Hathwell Heritage, and neither Gideon nor Everleigh could bear to dash her dreams. When Hathwell had leapt at the chance to retain her for the post, she had eagerly accepted. Gideon had held Everleigh as she had wept that night in their bedchamber. She considered the lady to be like her sister and held great love for her. The feeling was visibly mutual. It was easy to discern the camaraderie the women shared. Her former governess and companion deserved to forge her own path, and Everleigh was happy for her even if, at times, she became a hopeless watering pot. Who could blame her?

"I know. It's just that I will miss you dreadfully." Everleigh took the lace handkerchief Gideon offered her and dabbed at her eyes. She smiled her gratitude to him for the kind gesture. He was always at the ready to offer her aid. He rose and leaned forward into her bonnet to place a delicate whisper of a kiss upon the tip of her nose.

"Let us think of happier times ahead!" Gideon cheerfully exclaimed.

"We are to meet at Fairfield in three weeks' time with the families of the Earls of Bramley and Hathwell. Do you not find it curious that your dearest friends are both earls and you, too, have joined their ranks?" Everleigh blinked at him.

"The Lord leads us where he would have us. I am just thankful that I was eventually able to gain the goodwill of your father. 'Twas wonderful to spend the winter holidays with him and my grandfather. Our ever-growing family proves my motto," Gideon stroked his jaw.

"And what motto is that, my love?" Everleigh tilted her head to the side.

"Love holds true. No matter what is put before one, no matter how everything seems to be stacked against one, love holds true. Whether 'tis the love one possesses for a sibling, parent, other relations, or a bride-"

"Or a beloved friend. Love holds true." His countess interrupted him with a teasing smile for him and a beaming smile at her friend. Miss Owens took Everleigh's hand in hers and squeezed it, looking rather weepy herself.

"Yes, love holds true, and it's just us mortals that put constraints on it. Well, I am extremely thankful the love of God holds true as well; he brought me through the storm a better man, doctor, friend, and husband. And soon-to-be-father. What could one strive for that could possibly mean more?" Gideon raised his brows and nodded his head. Yes, the Lord had carried them all, showing that His love holds true if only one will follow the path He presents to them.

A NOTE FROM THE AUTHOR

Dear Reader,

Thank you for reading this book. It means so much to me that you did. I hope that you've enjoyed your time getting to know these characters and have fallen in love with one or two of them.

Please keep an eye out for the next Shades of Bramley standalone that will be about... how Mr. and Mrs. Morten met and fell hopelessly in love!

Supporting indie authors is important and appreciated. Self-publishing is a huge endeavor and the best way to support an author is to leave a review. Honest reviews can help others decide whether a book is right for them or not. Also, if you love a book, shout it out to the world. Share it with your friends and family and even with your book club. Books make wonderful gifts, too. Sharing your love of reading inspires others and may even assist another with finding their new favorite author.

Happy Reading,
Michelle Helen Fritz

ACKNOWLEDGEMENTS FROM MICHELLE HELEN FRITZ

Thank you so very much to you, dear reader! That you've made it this far means so very much to me. Gideon and Everleigh had a darker path to walk. I feared how their story would be received, and if you enjoyed it, please let me know!

Thank you as always to Ericka! Your time and patience that were so freely given was a gift that I will always treasure. Thank you for reading this before anyone else and offering suggestions. You are my forever bookish bestie and I love you!

Thank you to Brittany who bore with me through the rough patches as the story progressed! You are pure gold and I treasure you, bunches!

To Cathey who so generously gave me her time and feedback, thank you! I cherish you!

This would be a huge mess without the expert eye of Paullett Golden! My Lady, I adore you! Thank you for allowing me to take this journey by your side. Your steadfast friendship has meant the world to me!

I can't say thank you enough to Heather! She is the best boss and mentor that a girl could ever wish for. Thank you for all the things! I love you endlessly!

To Faith and Hailey from Fandom Fealty, you ladies are insanely creative and take my breath away with each piece I bring home. Thank you for creating the custom dollie pops of Gideon and Everleigh. I love them, and you too!

A huge well of gratitude to my editor, who took this and made it shine! I am forever grateful for the attention to detail and fact checking. You have made this what it is! My heart is overflowing with appreciation.

Isn't this book's cover just gorgeous!? Thank you to my fabulous cover designer, Wanderlust Ink & Tome LLC. Alexis is such a joy to work with!

To my Handsome Hubby who makes all my dreams come true, thank you! I couldn't tell these love stories without you, being you.

Thank you to my four children who challenge me daily. I hope that one day you'll find a comfy spot and meet these characters. Thank you for your creativity and allowing me to share all of the bookish things with you.

And to my Creator, thank you for giving me the words to write what is in my heart.

ALSO BY MICHELLE HELEN FRITZ

A Bramley Hall Regency - Clean & Sweet Regency Romance

Love At Last

Love That Lasts

Love Ever Lasting

Shades of Bramley Hall Regency - Clean & Sweet Regency Romance

Love Holds True

Courts & Curses - Clean Regency Fairy Tale Retelling

A Court of Broken Dreams & Curses

ABOUT MICHELLE HELEN FRITZ

Michelle Helen Fritz was born in Maryland and raised in Arizona with lots of traveling throughout the States. She began her literary career as a personal assistant to Indie authors and loves to see the process of an idea turn into a finished book. Michelle loves to write about dashing heroes and the compelling women that tempt them with a dash of intrigue, an abundant amount of romance, and scenes that hopefully make her readers swoon. She is the mother of four children whom she homeschools and currently resides in Maryland with her own jaunty hero who makes all of her dreams come true.

You can follow Michelle on:

Amazon Author Page: https://www.amazon.com/author/michellehelenfritz

Facebook: Author Michelle Helen Fritz

Instagram:@authormichellehelenfritz